Dinner Most Deadly

ANOTHER JOHN PICKETT MYSTERY

DINNER MOST DEADLY

SHERI COBB SOUTH

FIVE STAR
A part of Gale, Cengage Learning

GALE
CENGAGE Learning®

Farmington Hills, Mich • San Francisco • New York • Waterville, Maine
Meriden, Conn • Mason, Ohio • Chicago

GALE
CENGAGE Learning·

LIBRARY OF CONGRESS CATALOGING-IN-PUBLICATION DATA

South, Sheri Cobb.
    Dinner most deadly : another John Pickett mystery / Sheri Cobb South. — First edition.
        pages ; cm
    ISBN 978-1-4328-3096-0 (hardcover) — ISBN 1-4328-3096-1 (hardcover) — ISBN 978-1-4328-3090-8 (ebook) — ISBN 1-4328-3090-2 (ebook)
    I. Title.
PS3569.O755D56 2015
813'.54—dc23   2015008990

First Edition. First Printing: September 2015
Find us on Facebook– https://www.facebook.com/FiveStarCengage
Visit our website– http://www.gale.cengage.com/fivestar/
Contact Five Star™ Publishing at FiveStar@cengage.com

Printed in the United States of America
1 2 3 4 5 6 7 19 18 17 16 15

DINNER MOST DEADLY

CHAPTER 1

In Which an Entertainment Is Proposed

In an elegantly appointed drawing room in Audley Street, Julia, Lady Fieldhurst, sat watching raindrops race one another down the window pane. Beyond the glass, the few pedestrians hardy enough to venture out into the inclement weather tugged hats down and collars up to protect themselves from the elements. The dreary scene reminded her all too clearly of Scotland on the day of her departure some weeks earlier. She had been prone to melancholy in the days since then, a depression of spirits that had little to do with the November weather and still less to do with the violent death of her husband six months previously.

"A penny for your thoughts," said her companion, a rather dashing young matron in her mid-thirties, a decade older than Julia herself.

Lady Fieldhurst made a feeble attempt at a smile. "You would find them overpriced, I fear."

"Julia, I wish you would tell me what is troubling you," urged Lady Dunnington. "I vow, I've never known you to be so distracted."

"I beg your pardon, Emily." Lady Fieldhurst gave her head a little shake, as if to clear it. "I have had much on my mind of late. The sale of Frederick's house in Queens Gardens, and the hire of one in Curzon Street while I look for something to buy—"

7

"Balderdash!" declared the Countess of Dunnington inelegantly. "Oh, I don't blame you for selling your husband's little love nest and purchasing something for yourself with fewer unpleasant associations, but that is *not* the reason for your current preoccupation. You've been this way ever since you returned from Scotland, and *that* was two weeks ago. When are you going to give in and tell me what happened there?"

Lady Fieldhurst glanced about the room rather wildly, but there was no support to be found in Lady Dunnington's graceful Hepplewhite furnishings. "I told you," she insisted. "I disgraced myself with the Fieldhursts—again!—and was exiled to Scotland for my sins, with George's three sons in tow. At the last minute, we—the boys and I, that is—decided not to rusticate at the Fieldhurst estate as ordered, but stopped instead at a very pleasant inn overlooking the sea. The boys had a lovely time, but neither George nor Mother Fieldhurst was best pleased with our defection."

Lady Dunnington set down her empty teacup with perhaps more force than was necessary, and made a noise that in a less aristocratic female would have been called a snort. "Faugh! Frederick has been dead for six months now, Julia. When are you going to stop letting his mother and his heir browbeat you?"

"I don't let them browbeat me," Lady Fieldhurst said without much conviction. "I have gone into half-mourning, knowing quite well that they do not approve," she pointed out, gesturing toward her grey gown.

"Yes, and very pleased I am to see it," Lady Dunnington said, nodding in approval. "I should be happier still to see you in colors, but I know you dare not flout convention to such a degree, at least not yet. Be warned, though, on the anniversary of Frederick's death I intend to present you with a bright red bonnet!"

Julia had to laugh. "If you wish me to appear hag-ridden, by all means do so! I haven't the coloring to wear bright red, as you well know. I fear I must leave the red to you, my dear."

"Very well, then," acknowledged the dark-haired countess, regarding her friend with an appraising eye. "Celestial blue, or perhaps pomona green. Something besides unrelieved black or grey, in any case—not that you don't look disgustingly lovely even in mourning. If I were ten years younger, I should be quite mad with jealousy."

"And I shall be happy to wear either blue or green," promised Lady Fieldhurst, "when the time comes."

"Still, there are other ways you might rebel," Lady Dunnington said, leaning forward confidingly. "Things the Fieldhurst cabal need know nothing about."

"Emily—" Julia shook her head, having a very fair idea of what sort of "things" her friend had in mind. She picked up the teapot to fortify herself against the inevitable harangue, but when she tipped it over to pour, she found herself deprived of even this small comfort. The teapot, it seemed, was empty.

"Begging your pardon, my lady," put in a pretty little housemaid hovering discreetly in the background in case of just such an emergency. "Shall I bring more tea?"

Emily nodded. "Thank you, Dulcie." Once the girl had absented herself from the room, Lady Dunnington returned to the original subject with all the tenacity of a dog with a bone. "What you need, Julia, is a good tumble with a man who knows how to do the thing right."

"Emily, the things you say!" cried Lady Fieldhurst, coloring to the roots of her hair.

"In other words, my dear," Lady Dunnington continued, unfazed, "what you need is a lover."

Julia made a faint noise of protest, having covered this familiar ground more than once.

"As it happens, I am currently in the process of acquiring a lover of my own," Lady Dunnington went on, "so it seems a good time to find one for you while I am about it. I shall give a dinner party, a very select affair with half a dozen or so eligible gentlemen. You may look them over and, at the end of the evening, you have only to drop your handkerchief for the favored one to pick up."

"Emily," said Lady Fieldhurst with some asperity, "I wish you would rid yourself of the notion that every man I meet is clamoring to—to—"

"To bed you?" Lady Dunnington concluded, seeing that words had failed her friend. "But my dear Julia, past experience has taught me that at any given moment, most men *are* clamoring to bed someone, so why should not you be the one to oblige them?"

" 'Most,' perhaps, but not all," murmured Lady Fieldhurst.

If Lady Dunnington heard this qualifier, she made no sign. "Now, I have been giving it a great deal of thought, and I've come up with several promising candidates—"

Dulcie the maid entered at that moment bearing a steaming teapot. Lady Dunnington's plans were suspended temporarily while teacups were refilled with the fresh brew.

"Several candidates, I say, for the position of particular gentleman friend," she concluded, after the requisite additions of sugar and milk had been made.

"You make it sound like an advertisement one might place in the *Times*," Julia said.

"No, my dear, too vulgar by half." Lady Dunnington dismissed this notion out of hand. "Now, back to my dinner party. You will want Lord Rupert Latham there, I have no doubt—"

Lady Fieldhurst held up a restraining hand. "Spare me Lord Rupert, I beg of you! If you will recall, the one time I attempted a tryst with Lord Rupert, we discovered Frederick dead on the floor of my bedchamber. It rather destroyed the mood, to put it mildly."

"Yes, I can see how it might. Truth to tell, Julia, I have had my doubts about you and Lord Rupert. It seems to me that your dithering on the subject—"

"I don't 'dither,' surely!" Lady Fieldhurst objected.

"Very well, call it vacillating. Or shilly-shallying. Or wavering. By whatever name one chooses, your inability to make a decision regarding Lord Rupert suggests that something important is missing there. Still, he will do as a pattern-card by which you may measure the others, since we know that he, at least, *is* clamoring to bed you. Now, besides Lord Rupert, there is Sir Reginald Montague—have a care, Dulcie!" she scolded, as the tray of tea cakes the maid offered tilted dangerously in the direction of Lady Dunnington's lap.

"But I scarcely know Sir Reginald Montague!" Lady Fieldhurst protested.

"My dear Julia, who said anything about you? I have had my eye on Sir Reginald for the last fortnight. Then there is Mr. Brantley-Hughes, of course, and Captain Sir Charles Ormond—we should be taking down the names, lest we forget someone promising. Dulcie, will you fetch paper and ink from my writing desk? There's a good girl. What a pity Town is always so thin of company in November!"

Dulcie crossed the room to the elegant rosewood writing desk and soon returned bearing paper, quill, and inkstand.

"Now, where were we? Mr. Brantley-Hughes—"

"I thought Mr. Brantley-Hughes was *your* lover," Julia pointed out.

" 'Was' being the operative word," Lady Dunnington noted, writing down the name. "He and I are quite exploded, but if you have an interest there, I've no objection to your taking my leavings."

"But Mr. Brantley-Hughes is married!"

"So?"

Julia's expression grew mulish. "I will not force another woman to endure what I went through with Frederick."

Lady Dunnington's brow puckered in a thoughtful frown. "That will narrow the field considerably."

"Then perhaps you had best abandon the notion altogether."

"Never!" Lady Dunnington declared, jabbing the air with her quill for emphasis. "I shall merely have to dig a bit deeper. Captain Sir Charles, as I recall, is a confirmed bachelor, and then there is Lord Dernham, whose wife has been dead these past three years. Who knows? If you've a mind to marry again, you might persuade him to dip his toe once more into the waters of matrimony."

"And once again face the pressure of providing a titled husband with an heir? I thank you, Emily, but no!"

"Forgive me, my dear," said Lady Dunnington with unwonted seriousness. "I wasn't thinking. But you must know that the same barrenness you so deplored in your marriage must be considered an advantage when seeking an attachment of this sort. No danger of a cuckoo in the nest. Now," she added on a brighter note, "what think you of Lord Edwin Braunton? He is the younger son of a duke, and as his elder brother already has two sons, he is under no pressure to marry and ensure the succession—"

"Why, Lord Edwin must be forty-five years old if he is a day!" exclaimed Lady Fieldhurst.

Lady Dunnington's eyebrows rose in surprise. "Forty-five is hardly old, my dear. Dunnington is still virile at fifty—not that it does *me* any good!—and Frederick was past forty when he died, was he not?"

"Forty-one, but still—" Lady Fieldhurst could hardly explain to her friend that her tastes of late had run toward younger men—one young man of four-and-twenty, to be precise, two years younger than her own twenty-six.

"I'm putting Lord Edwin on the list, nevertheless," Emily insisted. "Gentlemen of a certain age know better how to please a lady. But what think you of Mr. Martin Kenney? Not a day over thirty, I'll wager, and he possesses that roguish charm that Irishmen wear so well."

"Long on charm, but short on funds," retorted Lady Field-hurst.

Surprised, Emily looked up from her list. "I had no idea you were hanging out for a rich man. Are things as bad as all that?"

"No, for Frederick did leave me quite comfortably well off," Julia acknowledged, giving credit where it was due. "I have no need for a wealthy lover, but neither do I wish to support him—which would almost certainly be the case with Mr. Kenney."

"I shall add him to the list anyway," said Emily, suiting the word to the deed, "so that you may decide if he would be a sound investment."

It took some time, since Lady Fieldhurst raised some objection to almost every candidate presented for her approval, but at last Lady Dunnington announced herself satisfied. In addition to Sir Reginald, the roll contained the names of five other gentlemen whom Lady Fieldhurst found to be the least offensive of the lot.

"What of the ladies?" asked Lady Fieldhurst when the countess pronounced her list complete.

"I beg your pardon?"

"Who amongst the ladies of our acquaintance do you plan to invite?"

"Why, none of them!" declared Lady Dunnington in some surprise.

"You will not want your numbers to be so uneven," Lady Fieldhurst pointed out.

"My dear Julia, the entire purpose of this dinner is to find you a lover. Why on earth should we want to invite competition? If we were to invite other ladies, I should be obliged to choose the most tedious and haggish females of my acquaintance, the better to appear to advantage by comparison. My reputation as a hostess would be utterly ruined, and *that* I refuse to do, my dear, even for you!"

"It will look very odd, just you and me and half a dozen gentlemen sitting down to dinner," observed the viscountess.

"On the contrary, the gentlemen will be delighted, and the ladies will never know, since they will not be in attendance. Now, when shall we have this dinner? What about Wednesday? Almack's does not host assemblies this late in the year, so there will be no danger of conflicting schedules, and—oh, fiddle!"

"What is the matter?" asked Lady Fieldhurst, indulging the forlorn hope that the countess would be forced to abandon her scheme.

"My butler has gone to Shropshire to visit his sister, and Jack the footman is down with the ague. Did you not wonder why it was Dulcie who opened the door to you? Dunnington did not object to my setting up my own establishment, but he refuses to give me an allowance sufficient to staff it properly! I suppose there is nothing for it but to wait until the butler returns, but as his sister is said to be deathly ill, there is no telling when that might be." She gave a little huff, although whether her annoyance was directed at her estranged husband or the butler's disobliging sister was not immediately apparent.

The maid Dulcie cleared her throat. "Begging your pardon, my lady," she said softly, "but I should have no objection to admitting your guests, if you should have need of me. It might even be more fitting for the sort of party you propose, to have a female at the door."

Mistress scowled at maid. "Impertinent girl! When I need

your advice on hosting a dinner, I shall be sure to ask for it. Oh, but wait," Lady Dunnington said in quite another tone, her eyes growing round. "It might work. Yes, I see it now! We shall give it a classical theme, and our guests shall be greeted at the door by a female in Grecian draperies. Or do I mean Roman? Never mind, I'm sure I have something suitable left over from the Herrington costume ball last spring. It shall be altered to fit you, Dulcie."

"Yes, my lady." Dulcie's doe-eyed gaze dropped to the floor, and she smoothed the skirts of the starched white apron covering her black cotton frock, no doubt wondering what she had let herself in for.

Lady Fieldhurst knew exactly how she felt.

CHAPTER 2

In Which a Dinner Party Devolves into Disaster

Lady Fieldhurst could only hope Lady Dunnington's enthusiasm for the project would fade before the invitations were sent, even though she knew enough of that determined Society matron not to feel optimistic. It was not that Julia had sworn off men, precisely, although in the days following her unexpected release from a miserable marriage she had found the prospect of forming some new intimate connection with a male of the species unwelcome in the extreme. More recently, however, she found herself thinking about the pleasanter aspects of such a connection, at least where one particular man was concerned. Unfortunately, her two attempts at acquiring a lover had ended in disaster, albeit in very different ways. The first time, as she reminded Emily, she and Lord Rupert Latham had got as far as the door of her bedchamber, only to find it blocked by the dead body of Lord Fieldhurst. The second, more recent attempt had taken place in Scotland, where she had offered her favors to the one man in England (if Emily were to be believed) who did not want them. Now, faced with a dinner party in which almost half a dozen specimens would be presented for her approval, she found herself torn between dread of opening herself up once more to rejection and a rather desperate need for confirmation of her own desirability.

In either case, Lady Dunnington's mind was quite made up.

Within three days, half a dozen invitations had gone out, and as many acceptances had been received. Alas, the countess had been obliged to abandon the classical theme she had so eagerly embraced when it was discovered that the housemaid Dulcie looked entirely too fetching in the filmy Grecian drapery her mistress had once worn to the Herrington costume ball; as Lady Dunnington put it, she had no intention of excluding all the ladies of her acquaintance only to be outshone by a serving girl.

And so it was that, when the first guest arrived on the following Wednesday evening, he was announced by a prim housemaid in a starched white apron and frilled mobcap.

"Sir Reginald Montague, my lady," said Dulcie, her eyes meekly downcast.

"Ah, Sir Reginald!" exclaimed Lady Dunnington, gliding forward to meet him with hands held out. "How glad I am that you could come to my poor little party! I believe you are acquainted with Lady Fieldhurst?"

Julia found herself facing a tall, powerfully built gentleman in his mid-forties. His once-golden hair was liberally threaded with silver, and his pale blue eyes were rather cold. His mouth was bracketed with deep lines, which gave the appearance of a perpetual sneer. Taken as a whole, he gave the impression of a fallen angel. She tried to remember what her late husband had said about him. Bad *ton*, Frederick had called him, although he had certainly been in no position to cast stones. Although Sir Reginald's brand of slightly menacing good looks held no attraction for her (she having recently developed a marked preference for a very different type of masculine beauty), she could see how the air of danger that seemed to emanate from him might appeal to some women—Lady Dunnington apparently among their number.

"I am indeed acquainted with Lady Fieldhurst," Sir Reginald

said, turning his attention to Julia. "May I say how pleased I am to see you making public appearances again, my lady? Brighton this past summer was a veritable wasteland without your fair presence."

Thus addressed, Lady Fieldhurst rose from her chair and sketched a curtsy. "Sir Reginald," she murmured, wishing she could recall what Fieldhurst had said about him. Scarcely had she returned to her seat when Dulcie returned with two more gentlemen in tow.

"Lord Dernham and Lord Edwin Braunton, my lady," she announced, then betook herself discreetly from the room.

"Lord Dernham, how pleased I am that you could come," said Lady Dunnington, offering her hand to a soberly clad gentleman in his late thirties with thinning hair and light blue eyes that held a mournful expression. "May I introduce Lady Fieldhurst?"

"My lady." Lord Dernham bowed over her hand. "May I offer my sincerest condolences on your recent loss?"

"And I on yours, my lord." Although Lord Dernham's loss had taken place some three years previously, it appeared he still mourned his dead wife. Lady Fieldhurst mentally crossed him off the list.

"And Lord Edwin! How fortunate we are that you are not off riding with the Quorn or some such thing. Lord Edwin, you must know, is an avid sportsman," Lady Dunnington added as an aside to Julia.

Lady Fieldhurst, offering her hand, recognized him as that uniquely British breed of men, the Spare who has outlived his usefulness. The second son of a duke, Lord Edwin had become superfluous once his elder brother married and begat an heir and a spare of his own. Now, having no greater purpose for his life, he collected a generous allowance from his brother and spent most of it on horses and hounds. While her father, a

18

country squire with no shortage of horses and hounds of his own, might deem Lord Edwin a very good sort of fellow, Lady Fieldhurst saw nothing in him to tempt her. He too was crossed off her list.

"Lord Dernham, Lord Edwin," Emily said, gesturing toward Sir Reginald, "I trust you are acquainted with Sir Reginald Montague?"

The effect of this introduction was immediate. Both newcomers stiffened, their eyes narrowing as they made the briefest of nods in Sir Reginald's direction.

"Sir Reginald and I are old—acquaintances," Lord Edwin said, his jaw clenched.

"Likewise," said Lord Dernham, then turned abruptly away from Sir Reginald and began speaking with surprising animation to Lord Edwin.

"Lord Rupert Latham," announced Dulcie, returning with Lady Fieldhurst's longtime suitor at her heels.

Lord Rupert said all that was proper to his hostess, then took Julia's hand and raised it to his lips. "My dear Julia, I had no notion you had yet returned from Scotland! It was really too cruel of you to let me languish in ignorance."

"Have you been languishing for me, Rupert?" asked Julia *sotto voce*. "If so, I fear you have been wasting your time."

"Have I? I wonder. If half of what Lady Dunnington tells me about this evening's entertainment is true—" He cast a critical eye over his fellow guests. "Fortunately, I do not see that the present competition is insurmountable."

"Lord Rupert," Emily put in, "are you acquainted with Sir Reginald Montague?"

"Indeed I am. Your servant, sir." While no fault could be found with Lord Rupert's manners, his voice had cooled considerably. Before Lady Fieldhurst had time to wonder at it, however, Dulcie appeared with the last of the guests.

"Captain Sir Charles Ormond, my lady, and Mr. Martin Kenney."

It would have been hard to imagine two more different gentlemen than the pair now paying their respects to their hostess. Captain Sir Charles, dashing in the scarlet coat and gold lace of a Hussar regiment, clicked his heels and swept a bow with military precision. Mr. Kenney, on the other hand, wore a blue coat of slightly outdated design that showed unmistakable signs of wear at the elbows, and his linen (as well as one could judge such things by candlelight) appeared somewhat yellowed. As if to compensate for his sartorial shortcomings, he took Lady Dunnington's hand and lifted it to his lips with an air of exaggerated gallantry.

Having been presented to Lady Fieldhurst (and giving her such appraising looks that Julia wondered just how much of the purpose of tonight's entertainment Lady Dunnington had revealed to them), the new arrivals were then made known to the other gentlemen in attendance.

"Mr. Kenney," Sir Reginald said, addressing the shabbily dressed Irishman, "your absence at Brooks's has been most conspicuous. The tables are not the same without you."

Mr. Kenney's jaw clenched, but he said nothing, and Lord Edwin hurried to fill the uncomfortable silence.

"The play there has been dam—deuced flat lately, anyway," he told the Irishman. "You haven't missed much."

"And Captain," Sir Reginald nodded in his direction, but addressed his speech to the company at large. "You would scarcely credit it, but Captain Sir Charles and I once served in the same regiment. But I believe you had yet to achieve your captaincy at that point, sir."

"I was a mere second lieutenant at the time," the captain conceded with a nod.

"I sometimes wonder what rank I might have achieved, had I

20

not been obliged to sell out when my father died," Sir Reginald continued.

"A sad day for the Army, when you were allowed to sell out," the captain noted.

His words seemed flattering enough, but Lady Fieldhurst had the distinct impression that no compliment to Sir Reginald was intended. Indeed, it seemed to her there was another level of meaning passing between the two men that quite eluded the rest of the company. She cast a speaking look at Lady Dunnington, but the countess seemed oblivious to the undercurrents swirling about the room, or was so taken with her latest paramour that she simply didn't care if Sir Reginald were heartily disliked by his fellow men. Lady Fieldhurst became more than ever convinced that this dinner was a mistake, and breathed a sigh of relief when the gong sounded. Now that the evening had officially commenced, she could count the minutes until she and Emily could withdraw and abandon the men to their port and cigars. That the gentlemen would take their leave at the first opportunity she did not doubt, since they obviously found the presence of one of their fellow guests so objectionable.

"We will not stand upon ceremony, since our numbers are so uneven," Lady Dunnington declared, thus eliminating the need for them to pair off and parade into the dining room two by two, like animals boarding Noah's ark.

But however casual their procession to the dining room, it soon appeared that the seating arrangements had been painstakingly plotted. As hostess, Lady Dunnington naturally sat at one end of the table. She had placed Sir Reginald at the opposite end, apparently designating him as *de facto* host. As for Lady Fieldhurst, she found herself halfway down the table, flanked by potential suitors on either side and facing three more across the table. Surrounded on all sides, Julia discovered five of the six gentlemen in attendance regarding her with expressions ranging from admiration to speculation to expectation, and wondered anew just what Emily had told them regarding the nature of this particular gathering. She cast a glance of desperate appeal at her hostess, who lost no time in throwing her to the wolves.

"Before you gentlemen arrived, Lady Fieldhurst was telling me about her recent sojourn in Scotland," she addressed the company. "Pray continue, Julia! What did you find to amuse you in Scotland?"

"It was not for amusement that I travelled there," Julia corrected her hastily. "I was merely acting as chaperone to George Bertram's—Lord Fieldhurst's, I should say—three sons. His three sons by Caroline Deering Bertram, that is."

"Yes, yes, a bad business, that." Lord Edwin shook his head in silent sympathy with the boys. "Deuced hard on a bast—er, illegitimate child."

"And how much harder when one of the children in question supposed himself to be second in line to a viscountcy," remarked Lord Dernham.

"Ah well, at least their father is trying to do right by them." Lord Edwin's gaze slewed to the end of the table where Sir Reginald sat addressing himself to a thick slice of roast beef. "Would that all men were so ready to take responsibility for their actions."

"What?" demanded Sir Reginald. "Would you condemn a man to pay through the nose for the rest of his life, just because some chit can't keep her skirts down?"

Since Caroline Bertram had had every reason to suppose herself legally married to George, this charge could hardly be laid at her door. Once more, Julia was convinced that there were other things being said than mere words would suggest.

Lord Rupert, seated at her left, cleared his throat. "Really, Sir Reginald, this is hardly a suitable topic of conversation when there are ladies present." He turned toward Julia. "I, for one, would like to hear more of her ladyship's travels. Tell me, my lady, how did you find Scotland?"

Lady Fieldhurst hardly knew whether to be grateful for the change of subject or chagrined to be once again the cynosure of all eyes. "The weather was quite pleasant right up until the day we departed for England," she recalled. "Most unseasonably warm for so late in the year."

"Oh, bother the weather!" declared Lady Dunnington impatiently. "What did you find to do there? Did you finally escape Frederick's shadow by going so far north that no one would know you, and dancing all night in the arms of a gallant laird?"

This was actually much too close to the truth for Lady Fieldhurst's comfort, although the only dancing she had done was on the darkened terrace of a country house, in the arms of a man whom not one of those seated at the table would receive socially. "As I am still in mourning, it would be most unseemly of me to dance," she said with perfect, if incomplete, truth. "The boys and I did enjoy long walks along the seashore, however, and Harold, the eldest, conceived the fixed intention of joining the Royal Navy. I believe he is to report aboard the *Dauntless* as a midshipman in a matter of weeks."

"I confess to being rather partial to the Army myself," put in Captain Sir Charles, to a chorus of chuckles, "but the military is certainly a good place for any young man who finds himself in young Mr. Bertram's situation. I wish him well, and I hope he will be fortunate in his commanding officer." Again the sidelong glance at Sir Reginald at the end of the table.

"I fear the only seaside I have ever seen is that at Brighton," said Lady Dunnington.

"Why, Emily, you surprise me," exclaimed Lady Fieldhurst. "Have you indeed seen the seaside at Brighton? I should have thought you spent all your time there socializing at the Royal Pavilion."

All the gentlemen enjoyed a hearty laugh at the countess's expense, and Lady Fieldhurst felt a certain degree of satisfaction in even this modest revenge.

"Guilty as charged," confessed Lady Dunnington cheerfully, throwing up her hands in mock surrender. "I confess, I prefer congenial company to the beauties of nature. Fortunately, Brighton offers both."

"And then there is the running of the Brighton Cup, as well," put in Mr. Kenney. "I was pleased to pocket a tidy sum this August past, when my horse finished first."

"Do you own a racehorse, Mr. Kenney?" asked Sir Reginald, his voice filled with admiration. "I'd no idea your pockets were so deep."

Mr. Kenney flushed a dull red, which clashed with his auburn hair. "I don't own a racehorse, no, but I am accounted to be an excellent judge of horseflesh."

"Whatever keeps one solvent, I suppose," said Sir Reginald with a shrug. "For myself, I prefer a more active form of racing. Next year I hope to shave a few seconds off Prinny's London-to-Brighton time. I almost had it several years ago, but just as the goal was in sight, I came up behind a dashed great berline taking up most of the road. I tried to pass it, but came to grief."

"Why?" asked Emily. "What happened?"

Sir Reginald shook his head sadly. "To make a long story short, my racing curricle ended up as a pile of splinters, and one of my horses had to be put down."

"How fortunate that you were uninjured!" exclaimed the countess.

"Yes, I wonder if the passengers in the berline were so lucky?" put in Lord Dernham tightly.

"If they were not, perhaps it will teach them not to tie up

traffic on one of the busiest thoroughfares in Sussex," suggested Sir Reginald smoothly.

Anger flashed in Lord Dernham's usually mild blue eyes, but anything he might have said was cut short by the entrance of Dulcie, hands twisting the skirt of her apron in agitation.

"Begging your pardon, my lady," she said, addressing herself to Lady Dunnington, "but my Lord Dunnington is here, and insists upon seeing you."

"Oh, bother!" exclaimed the countess. "Tell him I am entertaining at present, and he must go away."

"I—I tried, ma'am, but he refuses to leave."

Lady Dunnington gave a little huff of annoyance. "Very well, I suppose I shall have to see him."

"Shall I show him in, my lady?"

"By no means! Shove him into the drawing room, and tell him I shall be there directly."

"Yes, ma'am." Dulcie bobbed a curtsy and left the room to carry out her mistress's orders.

"It seems my presence is required by my lord and master," Lady Dunnington informed the group, quite unnecessarily, as they had heard every word of the exchange. "I shall return shortly. Don't any of you say anything interesting in my absence!"

With a brilliant smile and a gleam in her eye that did not bode well for Lord Dunnington, she rose from the table and absented herself from the room.

A rather awkward silence descended on those seated at the table, broken at last by Mr. Kenney.

"I don't know about the rest of you," he said with a grin, "but I should put my money on her ladyship to carry the day."

"Let us hope, then, that your understanding of women is as felicitous as your knowledge of horseflesh," answered Sir Reginald, an observation that had the unhappy effect of causing silence to descend once more on the little group.

As the drawing room was adjacent to the dining room, it was perhaps inevitable that in a very short time the sound of raised voices might be heard issuing from that direction.

"You cannot dictate to me, Dunnington," Emily declared. "I won't have it!"

"I can, and I will!" her husband retorted.

Lady Fieldhurst smiled much too brightly and addressed Sir Reginald. "Tell me, Sir Reginald," she said with sufficient volume to mask the sounds of altercation in the next room, "did I not see an announcement in the *Morning Post* that there will soon be wedding bells pealing in the Montague household?"

"Aye, my eldest daughter, Caroline," said Sir Reginald, answering in kind. "The wedding will be three weeks hence at St. George's, Hanover Square. That's all my wife and daughters can speak of these days. Lady Dunnington's dinner invitation was a godsend, as it allowed me to escape from talk of orange blossoms and white satin, if only for one night."

"I'm pleased to see that you're sending your daughter off in style, at any rate," remarked Lord Edwin, regarding Sir Reginald with lowered brows. "I had not supposed you valued matrimony so highly."

"When entered into with mutual affection and respect, there is no happier state," put in the bereaved Lord Dernham.

Alas, this high-minded statement was promptly given the lie by the not-so-blissfully wedded couple in the drawing room.

"I have turned a blind eye in the past, Emily, but this I will not tolerate!"

"You, sir, have nothing to say to the matter!"

"On the contrary, madam, you will find I have a great deal to say—and do, if it comes to that. Mark my words, I will do whatever it takes to put a stop to this!"

"Very well, Dunnington—you may do your worst! Now, if

you will excuse me, I am neglecting my guests."

When the countess returned to the room only moments later, her color high and her eyes sparkling dangerously, she found her guests apparently deep in concentration on their own plates, eating with such enthusiasm that one might have supposed they were partaking of their first meal in a fortnight.

"No one is going to take your plate away, so you might as well slow down," she remarked, returning to her seat with a flounce. "A tiresome misunderstanding, nothing more. Now we may all be easy again!"

Unfortunately, no one had been easy before, and they were even less so now. After fifteen minutes that seemed more like two hours, Emily laid aside her linen serviette and rose from the table. "Shall we leave the gentlemen to their port, Julia? Sir Reginald, I shall leave you to pour."

The gentlemen stood respectfully as Julia would have followed Emily, but Lord Dernham raised a hand as if to hold the ladies back. "Thank you, my lady, but no port for me. I must be getting back home."

"Likewise," said Mr. Kenney.

Lord Edwin nodded. "My physician has advised me to cut back—nothing stronger than sherry after nine o'clock, meddlesome old busybody," he said, although his tone suggested gratitude rather than censure.

"I too must take my leave, as my regiment will be on review in the morning," Captain Sir Charles put in.

"I must be on my way as well," said Lord Rupert. "Your servant, Lady Dunnington. And yours, my dear," he added, taking Julia's hand with a proprietary air and raising it to his lips.

"Poor Sir Reginald!" exclaimed Lady Dunnington. "Are they all abandoning you?"

All five gentlemen hastily demurred with varying degrees of insincerity. Lady Dunnington rang for Dulcie, and there fol-

lowed several minutes of civilized confusion as carriages were
sent for and coats, hats, and gloves fetched. At last only the
ladies and Sir Reginald remained.

"I should hate to think of your drinking alone," Lady Dunnington told him. "Will you not take your port in the drawing
room with us?"

"I thank you, my lady, but I must be pushing off as well,"
said Sir Reginald, bowing over her hand. "I appreciate your
kind invitation, and hope to see you again under less crowded
circumstances." He glanced over Emily's shoulder at Lady
Fieldhurst, his cold eyes clearly wishing her at the devil.

"Very well, Sir Reginald," agreed Emily, reclaiming her hand
with obvious reluctance. "I shall look forward to it."

She reached for the bell pull to summon Dulcie, but Sir Reginald laid a restraining hand on her arm. "No, no, never mind
fetching your maid. I'll show myself out." He leaned nearer and
added, "I daresay I shall soon know the house very well indeed.
I might as well start learning it now."

Lady Dunnington said nothing to correct this assumption,
but smiled coyly as he took his leave of Lady Fieldhurst and
departed.

"Well!" Emily exclaimed brightly, turning to face Lady
Fieldhurst. "I thought that went rather splendidly, didn't you?"

Lady Fieldhurst stared at her friend in shocked disbelief.
There were many words she herself might have chosen to
describe the evening, but "splendid" was not one of them. "Emily, are you quite certain as to Sir Reginald's character? It
seemed to me that most of the gentlemen disliked him exces-
sively. Do you not think perhaps you ought to find out why,
before you enter into a more intimate association with him?"

Lady Dunnington dismissed her concerns with a wave of one
be-ringed hand. "The other men are merely jealous, my dear,
nothing more. Sir Reginald possesses that air of danger that all

women find irresistible."

Julia chose to disagree. "I find him easy enough to resist."

"Yes, but you have grown so nice in your requirements of late, I doubt the man exists who could please you."

"Oh, he exists," Lady Fieldhurst said softly, but if the countess heard, she took no notice.

"Now, I was thinking—"

But Lady Dunnington's thoughts were to remain unvoiced, for at that moment the quiet of the house was disrupted by a loud report coming from the direction of the front hall. Both ladies stared at each other in mutual consternation, then ran as one to the hall. The front door stood half open to the cold November night, but the room's sole occupant was undisturbed by the chilly weather.

For Sir Reginald Montague lay sprawled face down on the marble tiled floor in a pool of blood.

CHAPTER 3

Which Reveals a Rather Awkward State of Affairs

"Sir Reginald!" cried Lady Dunnington, kneeling beside him and shaking him by the shoulder in a futile attempt to rouse him.

Gingerly stepping around the body, Lady Fieldhurst crossed the hall to the front door and walked out onto the portico. She looked both right and left, but saw no sign of anyone; whoever had shot Sir Reginald had disappeared into the night.

"Emily?"

She stepped back inside and noted that the noise had roused the entire household. The service door to the servants' domain below stairs was open and Dulcie stood framed in the aperture, eyes wide and hands shaking as she clutched the door frame for support. Behind her, the stout cook dried her hands briskly on her apron, her breathing ragged from the exertion of climbing the stairs so quickly. On the formal staircase leading to the upper floor, Lady Dunnington's abigail leaned over the banister, while a bleary-eyed footman clad in a nightshirt and breeches blew his nose vociferously into a large handkerchief.

"Emily," Lady Fieldhurst said again, "is he—?"

Lady Dunnington had by this time ceased shaking Sir Reginald by the shoulder and progressed to striking him smartly on the cheek with the palm of her hand, but with as little effect.

"Yes," she said unsteadily. "Yes, I think he is."

Dulcie sobbed loudly at this pronouncement, and Emily looked up, seeing for the first time the servants gathered around. "Be quiet, silly girl! What was Sir Reginald to you, anyway? All of you, go on about your business. Not you, Jack," she said to the footman, who was turning to go back up the stairs to his attic bedroom. "Go and get dressed. I am sorry to send you out in this weather when you are ill, but I fear I shall need you to deliver a message."

Once the crowd was dispersed, Lady Fieldhurst looked down at the countess, still on her knees beside the body of the man who would never be her lover. "What—what sort of message do you have in mind, Emily?" she asked, very much afraid she already knew the answer.

"We must send to Bow Street," Lady Dunnington said resolutely as she rose awkwardly to her feet. "What was the name of that Runner who investigated Frederick's murder? Something that started with a 'P,' was it not?"

"No!" cried Lady Fieldhurst, turning quite pale. "Not him!"

The countess blinked at her friend's vehemence. "Why not?"

"We need someone with more experience," Julia said desperately. "Mr. Pickett is much too young to be trusted with a case like this."

"Pickett!" exclaimed Emily. "That's the name! I knew it was something with a 'P.' "

"But Emily, you yourself called him the man-child of Bow Street!"

"Why, so I did, but he must know what he is about, in spite of his lack of years. After all, he contrived to clear you of any involvement in Frederick's death."

"He was able to clear me of any involvement in Frederick's death because I was innocent," Lady Fieldhurst pointed out in some indignation.

"Very true, my dear, but would a jury have seen it that way, had you been obliged to stand trial? I think not! No, I shall send Jack to Bow Street to ask for your Mr. Pickett."

"He isn't mine," Julia murmured, then, as the countess reached for the bell pull, "Emily, no! Wait!"

"It may have escaped your notice, Julia," said Lady Dunnington with some asperity, "but there is a dead man in my house. I should like to fetch a Runner here without further ado."

Lady Fieldhurst sighed. "I see I shall be forced to tell you. You asked me what had happened in Scotland. I fear I made rather a fool of myself there."

"I feel for you, Julia, truly I do, and while I am pleased you have finally decided to confide in me, this is surely not the time—"

"No, no, hear me out, I beg you! I told you George's sons were there. What I did not tell you was that they found a woman lying unconscious on the beach. We sent to a nearby manor for assistance, and it turned out that the woman bore a striking resemblance to the long-lost daughter of the house. As the woman herself could tell them nothing, the family decided to send to London for a Bow Street Runner to investigate."

Lady Dunnington raised a hand to forestall her. "Do not tell me, let me guess. The Runner turned out to be your Mr. Pickett."

"He isn't mine," Julia said again. "But since I was there when the woman was found, I was obliged to work rather closely with him, and—well—"

"Yes?" prompted the countess, glancing at Sir Reginald's body as if she feared it might decompose before Lady Fieldhurst reached the end of her tale. " 'Well' what?"

She darted a quick glance around the hall to ensure that none of the servants remained within earshot. She saw no one, but lowered her voice nonetheless. "I recalled that you had been urging me to take a lover, so on the day Mr. Pickett was to return to England, I—I asked him."

By this time Lady Dunnington's eyes were as wide as saucers. "And?"

"He turned me down," she concluded miserably.

"And no wonder! You *asked* him? Julia, you shouldn't have *asked;* you should have *seduced* the boy!"

"Hardly a boy, Emily," Lady Fieldhurst protested. "He is four-and-twenty."

"I see now why you considered poor Lord Edwin and his forty-five years too old," the countess remarked. "But Sir Reginald has been shot, and in my house at that, so I must do all I can to see that his killer is found. Therefore, I am sending to Bow Street for your *enfant prodige.* I am sorry if you are made to feel uncomfortable, but perhaps it is no more than you deserve for bungling the thing so badly. You realize, do you not, that were the situation reversed and *he* made *you* such an offer, it would be considered an indecent proposition?" With that Parthian shot, she gave the bell pull a tug.

With a sinking feeling in the pit of her stomach, Julia realized her friend was right. Of course, the situation would never have been reversed, for Mr. Pickett was too—too—yes, too *gentlemanly,* in spite of his humble status, to have made such an offer, even if it had occurred to him to do so.

So what did that make her?

She had meant no disrespect. She only knew she wanted *more:* more than a stolen kiss or two, and not only when there was a dead body somewhere in the vicinity to throw them together. So she had asked. And in the process, she had destroyed a budding friendship that had come to be precious to her for reasons she could not quite comprehend, much less explain.

★ ★ ★ ★ ★

"Thank God that's done," grumbled Mr. Patrick Colquhoun, magistrate of the Bow Street Public Office, as he signed his name with a flourish and laid aside his quill. "I've never seen such a docket in all my years as a magistrate. Dinner will be cold by now, and my poor Janet ready to send out a search party."

"Things did rather pile up while we were in Scotland, sir," agreed John Pickett, a very tall young man with curling brown hair worn unfashionably long and tied at the nape of his neck in a queue.

"Ah well, the price of a holiday, I suppose." The magistrate bent a keen eye on his young protégé. "Speaking of which, I never did hear how that little business of yours came out. What did her ladyship have to say?"

Pickett's gaze slid away to fasten on the wooden railing that separated the magistrate's raised bench from the rest of the room. "I—I haven't told her yet, sir."

Mr. Colquhoun's bushy white brows rose. Pickett knew his magistrate and mentor expected an explanation, but he had none to give. How did one tell a lady that, through some quirk of Scottish law, she was accidentally married to him? *It's a funny thing, my lady, but while I quite sympathize with your desire to escape to Scotland under an assumed name, and I am honored to have lent my name to the cause, it is my duty to inform you that you are now wed to a thief-taker with no more than twenty-five shillings a week on which to support you.* It was impossible.

And yet that was not the worst of it. For the past three weeks he had held close to his heart the knowledge that he was secretly married to the Viscountess Fieldhurst—so secretly, in fact, that his "wife" did not even know of it. But once her ladyship was informed of her newly wedded state, the process of obtaining an annulment would begin. The illusion that he might be married to Lady Fieldhurst, whom he had loved from the moment of their first meeting over her husband's dead body, was only that—an illusion—which must dissolve in the face of reality.

"There's no time like the present, my lad," the magistrate pointed out, not ungently. "It's not likely to grow easier with delay."

Pickett glanced at the clock mounted on the wall above the magistrate's bench. "It's very late, sir, past nine o'clock. I should hate to interrupt her ladyship at this hour."

"They keep late hours amongst the fashionable set. Recall, if you will, that they don't have to get up early to go to work like the rest of us."

While Pickett struggled for an excuse to further postpone the inevitable, the door opened, admitting a gust of wind that ruffled the papers on Mr. Colquhoun's desk. Carried in on this wind was a footman whose scarlet livery was scarcely redder than his nose, which he dabbed at frequently with a large handkerchief. Mr. William Foote, at thirty-five years of age the unofficial head of the night patrol, came forward to meet him.

"Nasty weather to be out and about in," the senior Runner observed. "What can we do for you?"

"There's a man been shot at Lady Dunnington's house in Audley Street," said the footman, gasping for breath. "Sir Reginald Montague. He's dead, sir. I was told to—"

"Lady Dunnington, you say?" said Pickett, recalling the dark-haired, tart-tongued countess who had made more than one unflattering observation regarding his age, or lack thereof. "I know her."

"Yes, Mr. Pickett, we're well aware that you're thick as inkle-weavers with half the aristocracy," the senior Runner said impatiently, then turned his attention back to the footman. "Audley Street, you say? I'll be right there."

The footman glanced uncertainly from one Runner to the

other. "I was told to ask for Mr. Pickett."

Mr. Foote made a derisive noise in the back of his throat. "It's true that Mr. Pickett has succeeded in achieving a certain notoriety in a very short time, but—"

"A moment please, Mr. Foote." Mr. Colquhoun never raised his voice, but he had the full attention of one footman and two Bow Street Runners nevertheless. "I believe Mr. Pickett was going to pay a call in Mayfair in any case, were you not?" Seeing Pickett agree—for what choice did he have?—the magistrate turned back to Foote. "Since he is already going in that direction, and is acquainted with one of the principals involved, let him handle this one. You may report to me in the morning, Mr. Pickett."

"Yes, sir," said Pickett, and followed the footman out into the cold November night. He sighed. With any luck, the case would prove so complex that by the time he left Audley Street, Mr. Colquhoun would agree it was too late to call on Lady Fieldhurst even by Society's standards.

CHAPTER 4

In Which a Most Uncomfortable Reunion Takes Place

The loud blowing of his nose announced the footman's return to Audley Street. Lady Dunnington clutched Lady Fieldhurst's arm, her fingers gripping like talons even through the fine kid of her long white glove.

"Julia! Not one word about Dunnington being here tonight, on your honor!"

Before Lady Fieldhurst could agree to this demand, let alone question it, the footman appeared in the doorway of the drawing room, where the two ladies had retreated to fortify themselves with sherry while they awaited Bow Street's arrival.

"Mr. Pickett from Bow Street, my lady," the footman said, and stepped aside to allow Pickett to enter.

Lady Fieldhurst stood abruptly, like a marionette jerked upright on strings, and moved to the far side of the room. She had wondered if she would ever see him again; she had certainly not expected to come face to face with him only weeks after his rejection of her, and her subsequent removal from Scotland. Now, filled with shame at the memory, she could not look him in the face, but stood with her back to him, hugging her arms to herself and drinking in the sight of him afforded by his reflection in the window.

"Mr. Pickett!" Lady Dunnington drained her glass in a single gulp, then set it aside and came forward to meet him. "I daresay

37

you've seen poor Sir Reginald in the hall—you could hardly miss him, for you practically had to step over him to reach the drawing room. Jack, go down to the kitchen and tell Cook to give you a drop of brandy with lemon to chase away the chill, and then take yourself off to bed. Really, Mr. Pickett, I can't imagine how it happened. One minute we were enjoying a perfectly lovely dinner, Lady Fieldhurst and I and half a dozen gentlemen of our acquaintance—she was going to choose one of them to be her lover, you know—"

Pickett glanced at Lady Fieldhurst. What little he could see of her face was beetroot red.

"—And the next thing I knew, there was a gunshot, and Sir Reginald was lying dead on the floor."

"Thank you, your ladyship," said Pickett. "I shall have some questions for you and Lady Fieldhurst shortly, but first I should like to examine the body."

Lady Dunnington nodded. "Of course. Must I show it to you, or can you find your own way?"

"I'm afraid I must ask you to come with me, your ladyship. You might have information that could prove useful."

"But I don't know anything," protested the countess. "Whoever shot poor Sir Reginald was long gone in the time it took Julia and me to reach the hall."

Nevertheless, she led the way back to the hall, where Sir Reginald still lay sprawled upon the floor. Pickett knelt beside the body.

"Was he in this position when you found him, or has he been moved at all?"

Lady Dunnington frowned, trying to recreate the scene in her memory. "I daresay I may have moved him some. I do recall shaking him by the shoulder. I didn't yet realize that he was dead."

"Quite understandable, your ladyship."

Pickett pushed on Sir Reginald's shoulder until the body fell over onto its back. The brocade waistcoat that Sir Reginald had worn was heavily stained with blood, and in the center was a small round hole that had never been put there by his tailor. A thin trail of blood had leaked from his mouth and dried on his chin. His light blue eyes were open wide and wore a startled expression, as if he could not believe such a thing could have happened to him. He had clearly been shot at close range, but glancing around, Pickett saw no sign of a firearm.

"The coroner will have to be sent for as a matter of routine," Pickett said over his shoulder to Lady Dunnington, "but it's quite obvious how he died."

He received no reply but an unintelligible sound. Looking up from his examination of the body, he saw that Lady Dunnington had retired to the nearest corner, where she was engaged in depositing her dinner into a potted plant.

"Shall I fetch someone to assist you, your ladyship?" he asked, feeling rather out of his element. "Lady Fieldhurst, perhaps, or your maid?"

"No, no, I shall be fine," came her muffled reply. "Still, I should be grateful if you could question Julia first, and give me a moment to compose myself."

Pickett needed no urging to seek out Lady Fieldhurst, so he agreed to this suggestion and would have returned to the drawing room at once, had not Lady Dunnington called him back.

"Before you go, Mr. Pickett, there is one thing you should know," said the countess. Her voice was stronger now, and she somehow managed to convey an air of dignity in spite of the fact that she was on her knees before a rather pungent potted plant. "Julia told me something of what happened in Scotland. I have seen her break her heart over a rich man, and I do not intend to watch her break it again over a poor one."

He was rather taken aback by her implication that he possessed the power to break Lady Fieldhurst's heart, much less the desire to do so. "Lady Dunnington," he said with some asperity, "let me remind you that there is a dead man in your house, almost certainly murdered in cold blood by one of your acquaintances. Surely you have more pressing matters to concern yourself with than who is—is—"

"Who is warming Julia's bed?" concluded the countess, never one to mince words. "As you point out, Mr. Pickett, Sir Reginald is beyond any help I might render him. Lady Fieldhurst, however, is quite another matter," she added with a backward glance toward the drawing room where the viscountess waited.

Pickett sighed. "I assure you, your ladyship, the last thing I should want to do is cause Lady Fieldhurst pain."

She nodded. "Just so we understand each other."

With this warning—or was it a threat?—ringing in his ears, he returned to the drawing room. He found his quarry standing exactly where he had left her, as if she had been turned to stone. He wanted to set her at ease, but he had no idea what to say— not after the way they had parted in Scotland, and certainly not in view of the disclosures that had yet to be made. And so they stood there like strangers, he and the woman who was and yet was not his wife.

"My lady," he began, "I should like to ask you a few questions, if you please."

She nodded. "Yes, of course." She returned to her chair before the fire, but her eyes remained fixed on the floor.

He took a deep breath. "I realize I have offended you, my lady, but will you not at least look at me?"

She did so, although he recognized the effort it cost her. He thought there were shadows under her eyes, and that they held a hunted expression. "Yes, Mr. Pickett? What did you wish to ask?"

He withdrew his occurrence book and a pencil from the

inside pocket of his coat. "You can begin by telling me about the people who were in attendance tonight. I believe Lady Dunnington said she was hosting a dinner?"

The viscountess colored rosily, apparently recalling exactly what her friend had said about the purpose of that dinner. "Besides Sir Reginald, there was Lord Rupert Latham—I daresay you will remember him—Captain Sir Charles Ormond, Lord Dernham, Lord Edwin Braunton, and Mr. Martin Kenney. And Lady Dunnington and myself, of course."

"My lady—" he paused, not quite certain how to frame the request he felt compelled to make. "My lady, I must ask you—I hope you will oblige me by not making a decision regarding any one of these gentlemen as a potential lover until the investigation is complete."

She stiffened. "I believe, Mr. Pickett, that you have forfeited any right to address me on that particular subject."

Pickett flushed. "I am speaking merely as a keeper of the King's peace, my lady. In that capacity, I would caution any female against becoming intimate with a man who might be a murderer."

Except, of course, that it was more than that, much more. Pickett wondered wistfully if there was any way to prove a conspiracy of five, and thus hang the lot of them. Pushing aside this rather bloodthirsty train of thought, he decided he would probably never have a better opportunity to broach a very personal subject indeed.

"However," he began, choosing his words with care. "There is another matter, a personal one, on which I must speak with you privately. This is neither the time nor the place, but I will be in Mayfair again tomorrow for the purpose of interviewing the men who attended Lady Dunnington's dinner party. I should like to call on you while I am in the area, and to speak to you alone, if I may."

She hesitated, and for a moment he feared she would refuse him.

"Very well, Mr. Pickett," she said at last. "If you will call at two o'clock, you may be sure of finding me at home. I shall instruct Rogers to deny me to any other visitors."

"Thank you, my lady. Now," he added briskly, returning to the matter at hand, "Where were you when you heard the gunshot?"

"Lady Dunnington and I were still in the dining room."

"And the men?"

She shrugged. "They had already left."

His pencil stilled, and he looked up from his notebook. "What, all of them?"

"Yes. Dinner was finished, and Lady Dunnington and I were just withdrawing to leave the gentlemen to their port. One by one, each of the gentlemen—all except Sir Reginald, that is—gave some reason he could not stay, and they all took their leave."

"And this was unusual? Forgive me, my lady, but I have never been to a Society dinner, and so have no idea how they work."

"Yes, I see. Lady Dunnington received her guests in the drawing room—this room, as it happens—and once everyone was accounted for, we engaged in idle conversation until the dinner gong sounded. Then we all went into the dining room. At the end of the meal all the ladies—in this case that would be Lady Dunnington and myself—usually retreat to the drawing room while the gentlemen remain at the table drinking port and perhaps taking snuff."

"Except in this case they didn't—the gentlemen, I mean."

"Exactly." She hesitated, as if wondering what—or perhaps how much—to say. "Mr. Pickett, Lady Dunnington may say it was a lovely dinner, but I can assure you it was not!"

"I can imagine it was most awkward for you," he said, fighting back an entirely unprofessional sense of elation that Lady Fieldhurst had found the company less than enthralling.

"No, not that—well, yes, it was, but not *only* that."

She leaned nearer and met his gaze unashamedly now; it was almost as if the earlier awkwardness had vanished. Not quite, but almost. At any rate, it was a start.

"Some of the conversation," she continued, "had, I don't know, undercurrents, I suppose you could say—as if there was a great deal being said that *wasn't* being said, if you take my meaning."

"I think so," said Pickett, recalling certain barbed comments made by Mr. Foote that very evening. Yes, it was possible to convey a great deal within the most innocuous of phrases. "And would you say Sir Reginald was the target of these remarks?"

"They were certainly aimed at him, although for what purpose I cannot begin to guess. In any case, he appeared unfazed by them."

"That must have been frustrating for the gentlemen trying to provoke him."

"I suppose so. In fact, I had the distinct impression that the other gentlemen left immediately after dinner because they had no desire to remain any longer in Sir Reginald's company."

"Interesting," remarked Pickett, making a notation in his occurrence book. "Can you remember exactly what was said?"

She lifted her hands in a gesture of helplessness. "I fear the gunshot and everything that followed has driven most of it from my head."

"I can see how it would. But anything at all that you can remember might prove useful."

Her forehead puckered in concentration. "As I recall, there was some discussion regarding the marriage of Sir Reginald's daughter. There were also more than a few questions regarding my recent journey to Scotland. I did not feel your investigations there were mine to tell, so I fear I threw poor Harold and his brothers to the wolves for the sake of conversation. This led, not unnaturally, to some talk about the plight of illegitimate children, until someone—I think it may have been Rupert— pointed out that the subject was unfit for mixed company. There was a brief exchange of military reminiscences between Sir Reginald and Captain Sir Charles, who used to serve under him. And then the conversation turned to the subject of travel— Scotland, as I said, and then Brighton."

Seeing Pickett taking down her words, she felt compelled to add, "Of course, none of this is in its proper order. Most of it was merely idle chatter of the kind that may be heard at any dinner party—you know what I mean."

In fact, Pickett did *not* know, never having attended a dinner party before, but he was not about to draw her attention to the wide chasm between their respective stations.

"But wait!" exclaimed Lady Fieldhurst as a new thought occurred to her. "On the subject of Brighton, I believe there was some mention of the Brighton Cup—the horse race, you know, in which Mr. Kenney had apparently won a tidy sum—and of Sir Reginald's attempt at besting the Prince of Wales's time in a curricle race either to or from London. I remember that particularly, because Lord Dernham's wife and several members of her family were killed when a racing curricle collided with the carriage in which they were riding. That was three years ago, and while I never heard all the details, I had the impression that Sir Reginald may have been involved in some way. I do know Frederick used to call him a loose fish, but I daresay his opinion hardly counts as evidence."

"Since the late Lord Fieldhurst was fair and far off in his valuation of women, I should be cautious about setting too much store by his word where men were concerned," muttered Pickett.

Lady Fieldhurst nodded. "You are thinking of his mistress, who turned out to be a killer."

"Actually, I was thinking of his wife, who turned out to be a peach. You may be sure I would—" He broke off abruptly. *You may be sure I would be a better husband to you than he was, if only you would be willing to let this absurd marriage stand. What's that, my lady? Oh, didn't I tell you? It seems we are married.* Yes, that would set the cat amongst the pigeons.

"You would what, Mr. Pickett?"

He shook his head. "Nothing. But you were telling me about the conversation at dinner. Was anything said about Lady Dernham's death?"

"She was never called by name, but there was certainly a rather sharp exchange between Sir Reginald and Lord Dernham on the subject of private races held on public thoroughfares. The subject was dropped, though, for the maid Dulcie—that is, for Lady Dunnington was obliged to leave the table."

"Was she?" He looked up sharply. "For what purpose?"

Too late, she remembered Emily's urgent warning. "Oh, I don't know," she said with a shrug. "Some domestic calamity, I daresay."

Pickett saw something flicker briefly in her eyes, and knew she was lying, or at least equivocating. It was the first time she had been less than truthful with him, and it stung to know that she no longer considered him trustworthy.

"How long would you say she was gone?"

"Five minutes, perhaps as much as ten." Seeing him writing it down, she added quickly, "But that was long before Sir Reginald was shot."

He looked up from his notebook. "My lady, I hope you know me well enough to understand that I am not trying to build a case against your friend. I am merely trying to gain some understanding of the movements of the major players."

She nodded, but her gaze slid away from his to fix once more on the expanse of carpet between them. "Of course, Mr. Pickett."

"So, we have Lady Dunnington returning to the table after an absence of no more than ten minutes," Pickett reminded her. "What next?"

She shrugged. "Nothing, really. We had dessert—over which no one seemed inclined to linger—and at last Lady Dunnington rose and suggested that she and I retire to the drawing room while the gentlemen enjoyed their port. Sir Reginald was to act as host."

"And this was when the rest of the gentlemen decided to take their leave?"

"Yes, but you make it sound as if it were a collective decision, which it was not. I believe it was Lord Dernham who first declined to stay, then one by one the others concurred. Some offered excuses for their early departure—Lord Edwin said his doctor cautioned him against drinking strong spirits, and Captain Sir Charles made some mention of being on review in the morning—but others simply said their goodbyes and left."

"And what of Sir Reginald during all this time?"

She frowned thoughtfully, trying to remember. "If he was offended, he didn't show it. Of course, it could be that Captain Sir Charles really will be on review in the morning, and Lord Edwin really has been cautioned against drinking."

"Both excuses should be easy enough to confirm or disprove," said Pickett, jotting down a notation. "Did Sir Reginald enjoy his port in solitary splendor, then?"

"No, for he departed very soon afterward himself." She grimaced. "What an unfortunate choice of words!"

"But quite accurate, it seems, and in more ways than one. What of the butler who showed him out?" Pickett asked, having acquired some understanding of the rôles of servants during a brief stint incognito as Lady Fieldhurst's footman.

Lady Fieldhurst shook her head. "Lady Dunnington's butler has gone to Shropshire to visit his sister who is ill, and the footman is not in good health himself. It was one of the housemaids who had the responsibility of opening the door to guests."

"It was a footman who fetched me from Bow Street," Pickett pointed out.

"Yes, Emily was obliged to rouse poor Jack from his sickbed, for she could hardly dispatch a lone female on such an errand, particularly at so late an hour."

Finding nothing to dispute in this statement, Pickett made a note of it.

"In any case," Lady Fieldhurst continued, "Sir Reginald declined to have the maid summoned, saying he could show himself out."

"And then?"

"He left the room, and it was only moments later that we— Lady Dunnington and I, that is—heard the gunshot. We ran to the hall and found Sir Reginald lying facedown on the floor in a pool of blood. Oh, and the door was open."

Pickett, scribbling away in his occurrence book, paused and looked up. "Which door?"

"Two doors, actually. The front door—the one leading outside, that is—and the door leading downstairs to the kitchen, for the servants had been disturbed by the sound as well. I remember stepping out onto the front stoop, which Emily thought a foolhardy thing for me to do. She claimed I might have been shot myself."

"Only if the shooter had a second gun, or time to reload. In all probability, you were never in danger." It was very likely true, yet he disliked the idea of Lady Fieldhurst standing alone outside the door where a murderer had just made his escape quite as much as Lady Dunnington had.

"My lady, will you show me, as well as you can remember, just how everything looked when you and Lady Dunnington arrived on the scene?"

"Certainly," she said, rising to her feet.

"I should caution you that Sir Reginald's body is still there," he added apologetically.

"It will not be the first time I have seen a dead body," she reminded him, lifting her chin bravely. "In fact, it has become quite a common occurrence of late. I daresay I shall soon become accustomed to it."

He might have told her that one never became accustomed, but as he had no desire to remind her of past horrors, he said nothing. As they crossed the drawing room, the temptation to touch her became too great to resist, and he was emboldened to take her elbow. She started a little at his touch, but he was gratified to note that she made no effort to pull her arm away.

They found the hall empty save for Sir Reginald's body; apparently Lady Dunnington was still upstairs cleaning up from her bout of nausea.

Lady Fieldhurst wrinkled her nose. "It reeks in here! I don't recall any of the other bodies having such a foul odor."

"I'm afraid we must attribute the smell to her ladyship. When I turned the body over to examine it more closely, she, er, succumbed."

"I can imagine," said Lady Fieldhurst, carefully avoiding the sight of Sir Reginald in spite of her professed indifference. She pushed open the door to the servants' domain below stairs. "Dulcie, the maid, stood just inside the door, with the cook right behind her. And on the formal staircase leading to the upper floors, Lady Dunnington's abigail and Jack the footman had come down from their bedrooms in the attics. Although, now that I think of it, I don't believe I noticed the servants until after I stepped back inside. The harder I try to remember, the more confusing it all seems!" She pressed her fingertips to her forehead in agitation.

"Please don't distress yourself, my lady. I believe you said the front door was open as well?"

"Yes." As she stepped gingerly around Sir Reginald's body, she was certain of one point she had previously missed. "He wasn't lying like that. His face was turned to the floor."

"Yes. I was obliged to turn him over to examine the body," Pickett reminded her.

She shuddered. "Oh. Oh yes, of course. You said so, did you not, when you told me Emily had become ill." She opened the front door, pushing it wider until it was almost perpendicular to the wall. "There. It was about like that."

"It appears someone was in a hurry to get away," observed Pickett. He stepped out onto the front stoop and looked at the tall, narrow houses on the other side of the street, their darkened windows staring indifferently back like blinded eyes.

"Surely whoever shot him has long since run away," Lady Fieldhurst pointed out from just inside the door. "And if he has not, he has certainly had more than enough time to reload his gun by now. Will you not come back inside, Mr. Pickett?"

"Oh, I didn't expect to see him lurking about," Pickett assured her, pleased beyond all reason by her apparent concern for his safety.

"What are you looking for, then?"

"I'm looking at the houses across the street. I wonder if anyone may have heard the shot, or seen someone running away. I shall have to make inquiries."

"I am sorry to disappoint you, but most of the houses will be empty," she told him. "The Season is long since over, and most of the aristocracy have retired to their country estates for the winter."

"You are still here, and so is Lady Dunnington," Pickett

pointed out. "And so, for that matter, were half a dozen gentlemen."

She wrinkled her nose in distaste. "I am still here because the alternative is to join my mother-in-law at the Fieldhurst estate in Kent. Lady Dunnington lives in Town year 'round, as she is estranged from her husband. As for the gentlemen," she began ticking them off on her fingers. "Sir Reginald was still here because of his daughter's upcoming wedding at St. George's, Hanover Square. Lord Dernham is still in Town because Parliament is in session, and he occupies a seat in the House of Lords. Captain Sir Charles is obliged to remain here with his regiment. Lord Rupert is here because he prefers Town life to rusticating at the estate of his elder brother. I daresay Mr. Kenney is still here because he can't afford to travel anywhere else. Lord Edwin—" She stopped, arrested.

"Lord Edwin?" Pickett prompted.

"To tell you the truth, I can't quite fathom why Lord Edwin is still in Town. He is an avid sportsman, and now that the hunting season is open, I should think he would be off somewhere in the country." She frowned. "Unless he was more interested in hunting Sir Reginald than in running foxes to ground. Do you think he might have stayed in Town expressly for the purpose of killing him?"

To Pickett's way of thinking, it was infinitely worse. He very much feared that Lord Edwin had stayed in Town because he entertained hopes of becoming Lady Fieldhurst's lover.

"I couldn't say, my lady. Perhaps I shall know more after talking to the gentleman tomorrow."

"I wish you would come back inside," she said uneasily. "I can't help feeling that he is still lurking out there somewhere with his gun—not Lord Edwin necessarily, but whoever the killer is—ready to strike again."

"I don't think so, my lady," Pickett assured her, wishing for some reason to linger just so that she might continue to fret over his safety. He glanced up and down the street and then, finding no excuse to remain, turned to go back inside.

"Hsst!"

He froze in mid-stride, looking back to identify the source of the furtive summons, but saw no one.

"Hsst! Down here!"

Like most of the houses in the better parts of Town, Lady Dunnington's residence was fronted by wrought iron railings, which partially concealed a staircase descending to the servants' entrance below street level. Pickett glanced down into the stairwell and discovered Lady Fieldhurst's fears were not so far-fetched after all.

There at the foot of the stairs stood a wild-eyed young man brandishing a pistol.

CHAPTER 5

The Continuing Investigations of John Pickett

"Here now, stop waving that thing about," Pickett scolded. Rounding the wrought iron railing at a run, he hurried down the stairs.

"Shh!" The young man ducked back into the shadows, but at least he lowered the gun. "Don't let her ladyship hear you! I mustn't be found here."

Pickett wondered what possible threat Lady Fieldhurst might pose to a youth still in his teens. Then he realized the stranger referred to Lady Dunnington, the mistress of the house.

"Her ladyship is upstairs, well out of earshot. Who are you? What are you doing with that gun?"

"You're from Bow Street, aren't you? Someone was shot tonight, weren't they?"

Pickett nodded. "Sir Reginald Montague. What has it to do with you?"

"I found the gun." He looked down at the pistol as if wondering how it came to be in his hand. "I heard the shot, and a moment later, this thing came flying over the railing. It clattered down the stairs and landed almost at my feet."

"Who are you?" Pickett asked again. "And what were you doing down here?"

"Beg pardon, sir. My name is James Marlow. I'm a footman at the Fanshaw house three doors down." He jerked his thumb in the direction of the house in which he was employed.

"Yes? Then why are you here and not there?"

The footman's expression became rather hangdog. "The Fanshaws have gone to their country place, leaving naught but a skeleton staff at the town house. Seeing as how I'm not needed there, I thought it would be a good time to come calling on Polly, Lady Dunnington's kitchen maid. We've been walking out together since last Christmas. My intentions are honorable," he added quickly. "I mean to marry Polly as soon as I have enough money saved up."

"I see," said Pickett. Apparently the lovers' tryst was interrupted by the same gunshot that killed Sir Reginald. "So where is Polly?"

The footman gestured toward the door leading into the servants' hall. "I pushed her back inside as soon as I heard the shot." He ducked his head. "To tell you the truth, I thought at first it must be that someone found out about Polly and me."

"I take it Lady Dunnington, or the Fanshaws, or perhaps both, don't approve?"

"We're servants, aren't we?" James said sullenly. "We're not allowed to have lives of our own."

From his own brief stint as a footman, Pickett knew the young man had a point, but he had more pressing concerns at the moment than the thwarted ambitions of young lovers. "So someone shot Sir Reginald and then threw the gun down here while making his escape?"

"It looks that way, doesn't it?"

"Did you see anyone leave the house?"

James shook his head. "No, sir, not a soul."

Which was hardly surprising, thought Pickett. Besides the fact that James and his Polly had been standing well below street level, their attentions had been otherwise engaged. But at least the murder weapon had been found; the next step was discovering to whom it belonged.

"I'll take that, if you please," he said, holding out his hand for the pistol.

"You won't tell anyone it was me that found it, will you? It would likely cost me my position," said James, unwilling to relinquish the weapon without some assurance of his own anonymity.

"If you thought your position might be jeopardized if you were found here, why are you still here? I wonder you didn't take off for home long before now."

"I couldn't run off when my Polly might be in danger, could I? Besides," he confessed sheepishly, "never mind what they say about curiosity killing the cat, I just had to know what was going on. You see how it was, don't you? You won't tell anyone?"

"I can't make any promises," Pickett said, unwilling to raise false hopes. "But if I must bring you into it, I can assure you I'll present you in as heroic a light as possible. Surely the Fanshaws would be reluctant to part with a servant who was instrumental in maintaining the peace and safety of the neighborhood by turning in a dangerous weapon to the authorities."

James grinned. "Polly wouldn't mind it being known she was keeping company with a regular hero, neither."

So pleased was the footman with this rosy picture of his future that he surrendered his prize without further ado. Pickett took the gun and sniffed the end of the barrel, wrinkling his nose at the smell of burned powder. He tucked the pistol into the waistband of his breeches and went back up the stairs and into the house. He passed through the hall where Sir Reginald still lay, and thence into the drawing room. There he found Lady Fieldhurst along with Lady Dunnington, the countess still a bit pale but otherwise recovered from her earlier indisposition.

"I have returned, Mr. Pickett, and await your convenience," she announced with an air of bravado that did not quite ring true. "You may do your worst."

"You have nothing to fear from me, your ladyship, I assure you," Pickett said, then turned to Lady Fieldhurst. "You are free to go, my lady, if you wish." There was a chilling finality to the words, too suggestive of the ones he would have to speak to her in little more than twelve hours.

Julia glanced uncertainly at Lady Dunnington. "If you would prefer me to stay, Emily—"

"Nonsense!" declared the countess, reaching for the bell pull. "I daresay your Mr. Pickett will not eat me."

She gave the bell pull a tug, and a moment later a maid entered the room, a slender young woman in a starched white apron over a demure black frock. Ash blonde hair peeked from beneath her frilled cap. Her large brown eyes opened wide at the sight of Pickett, but it was Lady Dunnington to whom she addressed herself.

"Yes, my lady?"

"Fetch Lady Fieldhurst's cloak and then have her carriage brought round, if you please."

"Yes, ma'am." She bobbed a curtsy to her mistress and then, with one last glance at Pickett, left the room.

"I'll see you out, my lady, if I may," said Pickett, unwilling to make Lady Fieldhurst walk past Sir Reginald's body again on her own.

"Thank you, Mr. Pickett."

She allowed him to lead her back into the hall, where the maid was already waiting with her velvet evening cloak. Pickett wished he had the audacity to take the cloak from the maid and place it around his lady's shoulders himself. A month earlier, in Scotland, he would not have hesitated to do so; now, however, she seemed so uncomfortable in his presence that he dared not make any move that might be construed as taking liberties.

Having completed this operation, the maid excused herself to summon Lady Fieldhurst's groom with her carriage, leaving the two of them alone in awkward silence.

"I hope you will be gentle with Lady Dunnington," Julia said at last. "She—she is not so hardened as she appears. Or, I suspect, as she would like to believe."

"I will bear it in mind," he promised.

"Until tomorrow, then."

She hesitated for a moment, then offered her hand. He took it and held it uncertainly, as if he were not quite sure what to do with it. In any case, the decision was made for him by the return of the maid.

"Your carriage, my lady," she said and flung open the front door just as the equipage drew up before the house.

"Tomorrow," Pickett said, and relinquished his lady to the coachman.

"I'm sorry to keep you waiting, your ladyship," said Pickett, returning to the drawing room.

"Not at all," Lady Dunnington assured him, gesturing for him to take a seat. Apparently no longer content with sherry, the countess had confiscated the gentlemen's neglected bottle of port from the dining room and now poured herself a generous measure. Her hands, Pickett noted, shook so violently that she splashed several drops onto the carpet. "Will you have a glass?"

He shook his head. "No, thank you."

"Now, where do you want me to start?" Lady Dunnington took a long pull from her glass. "The dinner party, I suppose. Yes, well, Julia—Lady Fieldhurst, that is—has been curiously blue-devilled since her recent sojourn in Scotland. I thought she needed a lover, and I told her so. In fact, I organized a dinner party, inviting some half-dozen candidates for her consideration. I daresay she has already told you the names of all the gentlemen in attendance, so I shan't bore you by naming them all again."

Pickett flipped back a couple of pages in his occurrence book. "I believe I have all the names here, your ladyship." He should not ask; it had absolutely no bearing on the case, but he could no more stop himself than he could make his heart stop beating. "Who did her ladyship—that is, did Lady Fieldhurst express a preference?"

"Wouldn't you like to know?" she retorted, albeit without malice. "In fact, so would I, Mr. Pickett. Unfortunately, Sir Reginald was shot before I had an opportunity to ask."

"Can you think of a reason why any of the other gentlemen in attendance might wish to shoot him?"

She waved one hand in an expansive gesture. "Oh, I daresay any one of them might have been jealous. Sir Reginald has— had—a certain air of danger about him that women find simply irresistible."

Pickett had no cause to doubt it; he was aware of a distinct pang of jealousy himself. "Would any of them be jealous enough to want him dead?"

She shrugged. "How should I know? If they did, there was no sign of it over dinner. No one threatened to stab him with the butter knife, or anything of that nature."

"Lady Fieldhurst mentioned some unpleasantness—not an argument, but veiled hints of some sort."

Lady Dunnington's eyebrows rose. "Did she? I didn't notice any such thing."

"I believe she said you had been obliged to leave the room for a time, so I daresay you must have missed it."

"Yes, I remember now," Lady Dunnington said brightly. "I splattered soup over my gown, clumsy me, and was obliged to leave the room in order to clean it up before the stain set."

Another lie, Pickett thought. Lady Fieldhurst had spoken of

some vague domestic calamity. Aloud he merely noted, "It must have been a very light stain, your ladyship, or else you cleaned it very thoroughly."

"I will thank you, sir, to keep your eyes off my bosom," she said, fixing him with a stare almost as lethal as the gunshot that had felled Sir Reginald.

If she had meant to discompose him, she succeeded admirably. Flushing, he asked, "If there were no hard feelings between any of the other gentlemen and Sir Reginald, why did they all decline to take port with him?"

"Lord Edwin was following his physician's advice, and Captain Sir Charles will be on review in the morning. As for the others, I daresay they had their reasons, and felt no compulsion to share them with me. Or do you suspect one of them of lurking in the hall with pistol cocked until Sir Reginald took his leave? You will catch cold at that, you know, for Dulcie must have seen him, if that were the case."

"Dulcie?"

"The maid who showed them in. And out, for that matter."

As if on cue, Dulcie appeared at the door. "Begging your pardon, ma'am, but the coroner is here."

"I'll see him, your ladyship, if you'd rather not," Pickett said.

"Thank you, Mr. Pickett," said Lady Dunnington with real gratitude. "I should be obliged to you."

"And you, Miss—Dulcie, is it? I should like a word with you, if I might."

"You may remain here, Dulcie, and await Mr. Pickett's pleasure. As for me," she added, grimacing, "if you are done with me, Mr. Pickett, I suppose I must inform poor Sir Reginald's widow."

"I can relieve you of that task, if you will allow me," Pickett offered.

"And to think I once questioned your competence!" marveled

58

her ladyship. "I see now that you are a very useful sort of fellow to have about. Yes, Mr. Pickett, I would be only too happy to shove the unpleasant duty onto your shoulders, if you would be so kind."

Having reiterated his willingness to take on this disagreeable task, Pickett excused himself to the countess and her maid, then met the coroner in the hall for a brief consultation over Sir Reginald's body. Afterward he exchanged a brief nod with this worthy (whom he would no doubt see again in court, provided he could piece together enough of a case to bring someone to trial) before returning to the drawing room.

Lady Dunnington, correctly assuming that Pickett would wish to speak to the maid in private, had taken herself off to some other part of the house, leaving her servant in sole possession of the drawing room. Dulcie in her maid's costume looked very young and very out of place sitting on the same furniture she would no doubt be dusting the following day. She looked up at him with wide, frightened eyes. He thought she couldn't be more than eighteen years old, if that. Pickett, who endured many a slight due to his lack of years, felt gratified to be, for once, several years older than the person he was called upon to question. He smiled kindly at her.

"How do you do, Miss—?"

"Dulcie, sir."

"Yes, but surely you have a last name?"

"Monroe, sir, but here I'm just plain Dulcie."

"I very much doubt you could ever be 'just plain' anything," said Pickett, and was rewarded with a shy smile. "I'm John Pickett of the Bow Street Public Office. I understand you've had a busy night of it."

"Yes sir, what with the butler gone and the footman sick."

"I've done a stint as a footman myself. It's a demanding life, being a servant. I understand you had to answer the door in addition to your other duties."

"Yes sir, but I didn't mind, not with her ladyship being short-handed as she is."

Having succeeded in setting the girl at ease, Pickett withdrew his occurrence book and a pencil from the inside pocket of his coat. "Will you tell me what happened tonight, as much as you can remember?"

"Yes sir, but—I hardly know where to start."

"Start at the beginning. Who arrived first, and at what time?"

Dulcie smiled. "Oh, that's easy! Her ladyship the Viscountess Fieldhurst arrived at half past seven, a full thirty minutes before dinner was to start at eight. I guess she was that eager to meet the gentlemen vying for her favors, to be here so early."

"Hmph," Pickett grunted, not deeming this observation worthy of a response. "Who came next?"

"Sir Reginald Montague. Lord Dernham and Lord Edwin Braunton arrived just a few minutes after."

"They came together?"

Her forehead creased in concentration as she considered the question. "I don't believe they travelled together. It's just that they arrived at the same time, so I announced them together."

"I see," said Pickett, making a note of it. "And then?"

"Lord Rupert Latham." She blushed rosily. "He's quite the gentleman, that Lord Rupert. I took his hat, gloves, and greatcoat, only one of the gloves fell on the floor. Lord Rupert bent down and picked it up for me, and said I was much too pretty to be a beast of burden!"

"He would," muttered Pickett, scribbling in his book.

"And then came Captain Sir Charles Ormond and Mr. Martin Kenney. And I *know* they didn't come together, for the captain rode, and had just given his horse over to the groom to take to the mews when Mr. Kenney came walking up on foot. So I announced the two of them together."

"I understand the dinner ended rather abruptly," Pickett remarked.

"Yes sir, it did. I had gone down to the kitchen to help prepare for the staff's dinner, thinking it would be at least a couple of hours before the gentlemen would be leaving. But it was scarcely an hour later when Lady Dunnington rang for me. It seems all the gentlemen were ready to leave at once. All except Sir Reginald, that is. Her ladyship never rang for me, so I daresay he meant to show himself out. Except that he never got out, did he? Not alive, anyway."

"No, not alive," said Pickett, disappointed. If all the gentlemen had left at once (all except Sir Reginald, in any case), it would have been extremely difficult for any one of them to lie in wait for him. He wondered how much time would have passed between the time the other gentlemen left and Sir Reginald followed; perhaps there had been a sufficient interval for one of them to return to Lady Dunnington's house after making the others believe him to have gone. Dulcie would hardly know, since she had not been summoned, but Lady Fieldhurst might, and so might Lady Dunnington. He made a notation in the margin to remind himself to ask.

"Tell me, Miss Monroe," he continued, "did you hear anything at dinner that would suggest why all the gentlemen would wish to leave so soon?"

"Why, Mr. Pickett!" she cried, scandalized by the very suggestion. "I would never eavesdrop!"

"No, no, of course not," Pickett said hastily. "But one can't help overhearing things, and, well, sometimes they talk in front of the servants as if we were no more human than the furniture," he added, thankful for the brief experience as a footman that allowed him to talk to the household staff as if he were one of them.

"That's true," Dulcie conceded, "but most of the time I was

downstairs in the servants' hall. I couldn't have heard the conversation in the dining room even if I'd tried."

Pickett closed his notebook and returned it to his coat pocket. "Thank you, Miss Monroe. You've been most helpful. Now, if you could send the lady's maid to me, I would be most appreciative."

"Mrs. Winters? But she couldn't have been anywhere near Sir Reginald at the time! She came running down the stairs when the shot was fired. I remember seeing her and Jack Footman leaning over the banister."

"I don't suspect Mrs.—Winters, did you say?—of having a hand in Sir Reginald's death," Pickett assured her. "I merely want to follow up on something her ladyship said."

"Oh, I see. Yes sir, I'll send her down at once."

She hurried from the room, and a very short time later a stately looking woman of late middle age entered the room. From his brief stint in the servants' hall, Pickett knew she was one of the highest ranking of the servants, second only to the housekeeper amongst the female staff. He noticed that she looked down her nose at him, most likely offended at being questioned by a man no older than Jack the footman.

"I believe you wanted to see me?" she asked.

"You are Mrs. Winters, personal maid to Lady Dunnington?"

"I am."

"I believe there was some mention of her ladyship spilling soup on her gown at dinner tonight. As her lady's maid, you would have been called on to clean up the stain, would you not?"

Mrs. Winters looked mildly surprised. "I know of no such spill, nor stain neither."

"I see." Pickett, unsurprised, made a note of it.

"Of course, if the spill were a very minor one, she may have simply dabbed at it with her napkin."

"No, it was said that she left the table to attend to the matter."

"Perhaps she went down to the kitchen for water," suggested Winters. "It is true that some stains must be treated at once if they are to be completely removed."

"Thank you, Mrs. Winters, I will look into it," promised Pickett, and dismissed her.

Pickett descended the stairs to the servants' hall, where he was made privy to the utterly unsurprising information that her ladyship had not been below stairs since quite early in the evening, when she had descended to the kitchen to review the dinner arrangements with Cook. He was about to go back upstairs to take his leave of her ladyship when Dulcie fell into step behind him.

"Begging your pardon, sir, but what will you do now?" she asked, climbing the stairs in his wake.

"I'll spend tomorrow interviewing all the gentlemen you announced tonight."

She followed him into the hall and laid a hand on his sleeve. "Oh, Mr. Pickett—"

"Yes?"

"I'm—I'm frightened," she said, looking up at him with great doe eyes. "What if he comes back? The man who shot Sir Reginald, I mean."

Rather distractedly, he patted the hand resting on his arm. "I don't think you have anything to fear, Miss Monroe. I think whoever shot Sir Reginald knew exactly what he was doing and will have no reason to return. If you're frightened, lock your door when you go to bed tonight."

She nodded and allowed her hand to fall back to her side. "I will, sir. And thank you."

It was doubtful whether he ever heard her thanks, for he was already out the door and heading down Audley Street. Dulcie gave a little sigh and closed the door behind him.

CHAPTER 6

Which Introduces the Dead Man's Widow

For the next quarter-hour, Pickett made a nuisance of himself by knocking on the door of every house on the opposite side of the street, where he inquired of the inhabitants if anyone had been seen leaving the Dunnington town house, particularly anyone whose exit appeared to be furtive or hurried. His inquiries could not be said to have been productive, for although the tone of the various responses ranged from annoyed to indifferent to luridly eager, the essence remained the same: No one had seen anything that might be considered a promising lead. In fact, most of the households were, like the Fanshaws', reduced to a skeleton staff, and of those remaining in residence, most had already retired for the night (hence their annoyance at being roused from their beds) and had been in no position to see anything at all.

As a result of these fruitless efforts, it was quite late by the time Pickett arrived at Sir Reginald Montague's house in Grosvenor Square, and he feared Lady Montague might already have sought her bed, all unknowing of her newly widowed status. But upon his giving his name to her ladyship's butler, he was promptly ushered into the drawing room with no greater show of perturbation on the butler's bland countenance than a brief widening of the man's eyes upon hearing the words "Bow Street."

"Mr. John Pickett of Bow Street, my lady," the butler announced woodenly and then withdrew, leaving Pickett alone to face a faded woman in her early forties. Her puce-colored evening gown with its short demi-train and modest *décolletage* was obviously expensive, yet somehow she looked frumpy (at least when compared with Lady Fieldhurst, who somehow managed to look elegant even in the unrelieved black of mourning), and the discarded opera glasses lying beside her on the brocade sofa testified to an evening spent in cultural pursuits. Standing near the fireplace with their heads close together were a young woman and a gentleman, also in evening attire; this, clearly, was the pair whose approaching nuptials in St. George's, Hanover Square were about to be disrupted.

"Please forgive me for calling at so late an hour," Pickett began. "I would not have done so had it not been necessary."

"Yes, Mr. Pickett, what is it?" Lady Montague asked wearily. "Something to do with my husband, I daresay. What has happened to him?"

Pickett's gaze sharpened. "Why should you think so?"

She sighed. "I have been married to him for almost a quarter of a century. I assure you, there is very little you could tell me about my husband that might surprise me."

Privately, Pickett thought Lady Montague's assertion was about to be put to the test. "Yes, your ladyship, it does have to do with Sir Reginald. I am sorry to inform you that he is dead, ma'am."

The girl gave a little shriek and buried her face in her fiancé's shoulder, but the widow merely heaved a sigh.

"I cannot say I am surprised, Mr. Pickett. But how did it happen? A driving accident, I daresay? I fear he has always been reckless with a whip in his hands."

"No, ma'am. I'm afraid Sir Reginald was shot."

She nodded. "A duel, then."

Pickett shook his head. "No ma'am, no duel. It appears that your husband was murdered."

A quick intake of breath greeted this pronouncement but, aside from withdrawing a handkerchief from her beaded reticule, Lady Montague betrayed no other reaction to the news of her husband's violent end. Even the handkerchief, Pickett noted, was not raised to her eyes to dry tears, but was twisted in her ladyship's remarkably steady hands. The young woman, on the other hand, burst into tears, which the gentleman at her side did his best to quiet.

"Very well, Mr. Pickett, if you will tell me where my husband is—was—I shall send a couple of footmen to bring his body home."

Here was a delicate subject that Pickett had not previously considered. "He was at the home of Lady Dunnington, in Audley Street, when he died."

The widow nodded in resignation and gave the bell pull a tug. "I daresay he and she were lovers. Were they—" She glanced back at her daughter, still sobbing in the gentleman's arms, and lowered her voice. "Were they in bed together when he was shot?"

On this head, at least, Pickett could reassure her. "No, ma'am, it was not like that at all. Your husband was one of some half-dozen guests at a dinner party. In fact, he had just taken his leave of her ladyship and was in the hall when he died." It was not the whole truth, of course, but anything more would only cause Lady Montague unnecessary suffering.

"I see," she said, and Pickett had the feeling she saw a great deal more than he had told her. A pair of footmen entered the room in answer to Lady Montague's summons, and the conversation was suspended while she gave them instructions for bearing Sir Reginald's body back home.

"I am sorry to press you with questions at such a time," Pickett said after the footmen had departed on their grim task, "but I must ask you if you know of anyone who might wish your husband dead."

At these words, the young woman emerged from her affianced husband's embrace, her eyes sparkling with tears and indignation. "How dare you, Mr. Pickett!"

"Let him alone, Eliza, the man is only doing his job," said her mother wearily.

Pickett, seeing the young lady's face for the first time, was struck by the realization that she reminded him of someone, although he could not immediately place whom. Her hair was pale, but more flaxen than gold, and her blue eyes were so light as to appear almost colorless. She had a pleasingly heart-shaped face, and her figure was trim. Attractive without being beautiful, she was, he realized, a pale imitation of Lady Fieldhurst. And yet, that wasn't it either. Banishing the irrelevant train of thought, he bent himself to the task of smoothing the girl's ruffled feathers.

"I am sorry, Miss Montague," he said as gently as possible, "but I'm sure you want your father's killer to be brought to justice."

"I daresay my husband's killer thought he *was* dispensing justice," said his widow with resignation in her voice. "I fear there were many people who wished my husband ill, Mr. Pickett, and I suspect more than a few of them had good reasons for doing so. Gerald," she said over her shoulder to her daughter's intended, "pray take Eliza into the morning room, so that I may speak privately with Mr. Pickett."

"Of course, ma'am. Come along, my dear," the gentleman urged.

Eliza Montague made no protest, but allowed him to lead her from the room.

"Now then, Mr. Pickett, where shall I begin? My husband

has had numerous affairs, many of them with married women whose husbands might well object, perhaps violently. He has twice killed his man in a duel, and I believe there was once a very unsavory incident connected with his military career, although I never knew all the particulars."

Pickett thought at once of Captain Sir Charles Ormond. "But surely that was long ago, was it not? Whatever Sir Reginald might have done in the past, why would someone choose to seek revenge now?"

The widow shrugged her thin, puce-covered shoulders. "Who can say how the human heart works, Mr. Pickett? Perhaps some long-ago injustice preyed upon someone's mind until he felt compelled to take action."

Pickett withdrew his occurrence book. "I wonder if you can tell me if any of these men might have reason to do your husband harm." He flipped a few pages until he came to the list of Lady Dunnington's guests. "Lord Rupert Latham?"

She shook her head. "They were members of the same club, but there was no ill will between them, at least none that I am aware of."

Conscious of a pang of disappointment, Pickett read further down the list. "Lord Dernham?"

"There was a carriage accident some three years ago in which Lady Dernham was killed, along with several members of her family. Although such things are not discussed in the presence of women, I suspect Lord Dernham may have challenged my husband to a duel, but Reginald was injured in the accident himself—a broken arm, in fact—and was unable to meet him."

Pickett made a note of it. "Mr. Martin Kenney?"

Lady Montague shook her head. "I am unfamiliar with the name. If my husband knew Mr. Kenney, he never mentioned the acquaintance."

"Captain Sir Charles Ormond?"

"There was an Ormond in my husband's old regiment, but I believe he held the rank of lieutenant, at least at that time."

Pickett made another notation. "Lord Edwin Braunton?"

Something flickered in the widow's eyes. "Lord Edwin's daughter Catherine was a friend of my daughter's."

"Was?" Pickett noted her use of the past tense. "Are the two no longer friends?"

Lady Montague waved her hand, and her handkerchief fluttered. "They were school friends, and both were presented at Court this past spring, but the demands of the Season soon pulled them in different directions."

"I understand your daughter is to be married soon," Pickett said. "I trust Miss Braunton's Season was equally successful."

"Now that you mention it, I have heard no word of a betrothal," said Lady Montague. "In fact, I believe Miss Braunton left London scarcely halfway through the Season. It can be very draining on young girls, Mr. Pickett, with social engagements every night, often lasting into the wee hours. If you are thinking a quarrel between my husband and Lord Edwin was somehow responsible for her abrupt departure, I can assure you there was no such thing."

Having reached the end of his list no more enlightened than he was when he first began, Pickett once again expressed his condolences, along with his apologies for having disturbed her ladyship at so late an hour, and took his leave. As far as he was concerned, at least two of the gentlemen—Lord Dernham and Captain Sir Charles Ormond—had valid reasons to wish Sir Reginald dead, but both gentlemen's reasons seemed to lie in the past. Why should they wait until years after the fact to seek their revenge? And if Lady Fieldhurst were to be believed, further investigation might well reveal that the other gentlemen had their own grudges against Sir Reginald.

Pickett sighed. How was he to determine the killer of a man whom *everyone* apparently wanted dead?

CHAPTER 7

This Is the Army, Mr. Pickett

"And you say you found it where, Mr. Pickett?" asked Mr. Colquhoun, turning the pistol over in his hands.

"I didn't find it at all." Pickett leaned against the wooden railing that fronted the magistrate's bench. "A footman from one of the neighboring houses did. He was at the bottom of the stairs leading down to the servants' entrance, sparking with one of Lady Dunnington's kitchen maids, when the shot was fired and the gun thrown down the stairwell."

Mr. Colquhoun chuckled. "I'll wager that gave the lovebirds a rare turn."

"I daresay it did, sir."

"You are persuaded the young man is telling the truth, then?"

"I would swear to it. Let alone that he seemed thoroughly discomposed by the incident, I can't imagine what reason he would have to lie about it. If he was truly fearful of his employer finding out about him and the kitchen maid, he would have done better to have kept quiet and done nothing to call attention to his presence in a place where he had no business being."

Mr. Colquhoun nodded, seeing nothing to dispute in this reasoning. "And he says he saw no one leaving the house? A pity, that."

"I agree, sir. It would have been helpful to have a witness." He permitted himself a smile. "I suppose he had other things on his mind at the time."

"I should think the next step, then, would be to try and determine to whom this belongs," recommended the magistrate, surrendering the weapon to his most junior Runner.

"Yes, sir," agreed Pickett. "I should think Captain Sir Charles Ormond would be the one most likely to be in possession of such a weapon. I had thought to visit one of the gun dealers to see what he might be able to tell me about it. Only—" he broke off, frowning.

"Yes? What is it?"

"I confess to being ignorant of the ways of the Quality, sir, but would it not be unusual for a man, even a military man, to carry a firearm to a dinner party?"

The magistrate nodded. "I should think it would," he said, "unless, of course, he had every intention of using it before the night was over."

"In which case Sir Reginald's murder was premeditated," deduced Pickett.

"It would appear to be. Mind you, I can remember a time when a man was not considered to be well dressed unless he had a sword hanging at his side," the magistrate continued with a reminiscent gleam in his eye.

"I'm sure you must have looked very dashing, sir," noted Pickett, struggling to suppress a most insubordinate grin.

"Impudent young cub!" growled Mr. Colquhoun. "Get along with you, then. Can't you see I've got work to do?"

"Yes, sir," Pickett said meekly, then hesitated. "Mr. Colquhoun, sir—"

"Yes, what is it?"

"I shall be interviewing those at the dinner party today, including Lady Fieldhurst, since the gathering was in her honor, so to speak. I had made an appointment with her ladyship to broach the subject of our irregular marriage, but now that I have to discuss this matter of Sir Reginald with her, I confess I am reluctant to conduct personal business during working hours. I daresay it would be better if I were to wait until—"

Mr. Colquhoun cocked a knowing eyebrow. "Stalling, Mr. Pickett?"

Pickett grinned sheepishly. "As a matter of fact, yes, sir."

The magistrate leaned back in his chair. "Well, I'm sorry to disappoint you, but since the whole thing is mixed up with that Kirkbride affair, one might say it is a professional matter as well as a personal one. You have my permission to take up the matter with her ladyship while you are conducting your investigations."

"Thank you, sir," sighed Pickett, although gratitude was not the emotion uppermost in his mind.

"Oh, and John—"

His use of Pickett's given name, while not unheard of, was unusual enough to capture the young man's attention. "Yes, sir?"

"Good luck."

Pickett smiled uncertainly. "Thank you, sir," he said again, and turned to leave.

"I've a feeling you're going to need it," muttered Mr. Colquhoun as he watched him go.

Pickett left the Bow Street office filled with determination to accomplish as much as he could on the investigation before his meeting with Lady Fieldhurst; he had a lowering conviction that by the time that meeting was over, he wouldn't feel like doing very much of anything. With this end in view, he went first to Whitehall, where, if Captain Sir Charles Ormond had been telling the truth, that gentleman soldier's regiment would be on review.

That some regiment was indeed on review was apparent from

the moment he reached the Horse Guards Parade, a broad expanse of pounded dirt just east of St. James's Park. Dozens of mounted Hussars moved in formation, the scarlet and gold lace of their dress uniforms dazzling in the cold sunlight of early morning. The fact that Pickett was unacquainted with Captain Sir Charles Ormond had caused him some concern, as he would not recognize that gentleman even if he saw him. This, however, proved to be a moot point: all the cavalrymen looked identical from this distance, and civilians such as Pickett could not get near enough to make out individual riders in any case. If he had hoped to identify the captain by his lack of a pistol, here too he was disappointed: the review featured much prancing of horses and brandishing of swords, but no drawing of pistols.

In spite of the early hour, there were a handful of spectators situated along the perimeter of the parade ground. Most of these were female, probably mothers, wives, or sweethearts of the soldiers, Pickett deduced from the ladies' ages. Of the handful of men in attendance, Pickett suspected most had seen action themselves, if the presence of canes, crutches, and eye patches was anything to judge by. He watched the proceedings on the parade ground for a few minutes, wishing he knew enough about military matters to enter into a reasonably intelligent conversation with one of the veterans, then strolled idly along the edge of the parade until he drew abreast of a grizzled veteran leaning heavily on a crutch. The weather, Pickett decided, was usually a safe bet.

"Fine day for a review, especially one so late in the year," he observed, nodding toward the sun riding low in the east.

The gambit did not disappoint him. "Aye, we can't have the Hussars parading in the rain; might soil their pretty uniforms," scoffed the old man. "Have you ever seen such a collection of jack-a-dandies? Faugh!"

"Not your former regiment, then," remarked Pickett, hazarding a guess.

"Mine? Nay, I was one of the death or glory boys." Seeing Pickett's bewildered expression, he added, "Dragoons, my lad! *We* didn't wear yellow boots! Who ever heard of such a thing? *Yellow boots!*" He spat on the ground in a demonstration of contempt for the Hussars' colorful footwear.

"I believe there used to be a captain of the Hussars, a Sir Reginald Montague," Pickett ventured.

The older man cast a furtive glance over first one shoulder, then the other. "Aye, but I wouldn't say that name aloud around here, if I were you. You'll find there's little love for Sir Reginald among the Hussars—nor any of the other regiments neither, come to that."

"So I had been given to understand." Pickett idly scratched at the ground with the toe of his boot. "Why not, can you tell me?"

"Well, it was all hushed up, but from what I understand, Captain Sir Reginald was to lead his men in an assault against the French at Masséna. The way I've heard it told, he'd been drinking heavily the night before—Dutch courage, some say—and was about half seas over when he led his detachment straight into an ambush. Sir Reginald contrived to escape without a scratch, but most of his men weren't so fortunate." He spat on the ground again.

"But surely Sir Reginald can't be blamed for a French ambush," Pickett objected. "I'll admit I am no expert on military matters, but I should think an ambush, by its very nature, would be impossible to adequately defend against."

"Aye, but in this case, all the signs were there, had the captain been sober enough to recognize them. Apparently one of his junior officers saw the danger, anyway, and tried to warn him. If Captain Montague, as he was then, hadn't been cast away at the time, he might have listened to his young lieutenant."

"Was the lieutenant's name Ormond, by any chance?"

"Aye, it was," said the veteran Dragoon in some surprise. "How did you know?"

"Lucky guess," Pickett said cryptically. "And you say there were heavy losses?"

"Aye, most of the detachment. Of those who survived, many were injured and left to languish in a French prison until their release could be negotiated. None of that for Captain Montague, though. He managed to show the French a clean pair of heels." A third stream of spittle demonstrated the veteran's opinion of Captain Reginald Montague.

"Surely he must have faced a court-martial for his part in the debacle," Pickett remarked.

"You would think so, but they say the devil looks after his own. His father died, and Captain Montague was allowed to sell his commission and go home to assume the baronetcy. Mind you, public support for the action was running low at the time; I daresay the War Office was afraid the spectacle of a court-martial might harm morale even further, and since they were getting rid of Captain Montague in any case . . ." The veteran shrugged.

The conversation grew more general after that, but Pickett had already learned what he needed to know. He watched as the cavalry regiment was put through its paces until at last they fell into retreat formation and returned to the stables on the north side of the Horse Guards building. Pickett excused himself to his new acquaintance and followed the horses from a discreet distance, picking his way cautiously around the droppings they left behind. Since he would not know the captain by sight, he was obliged to ask several times as to the officer's location. At last he located Captain Sir Charles Ormond, a tall figure resplendent in scarlet and gold, his chestnut hair topped with a feather-crowned shako. Pickett approached him as he dismounted his sleek black stallion and surrendered the beast to the enlisted man who served as his batman. Pickett's heart sank at the sight of him. The preference of ladies for a man in uniform was well documented, and the dashing captain seemed to embody all the most coveted qualities of the breed.

"Captain Sir Charles Ormond?" Pickett asked, hoping against all odds that he might yet be mistaken.

"Yes?" The captain frowned at the sight of a rather shabbily dressed civilian in the rarified domain of the Horse Guards.

"John Pickett of Bow Street. I believe you attended a dinner party in Audley Street last night?"

The captain inclined his head. "At the home of Lady Dunnington, in fact. What of it?"

"I should like to ask you a few questions about that evening, if I may."

The officer's frown deepened. "Why the devil should you?"

"In case you are unaware, Captain, a man died last night. Shot through the chest at point-blank range, in fact."

Captain Sir Charles hardly even blinked. "Who was it? Sir Reginald Montague, I daresay."

"And why should you come to that conclusion?" asked Pickett sharply.

"When the most hated man in England is shot to death, the only question one must ask is why it didn't happen sooner. I shall answer any questions you wish, Mr.—Pickett, was it?—but this is hardly the place for such a discussion. There is a coffee room inside the Guards building. If you will allow me a minute to finish up here, I shall attend you there directly."

Pickett agreed to this plan, and forsook the stables for the Palladian splendor of the Horse Guards building. A glance at the clock in its domed tower—long reputed to be the most accurate timepiece in London—showed the hour to lack a quarter to nine; more than five hours until the dreaded interview with

Lady Fieldhurst.

As a civilian within the very heart of the War Office, Pickett had expected to be glaringly conspicuous, but to his surprise (and yes, relief), none of the military men in their regimental uniforms of scarlet, green, or blue seemed to pay any attention to him. He located the coffee room by the simple expedient of following the aroma of the brew, ordered a cup, and sat down at a table along the wall to wait. And wait. And wait. He was beginning to wonder if the captain had given him the slip when Sir Charles appeared, full of apologies.

"I beg your pardon for keeping you waiting. My departure from the stables took rather longer than I expected. Now, what is all this about Sir Reginald Montague?"

Pickett sought recourse to the notes in his occurrence book. "He was the last to leave Lady Dunnington's house last night—"

"Yes, I daresay he would have been," observed the captain dryly.

Pickett looked up from his notes. "I beg your pardon?"

"My good fellow, all the *ton* knows of Lady Dunnington's determined pursuit of Sir Reginald—not, mind you, that her quarry was making any very noticeable attempt to elude her."

"Are you telling me that Sir Reginald had ambitions of becoming *Lady Dunnington's* lover?" Pickett began to feel a very real affection for the dead man; whatever his defects of character, Sir Reginald had apparently never entertained amorous intentions toward Lady Fieldhurst—an omission that, at least to Pickett's mind, must surely cover a multitude of sins.

"Oh yes, and he would undoubtedly have done so, had he lived long enough." Seeing Pickett's stunned expression, he added, "You are thinking of all that nonsense regarding Lady Fieldhurst, I daresay. Yes, I attended the dinner with the idea of, er, furthering my acquaintance with the viscountess, but by the end of the evening I had become convinced that Lady Dunnington was wasting her time in that regard. It should have been obvious to the meanest intelligence that Lady Fieldhurst had not the slightest interest in any of us poor blighters being trotted out for her inspection. Perhaps her marriage has soured her on the male sex in general, or perhaps she is pining for another—if the latter should be the case, then you may be sure the object of her frustrated affections is *not* the late Lord Fieldhurst."

Pickett found himself quite in charity with the good captain; in fact, if Sir Charles had confessed to the murder of Sir Reginald on the spot, he was not at all certain he could have found it in his heart to arrest him.

"But I interrupted you," continued Captain Sir Charles. "You say Sir Reginald was the last to leave?"

"The last of the gentlemen, in any case," Pickett corrected himself. "Lady Fieldhurst was still there. In fact, she and Lady Dunnington were in the drawing room when the shot was fired. They ran to the hall and found Sir Reginald lying there with a leak in his chest."

"And the killer?"

"Long gone. He did leave something behind, though." Pickett withdrew the pistol from the waistband of his breeches and laid it on the table. He intended to see a gunsmith later that morning, and was sure this individual would be able to tell him far more about the firearm than Captain Sir Charles ever could. In fact, he was less interested in hearing the captain's opinion of the gun than he was in gauging his reaction to it. "Can you tell me anything about this weapon?"

The captain picked it up and turned it over in his hands, examining it from all angles. "Perhaps. What do you want to know?"

"Is it yours?"

Sir Charles looked up, nonplussed. "My good fellow—!"

"I understand you had every reason for wishing Sir Reginald dead," Pickett said, not without sympathy.

"Oh, I'll not deny that."

"When did it happen?"

"Almost ten years ago." The captain's gaze grew unfocused, and Pickett suspected he was no longer in the coffee room at all, but on a battlefield far away. "They were good men, some of them little more than boys. And perhaps they would be alive today if their commanding officer had been less fond of the bottle."

"A heavy drinker, was he?"

"No more so than many others, I daresay. But most men know when to indulge, and when to keep a clear head. The good Captain Montague"—he all but spat the name—"obviously did not."

"I understand you tried to warn him of the ambush."

"I did. But what did I know? I was a mere second lieutenant, as the captain was quick to point out to me."

"I'm sure no one could blame you for wanting him dead," Pickett said. "Still, I'm afraid I must ask you for an accounting of your movements after you left Lady Dunnington's house last night."

"Certainly, Mr. Pickett. As I told Lady Dunnington at the time, I was obliged to leave early, since my regiment was on review this morning. Mind you, my premature departure was no great burden, as I had no desire to linger in Sir Reginald's presence. I left Lady Dunnington's house and came straight back to the barracks—as anyone in my regiment, as well as the sentry on duty last night, can attest."

"Thank you, Captain. I will look into it before I leave."

The captain nodded his approval of this scheme, and Pickett excused himself.

Unlike the parade ground, which was open to St. James's

Park on the west, the barracks were guarded by two sentry boxes on the Whitehall side to the east. Pickett approached one of these and spoke to the soldier on duty.

"John Pickett, Bow Street Public Office. I should like to speak to the sentries who were on duty last night, if you please."

The sentry's brow puckered. "Last night? Wilkinson would be one of them, but as for the other, I don't know. Lieutenant Carson is the officer who assigns sentry duty; he's the one you'll want."

"Carson, you say?"

"That's right, Second Lieutenant Andrew Carson. I'd take you myself, but I'm not allowed to leave my post. Bow Street, eh? Go on through, sir, and if anyone stops you, tell them Private Watters let you in."

Pickett nodded. "Thank you, Private."

He passed through the gates into the barracks where, after some questioning, he was able to locate Lieutenant Carson. The lieutenant proved to be no older than Pickett himself, but aristocratic breeding combined with military discipline had given him an air of command that Pickett could only envy; he suspected Lieutenant Carson did not have to endure disparaging remarks on his age, even from the enlisted men under his command who were many years his senior.

Upon hearing his request, the young officer nodded. "Last night? That would be Collins and Wilkinson." He turned to bark an order. "You, there—Simpson! Go fetch Collins and Wilkinson, and have them report to me."

Private Simpson hurried off to obey this command, and within minutes two soldiers stood saluting Lieutenant Carson.

"Wilkinson, Collins, this man is from Bow Street," said the lieutenant, gesturing toward Pickett. "He has some questions for you regarding your sentry duty last night. You will give him any assistance you can. Mr. Pickett, if you need anything else, you have only to send for me."

"Yes, sir. Thank you, sir," said Pickett, resisting the urge to salute. Alone with the two sentries, he said, "I understand you were both on guard duty last night. Do either of you recall Captain Sir Charles Ormond returning to the barracks?"

The man called Collins shook his head in the negative, but the other man, Wilkinson, nodded. "Aye, he came past my sentry box."

"Do you recall what time it was?"

Wilkinson scratched his head. "Let me see, the clock on the Guards building had just struck nine-thirty . . . Captain must have returned at about twenty-five to ten, no later than a quarter till. Well, it stands to reason he wouldn't have been out too late, would he, with the review this morning."

"Thank you," said Pickett, making a note of it. "You've been most helpful."

Thirty-five minutes, forty-five at the most, to walk from Audley Street to the Horse Guards. It seemed a reasonable time for a man in good physical condition with a clear conscience and therefore no need to hurry, thought Pickett, although he might wish to confirm it by walking the route himself. Not now, of course, when the streets of Mayfair and Whitehall bustled with fashionables and government officials, respectively, but later, between the hours of nine and ten. Barring any contradictory evidence, it appeared that Captain Sir Charles, however great the provocation, was innocent of any part in Sir Reginald's death.

CHAPTER 8

In Which John Pickett Traces the Provenance of a Pistol

Experience had taught Pickett that the *beau monde* rarely rose from their beds before noon, so he saw no point in trying to interview any of Lady Dunnington's dinner guests before that hour. In the meantime, he decided to call on Joseph Manton, premier gunsmith to the *ton,* at his popular shooting gallery in Davies Street. As he had expected, there were few of the fashionables about at this early hour. Only three or four gentlemen were present, taking turns shooting at wafers and laying bets as to their success (or lack thereof) at this endeavor. None of them had any attention to spare for a young man in an unfashionable brown serge coat, his curly brown hair tied back in an outmoded queue.

The proprietor, however, had had professional dealings with Bow Street before. Granted, these experiences were before Pickett's time, but that young man's reputation had preceded him, and so Mr. Joseph Manton abandoned his aristocratic clients and came forward at once.

"Good morning, sir," he said, "and what may I do for you?"

"John Pickett of Bow Street. I should like to know what you can tell me about this weapon." He withdrew the pistol from the waistband of his breeches and presented it to the gunsmith.

"Hmm, not one of mine, I can tell you that already."

"Is it the sort of firearm a captain of the Hussars might carry?"

"Yes and no," said Mr. Manton, turning the pistol over in his hands with the ease of long practice. "Unlike the enlisted men who are issued muskets, officers supply their own pistols, and they may purchase whatever type they prefer. I suspect more than a few of my own have seen service on the Peninsula."

"And this one?"

Pickett's knowledge of firearms was strictly utilitarian, and Mr. Manton very quickly took him out of his depth with his talk of swamped barrels, frizzen springs, back-sights, and half-stocks, concluding at last with, "This particular piece was made by Rigby of Dublin."

"*Dublin,* did you say?" demanded Pickett, seizing upon the one tidbit in this lengthy discourse that made sense to him. "Dublin, as in Ireland?"

The gunsmith's eyebrows rose. "If there's another Dublin where Rigby operates a gunworks, I'm not aware of it."

Pickett shook his head as if to clear it. "No, of course not. Thank you, sir, you've been most helpful."

He left Manton's shooting gallery with the fixed intention of paying a call on Mr. Martin Kenney, lately of Ireland, until it dawned on him that he had no idea where to find the man. Nor, for that matter, was he familiar with the residences of any of the other gentlemen present at Lady Dunnington's dinner, with the notable exception of Lord Rupert Latham, whom he'd had the dubious privilege of interviewing once before; he had been so distracted by the presence of Lady Fieldhurst, and so daunted by the prospect of the coming interview with her, that he had failed to obtain the information. Clearly, there was nothing for it but to return to Lady Dunnington's house and request to be enlightened—an exercise that would hardly raise the countess's opinion of his competence. Seeing no alternative, he set out for Audley Street, where the door was soon opened to him by a red-eyed and sniffling Dulcie.

"Miss Monroe?" he said, taking off his hat. "What's wrong?"

"Nothing, Mr. Pickett, sir." Giving the lie to this statement, she dabbed at her eyes with one corner of her apron.

"Has something happened?" he asked, growing increasingly alarmed. "Lady Dunnington—?"

"Her ladyship is fine, sir. It's—it's nothing that need concern you."

"At the moment, I'm afraid anything that happens in this house concerns me. Come, Miss Monroe, won't you tell me what is the matter?"

"Call me Dulcie, sir. If you must know, it's—it's the shepherd-ess."

"The shepherdess?" echoed Pickett, conjuring up bizarre images of flocks of sheep wandering aimlessly through London following the violent death of their keeper. "What shepherdess?"

"The Dresden shepherdess that used to stand on the drawing room mantel. Porcelain," explained Dulcie, seeing him still at a loss.

"Oh! Porcelain," said Pickett, relieved to have one mystery solved, at least. "What about it?"

"That's just what I don't know, Mr. Pickett," confided Dulcie, seeking recourse once again to the hem of her apron. "Her ladyship noticed this morning that it was missing, and she thinks—she thinks I stole it."

"Is it possible that someone—another servant, perhaps, knocked it off the mantel by accident while dusting or some such thing, and disposed of the pieces in the hope that Lady Dunnington wouldn't notice?"

Dulcie took instant exception to this theory. "*I* do the dusting in the drawing room, sir, and if I'd done such a thing, I would have told her ladyship at once, and never mind the punishment!"

"Of course you would have," he assured her hastily. "I'm sure her ladyship didn't mean anything by it—she's probably still upset about what happened here last night." He wasn't at all certain he believed it himself, but it seemed to make Dulcie feel better.

"Thank you, sir. I hope you're right."

"I should like to see Lady Dunnington, if I may."

"Of course." Recalled to her duties, she relieved him of his hat and gloves and set them on the side table near the door. "If you'll wait here, I'll inform her ladyship."

She bobbed a quick curtsy, then suited the word to the deed. Pickett had not long to wait until she returned, gesturing for him to follow. "If you will come with me, sir."

"Thank you. And Dulcie"—he hesitated, wondering if he were overstepping his authority—"if you would like for me to speak to her ladyship on your behalf, I would be glad to do so."

He was rewarded with a grateful smile from the chambermaid. "That would be most kind of you, Mr. Pickett."

She led him, not to the drawing room as he had expected, but to the breakfast room, where Lady Dunnington sat at the table sipping her morning chocolate. She still wore her dressing gown, and the shadows under her eyes testified to a night of very little sleep.

"I beg your pardon for interrupting your breakfast," Pickett said, taken aback by her haggard appearance. "I can come back later if you would prefer—"

"No, Mr. Pickett, if it is all the same to you, I would rather have done with it," said her ladyship. "Would you care for coffee? Dulcie, fetch a cup for Mr. Pickett, if you please. I daresay he has thought of a hundred questions to ask me."

"Not at all, your ladyship," Pickett demurred hastily. "And

no coffee, if you please. I shan't impose on you that long. I only realized this morning that, while I asked you for a list of the men who dined here last night, I failed to ascertain their directions."

"You disappoint me! Here I thought a Bow Street Runner would have no difficulty in running his quarry to ground." Her tone was playful, a circumstance jarringly out of place given her obvious distress.

"Perhaps not, but it usually helps to have some idea of where to look for him," Pickett said.

"Very well, Mr. Pickett, if you insist. Dulcie," she turned to address the maid, "fetch the invitation list from my writing table—you will know where to look."

"Yes, ma'am."

Dulcie left the room, and Lady Dunnington regarded Pickett across the breakfast table.

"Well, Mr. Pickett, have you found our killer yet?"

He blinked at her in surprise. "I have hardly begun investigating, your ladyship."

"I am sadly disillusioned. I thought surely you must be on the verge of making an arrest. Who will it be, I wonder? Lord Rupert Latham, perhaps? I daresay you would enjoy that, wouldn't you?"

Pickett flushed, well aware that such a thought had occurred to him more than once during his investigation into Lord Fieldhurst's death. "I only want to discover the truth, your ladyship. Whether I find any enjoyment in it or not is entirely beside the point."

"More's the pity, hmm?" she put in, cocking one delicately arched eyebrow suggestively.

Pickett was thankful for the interruption of Dulcie, returning at that moment with a single sheet of vellum in hand.

"Here is the invitation list, your ladyship."

"Give it to Mr. Pickett, if you please," said Lady Dunnington, gesturing toward him. "Mr. Pickett, you may keep it if you wish."

He took the list from the maid, then nodded to her in acknowledgment as she bobbed a curtsy and betook herself from the room.

He glanced down the list. The men Lady Fieldhurst had mentioned were all accounted for, along with the direction of each man's London residence. He noted with some disappointment that while most of the men lived in Mayfair, Mr. Kenney (the man he was most interested in questioning, given the provenance of the pistol) had his residence some distance away in the none-too-savory section of Town known as St. Giles. Pickett decided to interview as many of the men as he could before his two o'clock appointment with Lady Fieldhurst, then call on Mr. Kenney on his way back to Bow Street.

He thanked Lady Dunnington, then rose to take his leave. As she reached for the bell pull to summon Dulcie to show him out, he recalled he had an obligation to discharge where the girl was concerned.

"Your ladyship, Dulcie tells me you've noticed a piece of porcelain missing."

"Yes, it is the most tiresome thing, coming on top of everything else that has happened here."

"She seemed to be under the impression that you thought she had stolen it."

She shrugged, then regarded him with a surprisingly charming smile. "I daresay I might have said something to that effect. It has been a most distressing night, Mr. Pickett, and my tongue sometimes has a tendency to run on wheels. Those who are well acquainted with me know to disregard half of what I say."

From his own experience as a footman, Pickett knew a servant did not have the luxury of disregarding anything his mistress might say, but he suspected that pointing this out to Lady Dunnington would be a waste of breath. "Then you don't intend to discharge her?"

"Heavens, no! Good help is too hard to come by to dismiss a servant so lightly. I daresay the girl knocked it off and broke it, and is afraid to tell me."

The same thought had occurred to Pickett, but he believed Dulcie when she had denied it. Still, at least he could assure her that her position was not in danger. That, he supposed, would have to do. He thanked Lady Dunnington again, then when Dulcie came in answer to her mistress's summons, he followed her to the front door.

"Thank you, Dulcie," he said when she handed him his hat. "I am pleased to report that it was just as I expected, and Lady Dunnington spoke out of her own distress, given the events of last night. At any rate, I can assure you that you are not on the verge of being given the sack."

"You're very kind, Mr. Pickett," she said shyly, tucking her chin and looking up at him through her lashes. "I thank you for taking the trouble."

"It was no trouble at all," he assured her. "Good day to you, Dulcie."

"And to you, Mr. Pickett," she said, and stood at the door gazing after him until he disappeared down the street.

Pickett stopped first at Lord Edwin Braunton's town house in Portman Square, where he gave his card to the butler.

"I shall inquire if Lord Edwin is at home," intoned this individual, leaving Pickett to cool his heels in the foyer. He returned a few minutes later with the information that Lord Edwin would receive him in his study. The butler led the way upstairs, then paused at the study door to announce, "Mr. John Pickett of Bow Street, my lord."

Pickett, who lived in fear of discovering that at least one of the gentlemen vying for his lady's favors represented every woman's *beau ideal*, was relieved to find himself facing a tweedy gentleman fully two decades older than his own four-and-twenty years. Lord Edwin looked up from his desk, where he was engaged in cleaning what appeared to be, judging from the pieces littering its surface, a fowling piece. Several other specimens of the gunsmith's art were mounted on the wall behind the desk; apparently Lord Edwin was a collector. Pickett filed this information away for future consideration.

"Come in, sir, come in," Lord Edwin urged, waving him forward. "What brings you here, if I may ask?"

He waited until the butler had withdrawn and closed the door behind him to answer. "I am here at Lady Dunnington's behest, Lord Edwin. One of you gentlemen in attendance at her dinner last night appears to have left something there. I wonder if you have noticed any of your personal belongings missing."

"No, I've not lost anything that I'm aware of." Lord Edwin frowned and laid aside his cleaning cloth. "Look here, I've had no dealings with Bow Street before, but it's my understanding that you fellows wouldn't be called out to search for a missing glove or a watch. Unless you've recently opened a children's division?"

Pickett's jaw clenched, but he allowed the inevitable reference to his age to pass unchallenged. "No, sir, no missing glove or watch." He withdrew the pistol from the waistband of his breeches and laid it on the desk. "I see you have an interest in firearms. Does this one look familiar?"

"Hmm, Rigby, eh?" Lord Edwin picked up the pistol and studied it. "Not mine, I'm afraid. I prefer Manton, myself. You say someone left it at Lady Dunnington's house last night?"

"Yes, right after shooting Sir Reginald Montague in the chest with it."

"Good God!"

"Do you know of any reason why someone might want Sir Reginald dead?"

Lord Edwin laid the pistol on the desk and pushed it away. "You might do better to ask for some reason anyone might want him alive. The fellow was a bounder. I didn't kill him, but I can't say I'm sorry he's dead."

"Why not?"

Lord Edwin made an expansive gesture. "Any number of reasons. Ask anyone! That Captain Sir Charles, for instance. He had no reason to love Sir Reginald."

"Why? What happened between Sir Reginald and the captain?" asked Pickett, groping in his inside coat pocket for his occurrence book and pencil. He was, of course, fully aware of the captain's tale, having heard it straight from the horse's mouth, so to speak, but it would not hurt to have it confirmed by another source.

"Oh, I couldn't say, exactly—something on the Continent, if rumor is to be believed. It was all hushed up, but it is very likely Sir Reginald would have faced a court-martial, had his father not chosen that moment to die. The Army scotched the scandal by allowing him to sell out, when there were plenty of folks wanting to see him swinging at the end of a rope." He sighed. "Either way, it wouldn't bring those poor lads under his command back to life."

"And Captain Sir Charles knew about this incident—whatever it was?" asked Pickett, checking Lord Edwin's account against the one provided only a few hours ago by the captain himself.

"Knew about it? My good fellow, he was there! A mere second lieutenant at the time, however; who would take his word over that of his commanding officer?"

"Am I to understand that Sir Reginald Montague was his

commanding officer?"

"Didn't I just say so? No, if you're wanting someone who'd have reason to kill Sir Reginald, you need look no further than Captain Sir Charles. Unless, of course, it's Lord Dernham."

"Why? What did Lord Dernham have against him?"

Lord Edwin leaned back in his chair and fixed his gaze on the ceiling while he performed a series of mental calculations. "Let's see, two years ago it was, no, make that three. Mind you, I'm a sporting man myself, but I don't hold with using one of the busiest thoroughfares in the country as one's own private racecourse!"

"I gather that is what Sir Reginald did?"

"Aye, he had a mind to best the Prince of Wales's London-to-Brighton time. Curricle racing," he explained, seeing Pickett's blank expression.

"So what happened?"

"The way I heard it was that Sir Reginald came up on a big berline and took it into his head to pass it where the road wasn't wide enough."

"And?" prompted Pickett, suspecting he already knew the answer.

"Sir Reginald was thrown clear—they say the devil protects his own—but several of the berline's passengers did not survive the crash. Among them was Lord Dernham's wife."

Pickett looked up from writing in his occurrence book. Here was motive, indeed. But why would Lord Dernham—or Captain Sir Charles, for that matter—wait until years after the event to exact his own brand of justice?

"What about the other guests?" Pickett asked. Lord Edwin Braunton was as gossipy as an old woman. Was he hoping to divert suspicion from himself, or was he merely envious of the other men competing for Lady Fieldhurst's favors, and hoped to narrow the field? If the latter were the case, Pickett could sympathize wholeheartedly; either way, he intended to take full advantage of Lord Edwin's loquaciousness. "Had any of the others a reason to wish Sir Reginald dead?"

"I don't know about wishing him dead, but Mr. Martin Kenney had no reason to love him. Sir Reginald practically accused him of cheating at cards one night at White's, and although nothing was ever proven there, Mr. Kenney's membership was revoked."

Mr. Pickett could hardly see the loss of one's club membership as a justification for murder, but he knew the aristocracy tended to view things differently.

"And what about yourself, Lord Edwin?"

"Me?" Lord Edwin bristled. "I'll admit I didn't like the man—orange blossoms and white satin, indeed!—but I'd no reason to kill him!"

"Orange blossoms and white satin?" echoed Pickett, bewildered.

Lord Edwin sighed. "Sir Reginald's oldest girl is—was— getting married in a few weeks. He said he came to Lady Dunnington's dinner to escape his womenfolk's wedding chatter."

"Lord Edwin, I'm afraid I must ask you for an accounting of your movements after you left Lady Dunnington's house last night."

"Very well, sir, I looked in at Boodle's, my club, for an hour or two—which the porter will attest to, by the way—and then I came home, went to bed, and slept soundly until morning."

Pickett made a note of it, thanked Lord Edwin for the information, and took his leave. It was now almost half-past noon, and he decided he had time for one more interview before the anticipated yet dreaded *tête-à-tête* with Lady Fieldhurst. He called next on Lord Dernham, and was shown into an elegantly appointed yet somehow sterile drawing room. Here he was joined shortly by a melancholic man in his late thirties, with pale blue eyes and light hair in rapid retreat from a high forehead.

"Bow Street, you say?" asked this gentleman, gesturing to Pickett to take a seat before the fire. "How may I help you?"

Pickett resorted once more to the opening gambit he had employed with Lord Edwin.

"I am here at the behest of Lady Dunnington," he began. "I believe you dined with her in Audley Street last night?"

"I was one of several in attendance, yes."

"One of her guests left a personal item there last night. I wonder if you have noticed anything missing."

Lord Dernham's brow puckered. "Not that I am aware of. I daresay it must be an item of considerable worth, if she saw fit to call in Bow Street."

"You might say it was worth a man's life." Pickett withdrew the pistol. "Have you ever seen this before, Lord Dernham?"

Unlike Lord Edwin, Dernham made no attempt to take the weapon. "Not that I am aware of," he said again, eyeing it with some misgivings. "And you say someone left it at Lady Dunnington's house last night? Why would anyone bring a pistol to a dinner party?"

"Apparently for the purpose of shooting Sir Reginald Montague," Pickett answered.

Lord Dernham flinched at such plain speaking. "Montague was shot, then? Is he—?" He choked off, unable to speak the word.

"Is he dead? As a matter of fact, he is."

"Well, well!" Lord Dernham's expression changed, but instead of registering horror as one might expect, his taut facial muscles relaxed, and suddenly he looked like a convicted man given an unexpected reprieve. "Well, well!" he said again.

"You appear to be pleased at the news," Pickett observed.

"I'll not deny it. No, Mr. Pickett, I did not kill him, but I will not pretend to regret his death. If you are looking to me for assistance in finding the killer, I fear you have come to the wrong place. You will get no help from me."

"Sir Reginald may have been a bounder and a cad, my lord, but even bounders and cads are entitled to certain rights under British law. I understand you have every reason to wish him ill, but justice demands—"

"Justice?" interrupted Lord Dernham. "Don't speak to me of justice, sir! Where was justice for my wife and her family? In my opinion, whoever shot Sir Reginald meted out that justice which the Crown either could not or would not dispense. I only hope you will inform me of the killer's identity before he is executed, so that I may shake his hand."

"And yet I suspect your gratitude to the avenger of your wife's death would not extend to taking his place on the gallows, my lord. If you wish to avoid such a fate, you would do well to cooperate."

Lord Dernham heaved a sigh, the fires of his righteous indignation extinguished by this unpleasant prospect. "Very well, Mr. Pickett. What do you wish to know?"

"I fear I must ask for an accounting of your movements after you left Lady Dunnington's house last night."

Lord Dernham lifted one hand in a helpless gesture. "There is very little to tell. I came immediately home and went straight to bed. I let myself in, as it was my butler's day off. The hour was not yet nine o'clock—early by *ton* standards—and I had told him he need not return until ten. As for the only other servant who might have seen me, I had told my valet he need not wait up for me—in fact, Mr. Pickett, I had expected to be much later in returning home."

Pickett, making a note of it, wondered if Lord Dernham had hoped to end the evening in Lady Fieldhurst's bed. He thanked his lordship for the information and rose to take his leave, noting as he did so that the clock over the mantel showed that the time lacked only ten minutes to two.

The hour of reckoning, it seemed, was at hand.

CHAPTER 9

In Which a Marriage Is Announced

After leaving Lord Dernham's house, Pickett set out on foot for the Fieldhurst town house in Berkeley Square, and reached that dreaded destination entirely too soon for his liking. He lifted the knocker and let it fall, and was taken aback when the door was opened by a butler whom he had never seen before.

"Yes?" said this worthy, clearly unimpressed with Pickett's somewhat shabby brown serge coat and unfashionably shallow-crowned hat.

"John Pickett, to see Lady Fieldhurst," he said, standing a bit taller, the better to look down upon this unwelcoming gate-keeper. "Her ladyship is expecting me."

The butler gave a sniff as if he rather doubted this, but stepped aside to allow Pickett to enter. He relieved Pickett of his hat and gloves (Pickett suspected the hole in the left thumb was yet another black mark against him) and gestured for him to follow. "If you will wait here, sir, I will notify her ladyship of your arrival."

Pickett seated himself on the straw-colored sofa in the drawing room. He had sat here beside Lady Fieldhurst many times before during his investigation into the murder of her husband, but the room seemed to have lost its welcoming atmosphere in spite of the warmth of the fire. He supposed the butler had something to do with it, and wondered why she had replaced Rogers.

He got his answer only a few minutes later, when a plump, middle-aged woman entered the room, followed by a glowering George Bertram, seventh Viscount Fieldhurst.

"Good day to you, Mr. Pickett," said the new Lady Fieldhurst, offering her hand to him as he rose at her entrance. "What brings you here?"

Her husband George was rather less courteous. "I'd like to know what the devil you're about, calling on my wife!"

Too late, Pickett realized that the Fieldhurst town house was now the property of the new viscount and his wife. Julia, *his* Lady Fieldhurst, would have removed to—where? She would be expecting him to arrive at any minute, and he had no idea where to find her.

"I—I beg your pardon," Pickett stammered. "I had forgotten—I wasn't thinking—I'm looking for your cousin's widow. Can you tell me where she is living now?"

"And why the devil should I?" demanded George, Lord Fieldhurst. "What can it possibly have to do with you?"

"There is something I must discuss with her ladyship," Pickett said. "If you will tell me where I might find her, I will trespass no longer on your hospitality."

"You can have nothing to say to Julia that cannot be said to me, as head of the family."

"It—it is rather personal in nature," said Pickett. "It concerns something that took place in Scotland."

"Hmm, I always suspected there was more to that Scotland business than Julia was telling," George grumbled. "Whatever you have to say, you may be sure I will pass it along to her—if I deem it necessary."

"What I have to say to her, sir, is none of your business!"

George bristled, and would no doubt have summoned the

butler to throw Pickett out on his ear had his wife not intervened.

"George, your Cousin Julia is a grown woman," the current viscountess pointed out. "Surely she can decide for herself whether or not to see Mr. Pickett and hear what he has to say."

"You do have a point, my dear, but I would be remiss in my duty to the family if I did not demand to know what personal matter this fellow could possibly have with my cousin's widow!"

Pickett would have preferred to cut out his tongue rather than betray Lady Fieldhurst by bearing tales to her husband's meddlesome family. Still, he knew enough of George from previous experience to recognize that he would get no information from that source any other way.

"Very well," he said with a sigh, recognizing his last forlorn hope that the irregular marriage might stand would die with the telling. "You know that while in Scotland Lady Fieldhurst and your sons took matters into their own hands, going to the seaside rather than the Fieldhurst estate."

"Yes, yes, I know that. What of it?"

"You may not realize that they attempted to preserve their anonymity by adopting an assumed name. And the name her ladyship chose—well, it was mine."

"The devil you say! Are you telling me my cousin's widow was capering about Scotland calling herself Mrs. John Pickett?"

"In all truthfulness, I do not believe my Christian name ever entered into the discussion, but as to her calling herself Mrs. Pickett, yes sir, she did."

George heaved a sigh. "Well, I can't pretend I like it, but I suppose it's all water under the bridge now. Least said, soonest mended, I daresay."

"Not exactly. I have it on good authority that under Scottish law such a declaration before witnesses constitutes a valid marriage."

George's face grew quite purple with rage. "Are you telling me that *you* of all people are now married to my cousin's viscountess? No, Mr. Pickett, I'll not have it!"

"I'm afraid what you will or will not have has very little to say to the matter," Pickett said.

"If you've so much as laid a hand on her, by God, I'll have you horsewhipped!"

In fact, Pickett had laid more than a hand on Lady Fieldhurst. He had kissed her at least twice, and with the lady's full co-operation. Still, he knew himself to be innocent of the charges George was implying. "No horsewhipping will be necessary, your lordship. I had an appointment with her ladyship to inform her of the accidental union so that she might take whatever steps are necessary to secure an annulment." Some demon of mischief (or perhaps it was mere wishful thinking) compelled him to add, "But if you will not allow me to speak to her, I suppose we will be forced to let the marriage stand."

"*I* will inform Julia of the matter, and I will notify my solicitor at once! *You,* sirrah, need not come into it at all!"

Pickett had almost forgotten George's wife's presence, until she spoke up softly. "Nonsense, George. Of course Mr. Pickett must tell her himself." To Pickett, she added, "You may find her in Curzon Street. Number twenty-two, if memory serves."

"Thank you, your ladyship. You are very kind."

He turned on his heel and departed, leaving a sputtering George Bertram to stare after him.

"You are late, Mr. Pickett," Julia chided him when Rogers announced his arrival some twenty minutes later. She had awakened early and spent the long hours of the morning in mingled anticipation and dread of his call. Had he had second thoughts, and decided to take her up on her offer after all? If so, should she give him a second chance? Her pride said no, but seeing him again at Lady Dunnington's house the previous night had been enough to inform her that her pride was sadly lacking where he was concerned; she very much feared that if he asked to be her lover, she would fall into his arms.

"I beg your pardon, my lady," he said, bowing over her hand. "I called first in Berkeley Square. I didn't realize—I forgot you would no longer be living there."

She rolled her eyes. "Which will probably bring George down on my head!"

"I beg your pardon," he said again. "I had not meant—"

"Never mind, Mr. Pickett, he probably would have found out in any case. But will you not sit down?"

He sat, and so did she. For a long moment they faced one another in uncomfortable silence, until she said, "I trust you had a pleasant journey home from Scotland?"

He nodded. "The trip was uneventful, which to my mind is the best one can look forward to, travelling on the Mail." Another long silence. "And the boys? I hope they are well?"

"Quite well, thank you. Harold has joined the Royal Navy, and will soon be taking a berth as a midshipman aboard His Majesty's frigate *Dauntless.*"

"Better him than me," Pickett said, grinning sheepishly at the memory of his own seasickness aboard a small fishing boat while Harold Bertram reveled in the experience. "When you next see him, please give him my best regards."

"I will," she promised. "I'm sure he will be gratified to receive them."

Having exhausted their supply of platitudes, they lapsed into silence once more, until Pickett was forced to conclude there was no excuse for delaying the inevitable. "My lady," he began, "if you recall, during that time you were registered at the inn under my name—"

"Which made things most uncomfortable for you, I fear," she

acknowledged contritely.

"Not half so uncomfortable as they're about to be for you," he predicted grimly.

"I beg your pardon?"

"My lady, it has come to my attention that—Mr. Colquhoun, my magistrate, is a native Scot, and he says—that is, it seems that under Scottish civil law—"

Julia listened to his stammering with growing unease, until she finally interrupted, putting an end to his ramblings. "Mr. Pickett, what is wrong?"

He took a deep breath and looked her squarely in the eye. "My lady, it appears there is a very good chance that we are legally wed."

Every drop of color drained from her face. *"What?"*

"Apparently there is such a thing in Scotland as marriage by declaration, which means that all it takes to make a valid marriage is for both parties to declare before witnesses that they are man and wife."

"Oh, dear," Julia murmured under her breath. "Oh, *dear!* I am so very sorry, Mr. Pickett. I should have known!"

He regarded her with a puzzled frown. "Nonsense! How could you?"

"My dear sir, every gently bred female over the age of fourteen is cautioned against the sort of roués and fortune-hunters who might attempt to persuade her to elope over the Border to Gretna Green, where a hasty marriage might be made with no questions asked!"

"Well, there's one bright side," Pickett said ruefully. "No one can accuse you of having designs on my fortune when you claimed to be Mrs. Pickett."

She smiled somewhat mechanically. It was true that she'd had no designs on his fortune (one could, after all, hardly covet what did not exist) but Mr. Pickett possessed other—assets—in which she had certainly expressed more than a passing interest. "Mr. Pickett, is that why you turned down—why you declined to—to—"

He hesitated for a moment before answering. He knew she had been wounded by his apparent rejection of her, and here was his opportunity to save face by claiming to have done so in a noble cause. And yet he could not be less than truthful with her, even at a considerable cost to himself. "No, my lady, it wasn't. In fact, I wasn't aware of the marriage myself at the time. There were—other reasons."

She gave a little laugh utterly devoid of humor, then rose from her chair and crossed the room to gaze unseeing out the window. "So you reject me as a lover only to find yourself tied to me as a wife. Poor Mr. Pickett! It appears you have gone from the frying pan into the fire."

Pickett grimaced. "I wish you would not dwell so much upon my supposed rejection of you, my lady. Truly, it was not what you think."

"Oh, but I must dwell on it! Lady Dunnington has pointed out to me—quite rightly!—that had you made such an offer to me, it would have been considered an indecent proposal. I am most sincerely sorry, Mr. Pickett. I had no thought of giving offense."

He had to smile at that. "My lady, the man who could be *offended* to know that you were interested in him in such a capacity must be above being pleased by anything."

Her answering smile was singularly bleak. "And yet I failed to tempt you, Mr. Pickett. I assure you, I would have said nothing had I not believed that you felt—that is, I imagined that you—"

He let out a long sigh, then rose and joined her at the window, where she stood looking down out onto the street. "You have been frank with me, and you deserve no less from me. In all honesty, my lady, your assumptions were quite correct: I yearn for you body and soul. But I will not be your lap dog, to be summoned for your amusement and then dismissed when you grow weary of the game."

"It wouldn't have been like that!" she cried, whirling away from the window to face him.

He gave a humorless laugh. "It would have been *exactly* like that." He kept to himself the lowering conviction that, due to his own lack of experience, the end would very likely have come sooner rather than later. "You should be glad I didn't take you up on the offer—you might have found yourself bound to me for life! As things stand now, we should at least be able to obtain an annulment—unless you *want* to be a thief-taker's wife and live on twenty-five shillings a week," he added grimly.

She was silent for such a long moment that Pickett indulged a wild hope that she might turn to him and say, *Yes, Mr. Pickett, as a matter of fact, I do.*

But no. "Well, Mr. Pickett, you are certainly full of surprises," she said briskly, offering her hand. "I thank you for stopping by to tell me privately, and in person. I suppose the next step must be consulting a solicitor to discover exactly where we stand and what must be done. If you will excuse me, I shall send a note to Mr. Crumpton, the Fieldhursts' solicitor, requesting that he meet with the both of us. Unless you have a solicitor of your own with whom you should rather confer?"

Pickett, having no connections of his own in that regard, agreed with Lady Fieldhurst's suggestion, albeit with a marked lack of enthusiasm.

"Very well, then," said her ladyship. "I trust a note sent to Bow Street will find you?"

"Yes, my lady, thank you."

He wasn't quite sure what he was thanking her for. He bowed

over her hand and left the room, stopping only long enough to collect his hat and gloves from Rogers.

And just that simply, the "marriage" was over.

Lady Fieldhurst stayed by the window long after he had gone, watching as he strode up the street heading east. Married! Married to Mr. Pickett! She had thought her deception innocent enough at the time, giving a false name at the inn so that she might escape for a time the scandal that still surrounded her six months after her husband's death. She had never dreamed that she, by claiming to be his wife, or that he, by going along with the ruse, might actually be bound by it.

Even more disturbing than the irregular marriage itself, however, was her reaction to it. There was a time not so long ago—in Scotland, perhaps, or in Yorkshire this past summer, while he was playing the part of her footman—that she and Mr. Pickett would have shared a hearty laugh at the suggestion that he might be her husband. But neither one of them was laughing now; in fact, she found nothing at all of humor in the situation, and Mr. Pickett seemed to share her lack of amusement. Still, there was no need to make a Cheltenham tragedy of the thing: it was an inconvenience, certainly, but surely nothing that Crumpton and Crumpton, solicitors to the Fieldhursts for generations, could not overcome. There was nothing in the news, nothing at all, to leave her trembling and weak in the knees. What had changed?

Even as she wondered, she knew the answer. She had been grateful to Mr. Pickett for saving her from the gallows, and she had come to respect him as a trusted friend, but now—now the genie that was physical desire had escaped from the bottle, and there was no stuffing it back inside again.

It occurred to her that if his birth had been higher, or hers lower, marriage to Mr. Pickett might have been a very pleasant prospect indeed. But he was who he was, and she was who she was, and there could be no common ground on which to build a marriage, or indeed any sort of permanent association. Even a lasting friendship between them was unlikely in the extreme, depending as it did upon the event of various members of her circle getting themselves murdered at regular intervals.

In retrospect, she feared Mr. Pickett had been correct when he had said there could be only one ending to any liaison between them. Eventually he would meet a female of his own class whom he would wish to marry, and of course he must be set free before the issue arose; to be rejected as a matter of principle, as she had been in Scotland, was surely less humiliating than being abandoned in favor of another woman. She should be grateful, as he had said, that he had turned her down, so that the marriage (such as it was) might be annulled. And yet gratitude was not the thought uppermost in her mind when she considered the opportunity she had lost. Was it possible to miss what one had never had?

As his tall figure disappeared in the distance, she pushed aside her melancholy reflections, then sat down at her rosewood writing desk and penned a note to Walter Crumpton, Esquire, of Crumpton and Crumpton, Solicitors, Lincoln's Inn Fields.

CHAPTER 10

Which Finds John Pickett in the Doldrums

It was a very discouraged John Pickett who left Lady Fieldhurst's house and trudged down Curzon Street, wondering how long it might be before he could expect to receive word from her of a meeting with her solicitor for the purpose of discussing an annulment. He had expected nothing less from this meeting; why, then, had he persisted in hoping against hope that it might somehow turn out differently?

Now that the dreaded interview was past, Pickett realized it was almost three o'clock and he'd had nothing to eat since breakfast. He would have preferred to wait until he returned to Bow Street to purchase a meat pie from one of the many street vendors who hawked their wares in the vicinity of Covent Garden; the fashionable coffeehouses and tearooms of Mayfair would consume rather more of his wages than he liked to spend on a single meal. But his stomach was by this time loudly protesting his neglect, and he still had two more interviews to conduct before reporting his findings to Mr. Colquhoun. He found a modest-looking tearoom, requested a table, and ordered the cheapest thing the establishment offered. The price of even this humble repast served as a further reminder to him of just how great a gulf lay between him and Lady Fieldhurst, and why an annulment of their accidental marriage was not merely desirable, but necessary.

As he ate his meager meal, he withdrew a folded piece of paper from his pocket and consulted Lady Dunnington's list. Somehow it was not surprising that his next stop must be at the bachelor abode of Lord Rupert Latham; a *tête-à-tête* with the man who had almost been Lady Fieldhurst's lover seemed somehow all of a piece with the rest.

After finishing his luncheon, he called at Lord Rupert's flat in the Albany. As he followed Lord Rupert's man inside, Pickett told himself he had no reason to envy Lord Rupert; after all, that gentleman had not yet contrived to worm his way into Lady Fieldhurst's bed, whereas Pickett himself had been invited there. No, if anything, it should be Lord Rupert who envied him, and not the other way 'round.

That encouraging thought, however, withered and died as Pickett found himself facing a gentleman dressed in the first stare of fashion, his dark blue double-breasted coat of Bath superfine clinging so closely to his shoulders that Pickett, painfully aware of his own workaday brown serge, suspected Lord Rupert could not get it on or off without the assistance of his manservant. Pickett sighed. He was never more conscious of his own lack of sophistication (or, indeed, of anything else held to be of value by the class to which Lady Fieldhurst belonged) than when in the presence of the man who but for the death of Lord Fieldhurst would have been her lover.

"So we meet again, Mr. Pickett," said Lord Rupert after his manservant had announced the visitor and left them alone. "What is it this time, if I may be so bold as to inquire?"

"I understand you were one of several gentlemen attending a dinner party at Lady Dunnington's house last night," Pickett said. "A personal item of considerable value was left there, and I am trying to identify its owner. I wonder if you have noticed any of your belongings missing?"

Lord Rupert's eyebrows rose in mild curiosity. "Missing? No,

I don't think so. What is this personal item, if I may ask?"

For the third time that morning, Pickett withdrew the pistol from the waistband of his breeches and laid it on the table.

"Not mine," Lord Rupert said. "Aside from the fact that I prefer Manton's, it seems to me to be shockingly bad *ton*, bringing a firearm to a dinner party."

"I daresay Sir Reginald Montague would agree with you, seeing as how someone used this one to put a ball through his chest."

"You don't say!" His interest now fully engaged, Lord Rupert picked up the pistol and turned it over in his hands, examining it from all angles. "If only it could speak, what tales this weapon might tell!"

"Quite so," agreed Pickett. "But since it can't, I must deduce what I can. Tell me, if you will, where did you go after you left Lady Dunnington's house last night?"

Lord Rupert chuckled. "I'm sorry to disappoint you, Mr. Pickett, but if you are still hoping for some excuse to send me to the gallows, I must confess that, while I had no particular love for Sir Reginald, neither had I any reason to hasten him off to the reward he no doubt richly deserves."

"If half the tales I've heard about Sir Reginald in the past twenty-four hours are true, you would appear to be one of the few men in London who could make such a claim."

"Given the purpose of Lady Dunnington's party, one might assume that someone brought this little plaything along for the purpose of, er, eliminating the competition," Lord Rupert continued, as if Pickett had not spoken. "Still, if that were the case, I flatter myself that I, and not Sir Reginald, would have been the target of choice, in view of my greater claim, so to speak, on the fair Julia's affections."

Pickett wisely held his tongue. Was Lord Rupert so sure of himself where Lady Fieldhurst was concerned, he wondered, or was he merely amusing himself at the expense of one whose admiration of the lady they both knew to be hopeless?

Lord Rupert handed the weapon back to Pickett. "I'm sorry I could not oblige you by getting myself killed. I realize how much it would mean to you, but I assure you my intentions toward Lady Fieldhurst are quite honorable. However much she may try to emulate Lady Dunnington, I fear Julia is not the kind of woman who may take lovers willy-nilly. Once she discovers this fact for herself, I fully intend to marry her."

Pickett was surprised to find himself in agreement with his lordship, up to a point. He, too, suspected that Lady Fieldhurst was not the sort of female who might bestow her favors casually on any man who happened to take her fancy—a discovery that raised a new question: If he had accepted her invitation to become her lover, would she have followed through with it, or would she have made some eleventh-hour excuse not to consummate the relationship she herself had proposed? If the latter were to have been the case, then he had hurt and humiliated her unnecessarily. It was a disturbing thought.

Seeing that Lord Rupert was awaiting a response, Pickett took no small satisfaction in giving him one. "I believe you are correct in your reading of her ladyship's character. But as far as marrying her, I fear you are a bit late to the fair. Her ladyship—" *Don't say it, don't say it!* Warning bells clanged inside his head, but Pickett could no more hold back the words than he could cease breathing. "Her ladyship is already married. To me."

Alas, the pleasure he might have been expected to feel at making this pronouncement was considerably diminished by the fact that Lord Rupert appeared more amused than enraged by the revelation.

"Come now, Mr. Pickett," he said, chuckling, "this is doing it much too brown! If you think to throw me off the scent, so to speak, you will have to do better than that."

"If you doubt my word, you may ask her ladyship. She'll tell you it's true." *And then she'll kill me for spilling the secret to the first person I meet,* he added mentally.

At least he had the satisfaction of seeing the condescending smile erased from Lord Rupert's face. "Nonsense! Why would she choose to marry a thief-taker with—forgive me!—neither birth, nor breeding, nor brass to recommend him?"

"In all honesty, Lord Rupert, I believe it was my very lack of those things that worked in my favor. On her recent sojourn in Scotland, her ladyship found it desirable to assume an incognito, for reasons I should not have to explain to you. She chose to call herself Mrs. Pickett, and when I arrived in Scotland myself shortly thereafter, I supported her in this claim. Not until much later did we discover that in Scotland such a declaration constitutes a legal marriage."

"I see," said Lord Rupert, and Pickett had the lowering feeling that he probably saw a great deal more than had ever been stated. "And do you flatter yourself, Mr. Pickett, that this irregular marriage will be permitted to stand?"

"I will, of course, defer to Mrs. Pickett's wishes in the matter." It was impossible, particularly in his present company, to resist the temptation to call her by the name just once.

"You had better, or she will find herself widowed for the second time," promised Lord Rupert ominously, reaching for the bell pull. "Hastings, Mr. Pickett is leaving now. Please have the goodness to throw—er, *show*—him out."

Having departed the Albany unceremoniously (albeit under his own power), Pickett had one more stop to make. In truth, his interviews with first Lady Fieldhurst and then with Lord Rupert had left him with very little interest in Sir Reginald's murder. He had a duty to perform, however, and so, with the slight hope that the execution of that duty might give his mind a more profitable direction, he called on Mr. Martin Kenney at his hired rooms in St. Giles.

The door was opened not by a servant, but by Mr. Kenney himself, who greeted Pickett with a disarming smile and welcomed him to what he modestly (though accurately) termed his humble abode.

And humble it certainly was, thought Pickett, accepting Mr. Kenney's invitation to take a seat in a faded and threadbare wing chair before the rather feeble fire. Surveying his surroundings, Pickett was taken aback to discover that the Irishman's lodgings were no better than his own two hired rooms over a Drury Lane chandler's shop. And yet Mr. Kenney was considered a suitable, if by no means brilliant, connection for Lady Fieldhurst, he thought bitterly, while he himself was not. And why not? His brain supplied the answer almost before he could frame the question. Lord Rupert's three B's, of course: birth, breeding, and brass. The Irishman might be no wealthier than Pickett himself, but he had the birth and breeding that Pickett lacked; two out of the three, apparently, was sufficient.

All these thoughts passed through his head in less time than it took to seat himself in the chair Mr. Kenney indicated and decline the man's offer of tea. "In fact, I am here at Lady Dunnington's behest," Pickett explained. "It seems one of the gentlemen in attendance at her dinner last night left behind a personal item of considerable value."

"I see," said Mr. Kenney in his soft Irish brogue. "And would that item by any chance be a pistol made by Rigby of Dublin?"

Pickett blinked. "As a matter of fact, it would." He withdrew the gun from his waistband and handed it to the Irishman. "Would this be yours, sir?"

"Aye, that it would." He took the pistol and looked it over carefully. "It's been fired since it was last in my possession."

113

"Yes. Into Sir Reginald Montague's chest, as a matter of fact."

Kenney let out a long, low whistle. "Can't say I'm surprised, not really. He had a gift for making enemies, did Sir Reginald."

"You'll forgive me for being unfamiliar with the ways of the Quality, Mr. Kenney, but do you make it a practice to carry firearms when making social calls?"

Mr. Kenney sighed. "Not before I moved to St. Giles, I didn't. But these streets are none too safe at night, Mr. Pickett. I feel better for having a weapon at my disposal, just in case it's needed."

"If you don't feel safe here, why don't you find rooms somewhere else?" asked Pickett, suspecting he already knew the answer.

"Oh, I didn't always surround myself with such luxury," Mr. Kenney said facetiously, making an expansive gesture that took in the small room and its shabby furnishings. "At one time, I had rooms in the Albany—only a few doors down from Lord Rupert Latham, in fact. I owe the sumptuousness of my present situation to the generosity of Sir Reginald Montague."

"Do you? In what way?"

"My family has always been what is frequently called 'land rich but cash poor,' Mr. Pickett. We have an extensive estate in County Cork, but very little blunt on which to run it. When my father died last year, I was obliged to settle his debts, which left me rather at *point non plus*. I made my way to London, where I have lived by my wits for the past year. Fortunately, they are good wits, and so I have been able to stay one step ahead of the constable."

"Until Sir Reginald took a hand?"

Mr. Kenney nodded. "As you say. I was having a prodigious run of luck at White's one evening, much of it at Sir Reginald's expense." His fresh, open countenance turned dark. "He all but

114

accused me of cheating at cards. Nothing was ever proven—how could it be, when I was innocent of the charge?—but the insinuation was sufficient to get me blackballed."

"But if one must gamble for a living, surely there are other places in London where one may do so," Pickett pointed out.

"Oh, there are any number of discreet little houses in Jermyn Street where one may play for stakes higher than any found at White's," acknowledged the Irishman, "but one is far more likely to find oneself up the River Tick. Then, too, there is the matter of respectability. A friendly game of whist with one's fellow club members is one thing, but what man wants to give his daughter to a fellow who is known to frequent gaming hells?"

"Daughter?" Pickett tried to recall exactly what Lord Edwin had said about Mr. Kenney's matrimonial ambitions. "Are you speaking generally, or have you a particular female in mind?"

Mr. Kenney gave a short, humorless laugh. "I see the gossips have been busy. I suspect you will not be surprised to learn that among the company present that night was the father of a young lady, a considerable heiress, whom I had hoped to marry, thus finding permanent relief from my straitened circumstances. Needless to say, the scandal put paid to my hopes of matrimony. I may have won four hundred pounds, but I lost forty thousand—a remarkable evening's work, as I'm sure you will agree."

"You had no reason to love Sir Reginald, then," observed Pickett.

"I may be a fortune hunter, Mr. Pickett, but I like to think I am a man of honor. Had Miss—never mind her name now, but had she agreed to marry me, I had every intention of remaining faithful to her; I would have owed her that, at least, for saving my family's estates and our heritage. But as much as I might regret the loss of her forty thousand pounds, it never crossed my mind to put a ball into the chest of the man who was instrumental in depriving me of them."

"What, never?" Pickett asked, mildly surprised. "It would appear that you were one of the few men in London devoid of murderous instincts where Sir Reginald was concerned."

"Oh, I'm no saint; I hated and despised the man—not only for what he did to me, but for what, if rumor is to be believed, he has done to others, as well. But I am not the one who killed him." Apparently fearing that Pickett was not convinced, the Irishman added hastily, "Look here, if I had shot the man, is it likely I would leave my pistol behind, knowing full well that it might identify me as the killer? It seems to me that someone else used my weapon and planted it there to divert suspicion from himself."

"You may be right." Pickett made a notation in his occurrence book. "When did you notice the gun was missing?"

"On my way home last night. I thought I was being followed—a false alarm, as it turned out—and reached into my pocket for my pistol. And damme if I didn't find *that* thing there instead." He nodded his head in the direction of a drunkenly leaning side table, on which was precariously perched a porcelain figurine of a shepherdess holding a crooked staff in one hand and cradling a lamb with the other. He gave a short bark of laughter. "A lot of use that would have been in a fight! I suppose I might have smashed the thing against an attacker's skull, but if he'd had an accomplice, I would have been out of luck."

"There's one mystery solved, at any rate," Pickett said, crossing the room to examine the piece more closely. "Lady Dunnington noticed a Dresden shepherdess missing from her drawing room mantel this morning. In fact, I believe she gave her downstairs maid quite a bit of grief over it."

"Accused the girl of stealing it, did she?" asked Mr. Kenney with a knowing grin. "As I recall, that maid looked to be a dainty little armful. By all means, return the thing to her, Mr.

Pickett, and be sure you claim a hero's reward. One of us might as well benefit from the switch," he added with a shrug.

"Then you have no idea how the piece came to be in your pocket?"

"None at all."

Pickett lifted the figurine and weighed it in his hands. "I assume it was placed there for the weight, so that you would not notice the absence of your pistol until the deed was done."

"I daresay you are right."

"I'm afraid this will have to be kept in evidence, at least for a while." Pickett tucked the pistol back into his waistband and picked up the Dresden shepherdess. "I'll see that it's returned to you as soon as may be."

Mr. Kenney nodded his agreement, and Pickett took his leave. By the time he returned to Bow Street, the afternoon was far advanced.

"What's all this?" asked Mr. Colquhoun, seeing his most junior Runner enter the Bow Street Public Office with a porcelain figurine under his arm.

"A curious thing, sir." Pickett set the shepherdess on the magistrate's bench. "I found out who the pistol belongs to—an Irishman named Martin Kenney. It seems the gun was taken from his pocket, and this thing placed there instead."

The magistrate picked up the figurine and examined it from all angles. "Curious, indeed. A counterweight, I suppose, to conceal the theft of the weapon."

"It would appear that way."

"Dare I inquire about that other little matter?"

Pickett took a deep breath. "I told her ladyship, sir."

"And?" prompted the magistrate.

"And she—"

At that moment a freckle-faced urchin entered the premises, waving a folded piece of paper and bellowing, "Pickett! Message for Mr. John Pickett!"

"Excuse me, sir," Pickett said, then called to the pint-sized messenger. "I'm John Pickett. You say you have a message for me?"

The boy held the note just out of Pickett's reach. "What's it worth to you?"

Pickett, suspecting he knew from whom the message had come and what it would contain, thought he would pay a great deal more not to have to receive it at all. Still, he dug in his pocket and gave the lad a tuppence.

The boy glared down at the copper coin in his hand, then back up at Pickett. "Is that all?" he grumbled.

"Take it or leave it," Pickett said with a shrug. "It makes no difference to me."

The boy wavered, apparently struggling with the question of whether to hold out for a less paltry recompense. The bleak expression on Pickett's face, however, led him to conclude that he was unlikely to receive a greater reward for what was obviously bad news. He surrendered the note, then turned and left the Bow Street office, presumably in search of more lucrative commissions.

Pickett, turning away from the magistrate's bench, broke the seal and unfolded the single sheet.

Mr. Pickett, it read, *my solicitor, Mr. Walter Crumpton of Lincoln's Inn Fields, has agreed to attend me on Thursday at ten o'clock to discuss the steps necessary for obtaining an annulment. Since the matter concerns you as nearly as it does me, I hope you will be free to call at that hour as well. If not, you have only to inform me, and I will request that Mr. Crumpton postpone his visit until a more convenient hour.* It was signed, *Julia Fieldhurst.*

Thursday. And today was Tuesday, so two days hence. His "marriage" had lasted less than forty-eight hours.

"Well, what of it?" asked Mr. Colquhoun, discerning by his

young protégé's countenance that the news was not good.

"It's from Lady Fieldhurst, sir. She—she has arranged a meeting with her solicitor for the purpose of discussing an annulment."

"I see," said the magistrate with unwonted gentleness. "I'm sorry, John."

Pickett, staring down at the note as if he could change its contents through sheer force of will, looked up and gave his mentor a brave little smile. "It's all right, sir. I—I never really expected anything else." He glanced once more at the note in his hand. "She asks me to call on Thursday at ten, and I have no idea how long such a meeting might last. May I have that morning free?"

"Take the whole day, if you wish," Mr. Colquhoun said, entertaining thoughts of Lady Fieldhurst that were far from loving.

"Thank you, sir, but I—I think I would prefer to stay busy."

Mr. Colquhoun nodded absently. Since ordering John Pickett's father transported to Botany Bay for thievery some ten years previously, he had felt a certain responsibility for the fourteen-year-old boy who had been left behind. Eventually he had found a place for the lad on the Bow Street force, first with the foot patrol and later among the Runners. As his affection for the young man had grown, so too had his conviction that John Pickett was destined for greater things. Precisely what those things were, he had no idea, but it should certainly prove interesting to see where his protégé would be ten or even twenty years hence. A self-made man himself, when Mr. Colquhoun had learned of Pickett's dilemma in regards to Lady Fieldhurst it had occurred to him that a well-born wife, if she loved him, might do much to facilitate the young man's rise. While in Scotland, he had hinted—no, he had more than hinted, he had practically accused her ladyship of toying with John Pickett's affections to gratify her own vanity. So great had been her ladyship's indignation on that occasion that he had begun to wonder . . .

But he knew enough of Society to know that it would be a very rare viscountess indeed who would settle for marriage to an impecunious young man without birth or breeding to recommend him, whatever that young man's personal charms. As tempting as it was to condemn Lady Fieldhurst for her haste in seeking an annulment, in all fairness he could hardly blame her for the ways of the world to which she belonged. And yet he had hoped that somehow the thing might be resolved in a manner that would not bring pain to one who had become as dear to him as his own son.

Heaving a dissatisfied sigh, he dismissed Pickett and called for the next case to approach the bench.

CHAPTER 11

In Which John Pickett Plans a Journey

The November days had grown short, and the lamplighters were making their rounds when Pickett left the Bow Street office and set out on the short walk to his hired lodgings in Drury Lane. Along the way he stopped at a bookstore, where he caused the proprietor considerable annoyance by studying the latest edition of Debrett's *Correct Peerage of England, Scotland, and Ireland* for fully ten minutes before leaving the shop without making a single purchase.

Night had fallen by the time he reached his own residence. Not being inclined toward conversation, he offered a diffident greeting to his landlady, Mrs. Catchpole, and then climbed the stairs from the chandler's shop on the ground floor to his own two rooms above. These were cold and dark when he entered, a situation he set out to remedy as quickly as possible. A single candle stood on a small table near the door and, having lit this so that he might move about the room without barking his shins against the furniture, he knelt before the grate and built a fire. Once the kindling had caught hold, he set a kettle of water to boil, then lit a lamp from the candle flame and took a long, hard look about the rooms he had called home for the last five years.

Perhaps it was because he had spent most of the day traipsing about the wealthiest and most fashionable part of London, but tonight his lodgings appeared even smaller, older, and shabbier than usual. It occurred to him that even Mr. Kenney, who appeared to be no plumper in the pocket than Pickett was himself, had an estate in Ireland to offer a wealthy bride; he, John Pickett, had nothing. Small wonder Lady Fieldhurst could not contact her solicitor quickly enough! He tried to picture her living here as his wife—heating water over the fire for tea, perhaps, or setting the small table for dinner—and failed utterly.

His gaze drifted to a door in the wall adjacent to the fireplace, and thence to the darkened bedroom beyond. While it was undoubtedly pleasant to imagine lying in the narrow bed with "Mrs. Pickett" at his side (or, better yet, underneath him), that scenario was the least likely of all; it would not have been that way, even had he accepted her invitation to become her lover. No, he thought bitterly, any such assignation (assuming Lord Rupert was mistaken, and her courage would not have failed her at the crucial moment) would have been conducted at her house in Curzon Street, on a thick, soft mattress with perfumed sheets, and as dawn approached he would have tiptoed down the stairs, carrying his shoes in his hand lest the servants hear him slinking away like a dog with its tail tucked between its legs.

The wisps of steam beginning to rise off the kettle told him the water was hot, and so, shaking off a thoroughly unproductive train of thought, he set about preparing himself a cup of tea. While it steeped, he shrugged off his brown serge coat and hung it over the back of one of the two chairs beneath the table, then pulled the other chair close to the fire and took up a tattered copy of *The Vicar of Wakefield* from the mantel. He sat down, tugged off his boots, propped his stocking feet up on the hearth, and opened his book.

Alas, his present mood was not conducive to reading. After

skimming the same paragraph four times without yet comprehending it, he closed the book and set it aside, then padded in his stocking feet to fetch his occurrence book from the pocket of his discarded coat. Returning to the fire, he flipped back in his notes to the beginning of the case and began to review them.

He had been at this task for perhaps twenty minutes when he saw something that made him sit up straighter in his chair and draw the lamp closer. He turned back five pages—no, six—and reread Dulcie's account of the evening. It was just as he had thought. Captain Sir Charles Ormond had stated that it had taken him between thirty and forty-five minutes to return to the barracks from Audley Street. At the time, Pickett had found nothing amiss with this claim. But the captain had not walked; according to Dulcie, he had ridden. And a horse should have been able to cover the distance in substantially less time, especially at so late an hour, when there would have been little traffic in the streets. What would account for those extra minutes? Had the captain stopped somewhere along the way? Or had he, perhaps, lingered in the mews out of sight until the other guests had departed, then returned to the house and shot Sir Reginald?

It appeared that Captain Sir Charles Ormond, whom Pickett had all but eliminated from his list of suspects, was now back on that list—and very near the top.

"There is one thing about this case that puzzles me," Pickett confided to Mr. Colquhoun the next morning, leaning against the wooden railing in front of the magistrate's bench.

Mr. Colquhoun looked up at him from beneath bushy white brows. "Only one?"

"Well, several actually, but one thing in particular stands out."

"And what is that?" asked the magistrate.

"Why would anyone choose to kill Sir Reginald now? As I see it, Lord Dernham and Captain Sir Charles Ormond had the most compelling reasons for wanting the man dead. But Lord Dernham's wife has been dead for three years, and the disaster involving Captain Sir Charles's regiment took place almost a decade ago. Why would either of them decide to kill him now, when they had managed to restrain themselves years ago, at a time when their losses were still fresh?"

"Have you eliminated the other suspects, then?"

"No, sir, not entirely. But Lord Rupert Latham appears to have no motive, while as for Lord Edwin Braunton, he makes no secret of his hatred for Sir Reginald, but the only connection between the two men that I can see is the fact that their daughters were at school together. Even Mr. Kenney's banishment from his club, and his loss of a wealthy bride, would seem to pale in comparison to the deaths of innocent persons at Sir Reginald's hands."

"And yet you and I have both known men to kill for less," observed Mr. Colquhoun.

Heaving a sigh, Pickett drummed his fingers on the railing. "Very true, sir. In the end, I suppose it doesn't really matter how compelling I might find the motive; the murderer's reasoning is the only one that counts. I keep asking myself what in Sir Reginald's recent history could recall someone's mind to past grievances to such an extent that they would be moved to kill him. If I could just discover that, I can't help thinking the rest would fall into place."

"Very well, and how do you intend to accomplish this?"

"With your permission, sir, I should like to make a brief visit to Leicestershire."

The magistrate frowned. "Why Leicestershire, if I may be so bold as to inquire?"

Pickett came up off the railing and began to pace, his hands clasped lightly behind his back. "I keep coming back to the same question: 'Why now?' And I keep getting the same answer."

"Which is?"

"As far as I can see, the only thing in Sir Reginald's life that has changed recently has to do with the marriage of his daughter."

"But Miss Montague is living in London, is she not?"

"She is, sir, but I don't think it would do me the slightest bit of good to question her in any case. To judge by Miss Montague's behavior upon learning of her father's death, she would seem to be very fond of him; apparently she has been shielded from any rumors regarding his unsavory reputation. I don't think she could tell me anything of value—or that she would, even if she knew anything."

"And you believe there is someone in Leicestershire who could?"

"Lord Edwin Braunton's daughter Catherine. The two girls were at school together in Bath, and both were presented at Court this past spring. Being familiar with the family and yet some distance removed from it, she might have insights Sir Reginald's own daughter would lack, or be unwilling to divulge."

"I gather this daughter lives in Leicestershire?"

Pickett nodded. "Lord Edwin has an estate there. I looked him up in Debrett's." Seeing his mentor was not convinced, he added, "Call it playing a hunch, sir."

Mr. Colquhoun performed a few mental calculations. "Almost a hundred miles each way. At least two days on the road north and another two back, not to mention overnight accommodations and meals along the way. Damned expensive hunch, don't you think?"

"Yes, sir, I suppose so," Pickett conceded with a sigh, then brightened as a new thought occurred to him. "I could save a little by purchasing a seat on the roof of the coach, if that would help."

But this suggestion found no favor with the magistrate. "In this weather? Much use you'll be around here if you catch your death of cold! Very well, Mr. Pickett, you have my permission to play your hunch. You may leave first thing in the morning."

"Thank you, sir. But—"

"Yes? But what?"

"The annulment, sir. I was to meet with Lady Fieldhurst and her solicitor tomorrow morning at ten."

"Her ladyship has survived being married to you for this long; I daresay another se'ennight won't kill her."

"No, sir," said Pickett, pleased out of all proportion at being able to keep his "wife" for another week.

Mr. Colquhoun's permission notwithstanding, there were several things Pickett needed to do before his departure the following morning. The first of these involved another visit to the Horse Guards; the second (and to his mind, by far the most important) concerned paying a call on Lady Fieldhurst in Curzon Street.

Upon arriving at the Horse Guards in Whitehall, Pickett entered the stables, blinking as his eyes adjusted from the bright autumn sun to the relative darkness within. Once the spots had faded from his vision, he began questioning stable hands, and soon located the groom responsible for the care of the captain's mount.

"I understand Captain Sir Charles Ormond left the barracks two nights ago to go to a dinner party in Audley Street," he began. "I wonder if you can tell me if he took out his horse that night, or if he went on foot."

To his surprise, the groom chuckled. "As a matter of fact, he did both. He rode to Mayfair right enough, but he came back on foot, leading poor Diablo by the reins."

"Why should he do such a thing?" asked Pickett, trying to see how this scenario might dovetail with murder, and failing to see any possible connection.

"Had to, didn't he? Diablo threw a shoe along the way. Ah well," said the groom with a shrug, "if it had to happen, better that it should happen the night before than during review the next morning."

"Yes, I can see how it would be," conceded Pickett.

It appeared, then, that Captain Sir Charles hadn't had an opportunity to kill Sir Reginald after all—unless, of course, he had done so with the full cooperation of the men in his regiment, who were now covering for him. Pickett sighed. He'd run up against government bureaucracy once before, during his investigation of Lord Fieldhurst's death. On that occasion, the government entity had been the Foreign Office, and he had not come off well from the encounter. He would take on the British Army if all else failed, but he would prefer a simpler solution to the case. He could only hope for better luck in his *tête-à-tête* with Lady Fieldhurst.

Alas, it was not to be. "Why, Mr. Pickett," she exclaimed, when he was shown into her drawing room. "I did not expect to see you until tomorrow morning. Are you so eager to be rid of me that you would arrive a full day ahead of time?"

This suggestion was so glaringly abroad that Pickett chose not to dignify it with an answer. "I'm afraid I will be unable to attend you tomorrow morning, my lady. I must undertake a journey in the morning, and will be away for at least a week."

"Oh. I see." Her face fell, and Pickett could not help hoping that it was the prospect of his absence, and not the delay of the annulment, that caused her mouth to droop. "It was thoughtful of you to let me know, Mr. Pickett, but you need not have come in person. Surely a note would have sufficed."

"In fact, my lady, there is another reason for my calling. It concerns the investigation."

"Of course, if there is anything I can do—but will you not sit down?"

"Thank you, my lady." At her urging, he took a seat on the sofa, and was gratified when she eschewed the chairs that flanked it and sat down beside him.

"Now we may be comfortable," she said, smiling at him. "I daresay you have thought of more questions for me. As Emily Dunnington says, you may do your worst."

Pickett took a deep breath. "Speaking of Lady Dunnington, I should like for you to tell me why she was obliged to leave the room during dinner that night."

Her smile faltered. "But—but I told you."

"You certainly told me *something*, and Lady Dunnington told me something else entirely. Correct me if I am wrong," he said thoughtfully, "but I believe it was the first time you have ever lied to me."

She lifted her chin, but her blue eyes held a hunted expression curiously at odds with the defiant little gesture. "How do you know it was I and not Lady Dunnington who was being economical with the truth? Surely Emily is more closely involved than I am; why don't you put your questions to her?"

"I doubt she would be any more forthcoming the second time than she was the first," he confessed.

"And yet you expect me to be. Why is that, Mr. Pickett?"

Because there is—something—*between us, something that refuses to be denied, no matter how many times I tell myself how impossible it is . . . Please tell me it isn't one-sided, that you feel it too . . .* No, this was hardly the time or the place for a declaration, if such a time and place existed at all. While he groped for an answer, the silence stretched uncomfortably between them until Lady Fieldhurst felt compelled to break it.

"I didn't lie to you, not really," she insisted. "I told you it was a domestic crisis of some sort, and so it was, but more than that I cannot say. Pray do not ask it of me, Mr. Pickett."

"My lady, you know I must."

"I am sorry, then, but I must decline to answer."

It occurred to her that if Lord Dunnington had indeed shot Sir Reginald, she was shielding a murderer by her silence. And yet this prospect was somehow less disturbing than the bitter knowledge that she must be at odds with one whose good opinion had become invaluable to her for reasons she could not fully explain, not even to herself. But Emily had been her dearest friend for six years, had consoled her and helped her cope with the late Lord Fieldhurst's infidelities when she was obliged to present a brave and smiling face to the rest of the world. Surely Emily was more deserving of her loyalty than a Bow Street Runner of scarcely more than six months' acquaintance, be he never so winsome.

"My lady," Pickett said gently, taking her hand and clasping it between both of his own, "after all we have been through together, have I not shown you that you can trust me?"

Her gaze faltered, and her free hand plucked at the skirt of her gray half-mourning gown. "It's not that I don't trust you, Mr. Pickett, I just—can't tell you."

He released her hand abruptly and rose to take his leave. "If that is your idea of trust, I don't think much of it."

"Please don't go," she begged, clutching at his sleeve. "Not like this. Sit down and I shall ring for tea, and we can talk about something—anything!—other than Sir Reginald Montague's murder. I hear Mrs. Church will soon be making her final appearance on the Drury Lane stage. Do you remember when—"

She was interrupted by Thomas the footman. "Begging your pardon, my lady, but Lord Rupert Latham is below."

She sighed. "Very well, Thomas, show him up," she said with

a marked lack of enthusiasm.

If Pickett had been inclined to linger, the appearance of his most hated rival was sufficient to put paid to the idea. "I really must go, my lady," Pickett said. "I leave at first light for Leicestershire, and my bags are not yet packed."

Her fingertips trailed down his forearm as she released his sleeve. "I see. I—I wish you a pleasant journey, Mr. Pickett. You—you will let me know when you return to London?" Lest he should read too much into this simple request, she hastily added, "So that I can inform Mr. Crumpton, of course."

Pickett, however, had more pressing concerns. "My lady— before Lord Rupert arrives—I should warn you—"

"Lord Rupert Latham," announced Thomas, returning at that moment with the gentleman in tow.

Lord Rupert entered the room with feline grace, raising his quizzing glass to his eye at the sight of Pickett apparently *tête-à-tête* with Lady Fieldhurst. He gave a curt nod in Pickett's direction, then took Julia's hand and lifted it to his lips. "My lady—or should I say Mrs. Pickett?"

Lady Fieldhurst went quite pale as she and turned to confront Pickett. "You—you told him!"

"I—I—I—" Pickett could not begin to explain his lapse; there was, after all, no defending the indefensible. "I—I'm sorry, my lady, I—I'd best be going," he stammered, and beat a hasty retreat.

"A wise man, our Mr. Pickett," observed Lord Rupert, watching his scrambling departure.

"I can't believe he told you!" she exclaimed to Lord Rupert after he had gone. "Oh, how could he?"

"Surely you cannot expect a man of his class to keep such a coup to himself," said Lord Rupert. "I suspect it is not every day that a member of the Bow Street force marries into the aristocracy, even by accident."

"No, but—did he tell you how it came about?"

"He did." Lord Rupert inclined his head. "I suppose I should be flattered that you deemed me not insignificant enough to warrant your calling yourself Mrs. Latham."

"Mr. Pickett is hardly insignificant," protested Lady Fieldhurst. "Still, his name is certainly less likely than yours to be recognized in polite circles. Naturally we intend to obtain an annulment as soon as it may be arranged. In the meantime, Rupert, it is imperative that you tell no one."

Lord Rupert bowed his acquiescence. "I daresay I can be at least as discreet as your artless young husband."

"That is hardly reassuring under the circumstances," she retorted. "Still, I don't understand why he told you. It seems at odds with what I know of his character."

"I fear I must shoulder part of the blame for Mr. Pickett's, er, fall from grace," confessed Lord Rupert.

"You? Why? What did you say to him?"

He shook his head. "The particulars of the conversation are not important. Suffice it to say that I seem to have goaded him into indiscretion."

She frowned at him. "By which you mean you were being horrid. Really, Rupert, it is unkind of you to taunt him. He hasn't your advantages."

"Yes, quite unworthy of me, I know. But my dear, all that earnestness! He makes it well nigh irresistible."

"Irresistible," she echoed. It was the right word for him. One look into those warm brown eyes, and she'd come within ames ace of offering up Lord Dunnington's head on a platter in spite of her promises to Emily. *I yearn for you body and soul* . . . "Yes, he is, at that."

Lord Rupert bent a sharp look at her, but Lady Fieldhurst, gazing abstractedly at the door through which Pickett had just left, didn't notice.

CHAPTER 12

Which Finds John Pickett in Leicestershire

Pickett left for Leicestershire by stagecoach the following morning, and was on the road for the next three days. At last, having reached the end of his journey, he procured a room in a clean yet unpretentious inn and, having deposited his battered portmanteau in this chamber, inquired of his host as to the location of Lord Edwin Braunton's estate and set out on foot.

Lord Edwin's country residence turned out to be a very pretty Tudor dwelling with half-timbered walls, diamond-paned windows, and ivy framing the door. He wondered anew at Lord Edwin's determination to remain in London when by all accounts he preferred the country. Pickett, himself London born and bred and therefore no great lover of rural life, thought even he could be happy living in such a place, especially if he were to share it with a certain lady of his acquaintance—a lady, he reminded himself sternly, who was impatiently awaiting his return so that they might begin the process of voiding their marriage.

He knocked on the door, and after some delay (during which Pickett began to fear the house was unoccupied, in which case his trip to Leicestershire was nothing more than a very expensive chase after mares' nests) it was opened to him by an ancient butler.

"John Pickett," he told the old retainer. "I have come from

London to see Miss Braunton."

The butler gave him a look filled with disapproval so acute it bordered on loathing. "From London, are you?"

Pickett nodded. "Bow Street, in fact. Now, if you will be so kind as to inform your mistress?"

"I shall inquire if Miss Braunton is at home," the butler informed him, then left him to wait on the front stoop. After a delay that seemed interminable but that was probably no more than two or three minutes, he returned. "If you will follow me?"

The butler led him into a wide hall with exposed beams on the ceiling and fine linen-fold paneling on the walls. Several doors opened off this central chamber, and the butler paused before one of these to announce, "Mr. John Pickett of Bow Street, miss."

Pickett entered the room, and thus had his first glimpse of Lord Edwin's daughter and Eliza Montague's erstwhile school friend. He noted at once that Miss Braunton was a beauty, much more so than Sir Reginald's daughter, who was hardly an antidote herself. Aside from a certain air of aristocratic breeding, the two young women looked nothing alike, for where Eliza Montague was fair, Lord Edwin's daughter was dark, with lustrous brown hair and sparkling dark eyes.

But their coloring was not the greatest difference between the two ladies. For where Eliza Montague was slender as a reed, Miss Braunton's belly was swollen with child.

"Miss—er—Mrs.—?"

"Yes, Mr. Pickett, it is 'Miss,' and likely to remain so," acknowledged the fecund Miss Braunton with a rueful smile. "Will you please sit down and tell me what has brought you to Leicestershire? Has something happened to Father?" Her voice rose on a note of alarm.

"When I last saw Lord Edwin, he was in perfect health," Pickett assured her, seating himself on the sofa she indicated and trying very hard not to let his eyes leave her face.

"What, then?"

"It concerns, at least indirectly, an old school friend of yours. I believe you are well acquainted with Miss Eliza Montague?"

The young woman nodded.

"It seems Miss Montague's father was killed a few nights ago."

Miss Braunton's hand went to her bulging abdomen, telling Pickett a great deal without saying a word.

"How—how did he die?"

"He was shot through the chest," Pickett said as gently as possible. "I am sorry if this upsets you."

She shook her head. "No, no, it is quite all right. Tell me, did—did Father kill him?"

Pickett frowned. "Do you know of any reason why he should wish to?"

Her gaze dropped to her belly. "Sir Reginald Montague is the father of my child."

Pickett sucked in his breath. He had already begun to suspect as much, but hearing it stated so baldly rendered him uncomfortable and embarrassed; he could only imagine how the confession must affect Miss Braunton. "I do not mean to pry, but will you tell me how it happened?" At the sound of his own words, Pickett flushed crimson. "That is, I know how it happened, obviously, but I should like to know—that is, I must ask—"

As he descended rapidly into incoherence, Miss Braunton took pity on him. "Sir Reginald did not force me, if that is what you are thinking. I fear I must shoulder much of the blame for my own ruin. I was at school with Eliza, as you said. Whenever her father came to fetch her—on holidays, or at the end of term—the other girls and I were all a-twitter. He is—was—a very handsome man, you see, and I fear we were as silly a collection of females as ever were assembled under one roof." She smiled a little at the memory. "He was most flatteringly attentive when I made my curtsy this past spring, and I was gratified that he should finally see me, not as a schoolgirl, but as a grown woman in long skirts and with my hair up—and that he apparently liked what he saw. I knew he had a wife, of course, but I was aware that even married people indulged in flirtations, and his attentions made me feel quite grown up and sophisticated. And then one evening at the Heatherton ball, he led me into one of the back bedrooms and kissed me. It was all very thrilling at first, although of course I knew it was wrong. And then when I realized he wanted more than a few kisses, it was—it was too late. I asked him to stop, I *begged* him to stop, but he— he—" She buried her face in her hands.

Pickett withdrew a handkerchief from the inside pocket of his coat and handed it to her.

"Thank you," she said in a muffled voice.

"Miss Braunton, I fear you take too much of the blame upon yourself. You say he did not force you, but it sounds to me as if that is *exactly* what he did. Not to put too fine a point upon it, what happened to you was rape."

"Yes, but I asked for it," she sniffled. "I had led him on ever since the Season started, and I accompanied him to the bedchamber readily enough."

"Is that what he told you?"

"Yes." She dabbed at her nose with the handkerchief. "When I told him there was to be a child."

"You might have led him on, but I can assure you that no man is a slave to his impulses. You did not—you *could* not— compel him to do anything he was not already of a mind to do. Furthermore, he was an adult, while you were hardly more than a child. No, Miss Braunton, it seems to me you were more sinned against than sinning."

She sniffed. "Thank you, Mr. Pickett, you are very kind. But tell me, do you think my father killed him?"

"To be perfectly honest with you, I don't have enough information at this point to form an opinion, much less make an arrest. He certainly had adequate provocation, but so did half a dozen others. You know him far better than I; do you think he would be capable of such an act?"

Pickett found it telling that she did not hotly defend her father against the very suggestion, but tilted her head at an angle and considered the question carefully before answering. "He was certainly furious when he learned about the baby—furious with me as well, for putting myself in harm's way, but more so with Sir Reginald. And as he is an enthusiastic hunter and a collector of firearms, he would have had both the weapon and the skill to do so." She shook her head. "More than that, I cannot say."

"As for the skill, Sir Reginald was shot at close range. No particular accuracy with a pistol would have been required. In fact, it would have taken a monumentally poor shot to have missed him at that distance," Pickett assured her. "But I am aware that your father is an avid sportsman; in fact, I am puzzled as to why he was still in London when there were foxes to be chased and grouse to be shot in the country."

She sighed. "Need you wonder, Mr. Pickett? He is still in London trying to persuade some poor gentleman to marry me before the child is born. I already had an adequate dowry, but when my uncle, the Duke of Wexham, heard of my dilemma, he more than doubled it in an effort to entice some man to the altar." She rested a gentle hand on her belly. "I fear it is a wasted effort. What man would be willing to take on the child of such a father? There is no telling what sort of monster the babe will grow up to be."

Pickett pondered this observation for a long moment, then

asked, "Miss Braunton, may I tell you a little about my own father?"

She looked rather nonplussed, but nodded. "If you wish."

"He was transported to Botany Bay for petty thievery when I was fourteen, but before he was arrested and sentenced, he had taught me well. I was already an accomplished pickpocket."

Miss Braunton made a faint noise indicative of surprise.

"I daresay he saw it as teaching me to support myself, and I don't blame him for it. Still, I don't know where I might have ended up—transported myself, I suppose, or hanged—had another man not taken it upon himself to stand in the place of a father to me." He smiled at the thought of his magistrate. "And he still does so, whether I want him to or not."

"I am glad for you, Mr. Pickett, but I do not quite understand what this has to do with me."

"What I am trying to say, Miss Braunton, is that blood is not necessarily destiny." Unless, of course, one was a thief-taker who aspired to marriage with a viscountess, but that was a subject for another discussion, and one in which Miss Braunton played no part. "Your baby's father may have been a scoundrel, but it does not follow that the child must be one as well. With the support of a good man, even though he might not necessarily be of noble birth, your child might well grow up to be a man or woman you can be proud of."

Miss Braunton arched an ironic eyebrow. "Why Mr. Pickett, are you offering your services?"

Pickett flushed. "I—I—I'm a married man."

She laughed aloud at his obvious discomfort. "Never mind, Mr. Pickett, I am merely roasting you. I can just picture my father's reaction—or, worse, my uncle the duke's!—were I to tell him I intended to marry a Bow Street Runner."

"Hilarious," muttered Pickett. She did not mean to be cruel, he reminded himself. She was no more than eighteen years old, and very much a product of her upbringing. And of course she had no way of knowing he had lately begun to entertain ideas above his station. "But tell me, are you acquainted with a Mr. Martin Kenney?"

"Why, yes," she said. "I danced with him a couple of times early in the Season, before—before I was obliged to leave London. He is a very charming gentleman, but every young lady in Town is cautioned not to encourage him, for everyone knows he hasn't a feather to—oh!" she broke off abruptly as she realized where the discussion was heading.

"Hasn't a feather to fly with," Pickett concluded for her. "Precisely. In fact, Mr. Kenney was wronged by Sir Reginald, just as you were. It occurs to me that in this instance, at least, two wrongs might well make a right. If you would not find the thought of such a match repugnant, I should like to suggest it to your father—provided, of course, that Mr. Kenney will not be obliged to stand trial for the murder of Sir Reginald."

She sighed. "Even if he were to do so, I fear I am in no position to be overly nice in my requirements. Beggars, as you know, cannot be choosers."

"So I have always heard," Pickett acknowledged, smiling, "but it cannot make for a happy marriage, the bridegroom going to the gallows as soon as the vows are said."

Miss Braunton laughed in spite of herself. "Very true. In fact, I rather liked Mr. Kenney, and hope he turns out to be blameless in Sir Reginald's death quite for his own sake as well as mine. Yes, you have my permission to suggest Mr. Kenney to my father as a possible husband for me."

"I shall do so as soon as I return to London," Pickett promised.

"Thank you. Do you know, Mr. Pickett, it occurs to me that Mrs. Pickett must be a very lucky woman."

A very lucky woman who was at that moment contacting her

solicitor in order to have the marriage annulled. Pickett's answering smile held more than a trace of sadness. "Thank *you,* Miss Braunton. It is my dearest wish that she should believe herself to be so."

While Pickett pursued his investigations in Leicestershire, Lady Fieldhurst found herself strangely blue-devilled. Restless and not quite sure what to do with herself, she called on Lady Dunnington with some vague notion of supporting her friend through the ordeal of having a man murdered in her home, she having been through a very similar experience herself some six months earlier with the death of her husband.

"And," she concluded, having pointed out this similarity to Lady Dunnington, "at least no one can suspect you of having killed Sir Reginald, since I can vouch for your presence in the drawing room when the shot was fired."

"Very true, my dear." Emily nodded, glancing toward the door as Dulcie entered with the tea tray. "How fortunate it is for me that your Mr. Pickett would never think of doubting your word!"

"I wish you would stop calling him mine," snapped Lady Fieldhurst, painfully aware that her word was no longer held in such high regard by Mr. Pickett, and that she had no one but herself to blame for this change in circumstances.

"Of course, things would be most unpleasant for Dunnington, if his presence that night should become known," continued Lady Dunnington, unaware of Julia's inner sufferings. "I trust you have made no mention of it?"

"No, I have not mentioned it," Julia said, her voice bleak.

"You are an angel!" declared the countess.

Lady Fieldhurst could think of other, more accurate descriptors, but she said only, "Emily, had you best not make a clean breast of the matter? It is bound to come out eventually, for everyone at the table heard what was said. Or allow me to tell Mr. Pickett, if you cannot bring yourself to do so. As you said, my—my word holds some weight with him."

"No, Julia, you must not! For Dunnington's words must appear most damning, in view of what happened later."

Lady Fieldhurst could not help wondering at the countess's determination to shield a man for whom she'd not had a kind word in the six years the two women had been friends. "Never fear, Emily. Mr. Pickett has gone to Leicestershire to follow up on some line of inquiry, so unless Lord Dunnington has some secret connection in the North, I believe he is quite safe."

"Thank God!" declared Lady Dunnington. "Yes, Dulcie, you may go now. There is no need for you to be lingering about."

The two ladies lapsed into silence until the maid had left the room, shutting the door behind her.

"Really!" exclaimed Lady Dunnington in an undervoice. "Did you see how the girl's ears pricked up at the mention of a certain someone's journey to Leicestershire? I do believe she is enamored of your Mr. Pickett! First there is Polly skulking about with the footman down the street—as if I did not know all about it, the silly girl!—and now this. I vow, at this rate I shall have no housemaids left by Christmas."

"I can assure you that whatever Dulcie's feelings toward Mr. Pickett may be, she will not be married to him by Christmas," said Lady Fieldhurst in a flat voice.

"Well, thank heaven for that! But how do you know?"

"Because Mr. Pickett is already married."

"Is he? I wonder who robbed the cradle."

"As a matter of fact," confessed Julia miserably, "*I* did. Mr. Pickett is married to me."

Lady Dunnington set down her teacup with a loud *clink*. "Julia! He refused you as a lover, so you married him instead? My, my, you *did* want the man-child from Bow Street in your bed, didn't you? I hope he was worth it!"

"Mr. Pickett has never been, nor will he ever be, in my bed!" Lady Fieldhurst declared, her cheeks flaming. "I tell you, it wasn't like that at all. It—it happened in Scotland."

"Everything interesting seems to, these days," drawled the countess. "Really, I must go there myself sometime. It certainly made a merry widow out of you!"

"I was not a merry widow! But I didn't want to molder away at the Fieldhurst estate, so we—George's boys and I, that is—stopped at an inn on the coast, and to make sure we couldn't be traced, I registered there under a false name."

Lady Dunnington held up a hand. "Do not tell me, let me guess: you called yourself Mrs. Pickett."

"It seemed harmless enough at the time," Julia insisted. "How was I to know that Mr. Pickett would turn up a week later?"

"Chasing you down to demand the return of his name, I daresay," observed Lady Dunnington.

"Of course not! In fact, he had accompanied his magistrate there. Mr. Pickett was investigating a case while Mr. Colquhoun, his magistrate, enjoyed a fishing holiday. I—I rather think Mr. Colquhoun may have dragged him away from London with the idea of getting him out of my clutches."

"I guess you showed him, didn't you?"

"It isn't funny, Emily! When Mr. Pickett arrived at the inn and gave his name, the proprietor assumed he was my husband, and put us in the same room. Of course we never actually shared the room," she added hastily, anticipating the countess's next question.

Lady Dunnington clicked her tongue disapprovingly. "No wonder Cousin George was beside himself! Gadding about Scotland, corrupting England's youth—"

"Nonsense! Thanks to their explorations along the shore, the boys went to bed exhausted every night long before the adults of the party turned in. Even if we had been occupying the same room, the boys never would have known. It was all perfectly innocent—until we learned that in Scotland, such a thing constitutes a legal marriage."

Lady Dunnington pursed her lips and let out a long, low whistle. "So what do you do now? Has it occurred to you that, had he accepted your, er, interesting proposition, you would be—"

"Yes, it has, many times," Julia put in quickly. "As it is, we intend to meet with my solicitor to discuss an annulment as soon as Mr. Pickett returns from Leicestershire. Until then, there is nothing I can do."

And this lack of progress, surely, was the reason for her low spirits. There could be no other reason why, in a city of a million souls, the absence of one should be so keenly felt.

CHAPTER 13

In Which John Pickett Receives a Most Unpleasant Surprise

On his last evening in Leicestershire, Pickett sat alone in his room at the inn from which he would take the southbound stage the next morning. He was not quite sure what to do with himself. His bags were packed in preparation for the journey, but it was still too early to go to bed. The public taproom downstairs held no appeal, and he hadn't thought to bring anything to read. He decided to write a letter to Lady Fieldhurst; she had, after all, requested him to let her know when he returned to London. Never mind the fact that it was her eagerness to set matters in train for the annulment that inspired this request; alone in a strange place, he craved some connection with her across the many miles that separated them. His mind made up, he tore a sheet from his occurrence book and set pen to paper.

Or at least he tried to. This task proved to be easier said than done. *Dear Mrs. Pickett,* he began, but quickly decided against this form of salutation; her ladyship might not understand that he meant it in jest. In fact, he wasn't quite sure he *did* mean it in jest. He wadded up the paper, threw it into the fire, and began another. *Dear Lady Fieldhurst,* he wrote, but then hesitated. Did the "dear" seem presumptuous? True, it was a standard greeting in written correspondence, but he would not want to be perceived as being overly familiar. This attempt at the epistolary arts joined its predecessor in the flames. *My Lady Fieldhurst,* read his third attempt, and this one he regarded with satisfaction. It was perfectly correct in form, and if he was a bit too fond of the possessive pronoun, surely no one but himself need ever know.

By the time this reaches you, the letter continued, *I will have returned to London. I await your instructions in regard to a meeting with your solicitor so that we might put an end to the*—Here he paused. He could not bring himself to use the word "marriage." To do so in this context would seem too final, too irreversible. *The awkward situation in which we now find ourselves,* he wrote at last. Having cleared this hurdle, he found he could discourse easily enough on such innocuous subjects as the weather in Leicestershire and the beauties of the Northern countryside as compared to those of Town. There had been a time when he would have brought her up to date on the progress (or lack thereof) of his investigation, but no more. Not when he knew her to be deliberately withholding information from him. It was probably just as well, he thought; the condition in which he'd found Miss Braunton was hardly the sort of thing one could discuss with a lady, even one who was nominally his wife. Heaving a sigh, he turned himself to the task of bringing his letter to a conclusion.

The closing phrase, however, gave him cause for further soul-searching. *Love, John Pickett* was clearly out of the question. *Respectfully submitted, John Pickett* seemed too cold and formal by half. At last he settled on *Yours, John Pickett.* Besides allowing him the opportunity to render on paper (however obliquely) the declaration he could never speak aloud, it had the additional advantage of being true: he was indeed hers by law, at least for the nonce, whether she wanted him or not.

★　★　★　★　★

Four days later, Lady Fieldhurst was reading in the drawing room when her footman Thomas entered, bearing a letter on a silver tray.

"The morning post, my lady," he said, bowing and simultaneously placing the tray within easy reach.

"Thank you, Thomas."

Setting aside her book, she took the letter and looked at her own name written on the front. She did not recognize the handwriting, but saw that the wax seal had been broken.

Thomas, noting the direction of her gaze, was quick to explain. "A tuppence had been placed beneath the seal to cover the postage, my lady. I took the liberty of removing it in order to pay the postman."

A wealthy correspondent, then, who wished to spare her the burden of paying postage, but not a nobleman, as the aristocracy enjoyed franking privileges and therefore had the luxury of sending letters at no charge. "Very well, Thomas. You may go."

Thomas bowed and betook himself from the room. Alone once more, Lady Fieldhurst unfolded the single sheet and began to read. The first sentence was sufficient to identify the sender, and she smiled a little at the idea of Mr. Pickett in faraway Leicestershire including tuppence with his correspondence so that she would not be put to the inconvenience of paying a trivial amount that she could no doubt spare far more easily than he. She read through the letter a second time and then a third, as if searching for some secret message hidden between the lines, and was vaguely disappointed to find none; she could not know what it had cost him to pen so carefully neutral a communication. At last, giving up this fruitless exercise, she rose and crossed the room to her writing desk, where she spent the next ten minutes composing a note to her solicitor. Having dispatched Thomas to deliver this missive, she read through Mr.

Pickett's letter once more, then refolded it and tucked it away in her desk drawer, although she could not have said precisely what it contained that might be worth keeping.

Her second attempt at arranging a meeting proved more successful than the first, and so it was that Pickett arrived at Lady Fieldhurst's house on Curzon Street and was admitted by Rogers, her butler, and ushered up the stairs to the small room that she had fitted out as a library.

"If you will wait here, Mr. Pickett, I will notify her ladyship of your arrival."

Left to his own devices, Pickett wandered over to the bookshelves and was perusing the titles when the door opened to admit Lady Fieldhurst, soberly clad in a grey half-mourning gown trimmed with black ribbons.

"Mr. Pickett, how good of you to come." She held out her hands to him as she approached; apparently he had been forgiven for his lapse where Lord Rupert was concerned. "I am sorry to take you away from your work in Bow Street."

He took her hands and gave them a little squeeze before reluctantly releasing them. "It's quite all right, my lady."

"I trust your trip went well?"

He shrugged. "It was informative, but I'm not sure I'm any closer to solving the case. I seem to be finding more suspects instead of eliminating them."

"It was kind of you to write, although you need not have paid the postage. I should have been happy to do so."

Pickett could hardly admit that his pride would not have allowed it, so he was not entirely sorry when the door opened once more to admit Rogers, with the solicitor in tow.

"Mr. Crumpton, my lady," announced the butler.

"Do come in, Mr. Crumpton," Lady Fieldhurst said.

"Your ladyship." Mr. Crumpton bowed from the waist, then

stood upright and regarded Pickett with professional interest. "I take it this is the, er, bridegroom?"

"This is Mr. John Pickett, of Bow Street," said Lady Fieldhurst. "I believe you met him briefly during his investigation into my husband's death."

"Of course, of course," said the solicitor with a nod. He shook hands with Pickett, then moved behind the large desk positioned before the window and withdrew a sheaf of papers from a leather satchel. "With your permission, your ladyship?"

This being granted, he began to spread out the papers. "Do have a seat, both of you, and we will see what we can do about extricating you from your present dilemma."

Lady Fieldhurst took a seat at one end of a green striped sofa that faced the desk, and nodded at Pickett, giving him to understand that he was welcome to sit beside her. He did so, having no intention of allowing such an invitation to go to waste.

He thought she looked most uncomfortable, and more than a little frightened. He could enter into her sentiments wholeheartedly, although he suspected she was most likely fearful that the marriage could not be nullified, where he was equally fearful that it could.

"Ah, yes, annulment of a Scottish irregular marriage," said Mr. Crumpton, seeking recourse to his papers. "While you were out of Town, Mr. Pickett, Lady Fieldhurst explained to me how you came to find yourselves in such a predicament, so we need not go through that again. In truth, the pair of you sent me back to my law books on this one. It seems most cases involving such marriages have to do with their being proven valid, not the other way 'round."

Lady Fieldhurst leaned forward eagerly. "Then there is a chance we are not truly married, after all?"

"I'm afraid it isn't as simple as that, your ladyship. Scottish irregular marriages are perfectly legal in England, but because of their, er, irregularity, they are more likely to be challenged and, if challenged, more likely to be overturned. As you might guess, such marriages are usually disputed by the families of the bride or, less frequently, the bridegroom, usually when a fortune or, in the latter case, a title is involved. Challenges are more likely to be successful if there are other discrepancies present as well: one party being underage, perhaps, or falsifying other pertinent information—being closely related by blood, for example, or already being legally wed to another. I gather none of these applies in this case?"

Pickett and Lady Fieldhurst exchanged looks, then turned back to the solicitor and shook their heads.

"A pity, that; it might have saved us a great deal of trouble," remarked Mr. Crumpton, consulting his papers once more. "Now, as you may not be aware, it is no easy thing to dissolve a marriage, even an irregular one. Marriages are meant to last 'until death do us part.' There must be grounds—compelling reasons, that is—why the marriage can and should be nullified."

"But—but we haven't *done* anything!" insisted Lady Field-hurst, blushing. "I mean—that is—we haven't—"

Mr. Crumpton permitted himself a smile. "It is a common misconception, your ladyship, that a lack of consummation constitutes grounds for annulment or divorce, but I fear it is rather more complicated than that."

"Then what are the possible grounds?" she asked.

The solicitor ticked them off on his fingers. "The first is fraud, which we have eliminated. The second is incompetence under the law, which includes being underage." He turned to look at Pickett. "I believe we have established that you are over twenty-one years of age, Mr. Pickett?"

"These three years and more," said Pickett, perhaps under-standably annoyed to have his lack of years dredged up yet again.

"Just so," said Mr. Crumpton, nodding. "Incompetence under the law also includes insanity, which I daresay we can also rule out," he added with an indulgent smile.

"I don't know about that," muttered Lady Fieldhurst. "I think I must have been insane to think of escaping to the Scottish coast under an assumed name in the first place."

Mr. Crumpton wagged his finger at her. "I fear you gave the Fieldhursts a rare turn over that escapade, your ladyship, but that in and of itself hardly suggests an unstable mind. No, I believe we can rule out insanity as possible grounds for annulment."

"What does that leave?" asked Pickett, weighing the wild hope that they would be forced to let the marriage stand against the bitter knowledge that his wife would hate him forever if it did.

For the first time in the interview, Mr. Crumpton's professional demeanor faltered. "The only possibility that remains is, er, that is, it involves consummation of the union."

"But you just said a lack of consummation did not constitute grounds," protested Lady Fieldhurst.

"No, but if either party should prove unable to—that is, to be incapable of—" He took a deep breath and started over. "Your ladyship, I must remind you that you and the late Lord Fieldhurst were married for six years. If, during that time, it had come to light that you were—were incapable of participating in the act that might have given your husband the heir he desired so desperately, he would surely have sought such an annulment for himself years ago." He turned to Pickett, his eyebrows raised expectantly. "Such being the case, that only leaves . . ."

As the solicitor's implication dawned, Pickett flushed a deep red.

Lady Fieldhurst was equally embarrassed, but considerably

more vocal. "You cannot ask Mr. Pickett to—to—" Words failed her. She broke off and tried again. "Mr. Pickett may not have been married, but I daresay there is a female somewhere who could destroy such a claim simply by coming forward and—and—"

"As a matter of fact," Pickett said miserably, "there isn't."

"There isn't?" echoed Lady Fieldhurst.

Pickett shook his head and prayed for the floor to open up and swallow him.

"There isn't," she murmured, regarding him with new eyes.

"But," he added hastily, "that isn't to say I couldn't—that is, I—I have no reason to suppose that—that all my parts are not—not in good working order."

"Oh, my." She snatched up one of Mr. Crumpton's legal papers and began fanning herself with it. "Oh, my." What must it be like, she wondered, to be someone's one and only? Even in the early days of her marriage, when she was still overawed by the wealthy and powerful man who had swept her off her feet, she had never flattered herself that there had not been others before her.

Small wonder that Mr. Pickett had rejected her invitation! He was saving himself for Mrs. Pickett—for the woman who would someday be the *real* Mrs. Pickett. She wondered fleetingly if he had a particular female in mind for the position, and recalled seeing him at Drury Lane Theatre in the company of a rather sharp-faced yet not unattractive young woman wearing a ghastly purple bonnet. Oh no, surely not! Then another memory intervened, this one of the two of them in her drawing room, standing awkward and ill at ease, yet near enough to touch. *I yearn for you body and soul* . . . No, they were not the words of a man already committed to another woman. And for some reason, she was glad.

"There will, of course, be a medical examination to be made," continued Mr. Crumpton, "but the physician is well known to the Fieldhursts, and will falsify the results for a consideration."

"A bribe, in other words," observed Pickett.

The solicitor shrugged. "Call it what you will, but his testimony before the bishop in ecclesiastical court is what will allow the annulment to be granted—or not."

"No!" protested Lady Fieldhurst. "You cannot ask such a thing of Mr. Pickett!"

"Now, Mr. Pickett," continued the solicitor as if she had not spoken, "I have taken the liberty of discussing the matter with Lord Fieldhurst—"

"*George?*" cried Lady Fieldhurst. "Mr. Crumpton, you had no right to discuss such a thing with him without my knowledge, much less my consent!"

"Now, now, your ladyship, of course Lord Fieldhurst, as head of the family, is entitled to know, and to have some say in the matter. In fact, he was already aware of the marriage—"

"But how could he have been?" she demanded.

"I'm afraid I told him, my lady," Pickett confessed, feeling as if he were sinking himself lower in his lady's esteem every time he opened his mouth.

"*You?*" Her voice rose on a note of hysteria. "Just how many people have you told, Mr. Pickett?"

"No one else," he said hastily. "That is, Mr. Colquhoun, my magistrate knows, but it was he who told me, not the other way 'round."

"But *George*, of all people!"

"Believe me, my lady, I had no choice. When I called on you at the Berkeley Square house, he insisted on knowing the nature of my business with you, and refused tell me where I might find you until I made a clean breast of the matter. I'm sorry, my lady. If there had been any way of avoiding it, I assure you I would have."

She sighed. "I cannot be angry with you, Mr. Pickett, for I know George all too well! But the very idea that he should expect you to—to—to debase yourself in such a way—"

"As I was saying, your ladyship," the solicitor put it, "Lord Fieldhurst is eager to settle the matter as quickly and as quietly as possible."

"I can just imagine," muttered Lady Fieldhurst.

"However, his lordship is well aware of the sacrifice Mr. Pickett is being asked to make. In fact, Mr. Pickett, you will be pleased to know that I have been authorized by his lordship to offer you a bank draft in the sum of two hundred pounds sterling as compensation for any indignities you might suffer."

"You may tell Lord Fieldhurst," said Pickett tightly, "that I have neither the need nor the desire for his money."

The solicitor had clearly not expected this response to his lordship's generosity. "But Mr. Pickett, consider if you will—"

"There is one thing, though," Pickett said. "If I understand you aright, you are asking me to perjure myself."

"Not at all, not at all," the solicitor assured him hastily. "You need never testify, nor even appear in court at all if you do not wish to do so."

"But—but this is positively *wicked*!" cried Lady Fieldhurst, aghast. "I am the one who got us into this mess, so I should be the one to get us out of it."

The solicitor shook his head. "As I pointed out, your ladyship, Lord Fieldhurst would have long since sought an annulment if such a—problem—existed."

"There must be a way," insisted Lady Fieldhurst. "Perhaps we might claim that the problem is of a more recent date."

"You cannot have thought of your reputation, your ladyship," the solicitor chided her. "If such a rumor should be bruited about, you would never have the opportunity to marry again."

In fact, that was the best reason Pickett could think of for allowing Lady Fieldhurst to bear the burden of proof. But chivalry won out, and he said woodenly, "I will do whatever I must in order to release her ladyship from a marriage she does not want. After all," he added with a twist of his lips that was no doubt intended to be a smile, "no one cares about my reputation but me."

She laid her hand over his. "*I* care, Mr. Pickett," she said softly.

"Excellent!" declared the solicitor, rubbing his hands together in glee at having so delicate a matter resolved so easily. "Very broad-minded of you, Mr. Pickett, if I may say so. And if your, er, little problem is resolved a respectable length of time after the annulment is granted, I'm sure no one will question the matter too closely."

With these assurances (if one could call them that), the solicitor stacked his papers and took his leave, promising to inform Lady Fieldhurst when a date had been set for their appearance in the ecclesiastical court.

Pickett and Lady Fieldhurst sat in stunned silence for a long moment after he had gone, Pickett, at least, feeling as if he had received a blow to the solar plexus.

Lady Fieldhurst found her voice first. "Mr. Pickett, I—I don't know what to say to you. When I appropriated your name, I never dreamed it might end like this!"

"I am equally to blame, my lady," he pointed out. "I did nothing to correct the misunderstanding when I had the chance." *I liked the idea too much to dispute it,* he might have added, but did not.

"Please believe that I would never have—I would never intentionally do anything to cause you to suffer," she insisted. "After all you have done for me, it is shameful that your kindness is to be rewarded so shabbily!"

He gave her a singularly bleak smile and rose to leave. "Please do not distress yourself, my lady."

She did not summon Rogers to show him out, but accompanied him down the stairs and to the front door herself. When they reached the hall, she laid her hand on his sleeve. "What you've consented to do, Mr. Pickett—"

He sighed. "Yes, what of it?"

"I think—I think perhaps you should accept George's offer, after all. Yes, I know what you told Mr. Crumpton," she added hastily, anticipating his objection, "but God knows you deserve *something* in return for what is being asked of you."

He shook his head emphatically. "You heard my answer. I said it, and I meant it. The whole thing is emasculating enough without being paid for my services like a cuffin-crack." He gave a bitter laugh. "But no, that won't wash, will it? I'm supposedly incapable of that sort of thing."

She looked up at him with wide, troubled eyes. "If you will accept no other compensation, Mr. Pickett, at least let me tell you that it is the most—the most *selfless* thing I have ever heard of, and that if only—if things were different—if it were not for—" She broke off and swallowed past the lump that had formed in her throat. "What I am trying to say, Mr. Pickett, is that I—I could envy the woman who will someday be Mrs. Pickett."

"There will never be another Mrs. Pickett," he said in a flat voice.

"I know it must feel that way now, but you are very young, Mr. Pickett, and someday—"

He jerked his arm from her grasp so abruptly that she started. "I am sick to the teeth of hearing how young I am! I'm old enough to know what I want, and old enough to know I can't have it, so please don't condescend to me as if I were some schoolboy with a youthful passion I've yet to outgrow!" He seized her roughly by the shoulders and kissed her hard and swift on the mouth, then left the house, slamming the door behind him.

Lady Fieldhurst had never seen him lose his temper before, and the sight was terrifying to behold—not because she thought herself in danger from his anger, but because she knew it to be entirely justified, and because she knew herself to be responsible for it. She stood alone in the hall for a long while after he had gone, the back of her hand pressed to her bruised lips.

She was still standing there some minutes later, when Lady Dunnington knocked on the door and let herself into the house with the ease of long acquaintance.

"Julia? What has just happened here?" she demanded. "First I see your Mr. Pickett striding down Curzon Street as if the devil were at his heels, walking right past me without so much as a by-your-leave, and then I find you standing here as if turned to stone." Her eyes grew wide as a new and terrible possibility came to mind. "Never say you told him about Dunnington!"

"What?" Lady Fieldhurst blinked. "Of course not! You urged me to keep silent on that point, did you not? Although why you insisted on summoning Mr. Pickett in the first place, when you refuse to give him the information that would allow him to exercise his unique gifts—"

This charge led not unnaturally to thoughts of what other unexercised gifts he might possess, and she pressed her hands to her flaming cheeks.

"If not Dunnington, then what?" asked the countess. "What was he doing here?"

"Oh Emily, we are in the very devil of a fix!"

"We are?" Her voice rose on a squeak. "Does he intend to arrest Dunnington?"

"For heaven's sake, Emily, pray disabuse yourself of the notion that Dunnington is in imminent danger of going to the gallows!" said Lady Fieldhurst with some asperity. "When I said 'we,' I meant Mr. Pickett and myself. It—it is rather more complicated than we ever expected. This morning we met with a solicitor to see how the thing might be annulled—"

"On what grounds?" Lady Dunnington interrupted.

"Grounds?" echoed Lady Fieldhurst in some indignation. "Does everyone know about these grounds except me?"

"My dear Julia, I doubt there is a married couple in existence who has not considered the possibility of annulment at some point—annulment, or divorce, or murder." She grimaced at her own words. "Pray forget I said that!"

"The good news, according to Mr. Crumpton, is that an annulment might be granted, provided such grounds could be shown to exist," Julia said slowly, choosing her words with care.

"What grounds?" asked Lady Dunnington again.

Lady Fieldhurst told her.

"Oh, the poor boy!" gasped the countess. "No wonder he turned you down!"

Lady Fieldhurst felt compelled to come to Pickett's defense. "It isn't true, of course!"

Lady Dunnington's left eyebrow arched suggestively. "How would you know?"

"Not from any personal experience," Julia assured her hastily. "I just—know. But he is allowing himself to be held up as an object of ridicule in order to release me. And yet—I wonder—" She broke off as a new and utterly unexpected thought occurred to her.

"Yes? You wonder what?"

"I wonder if being Mrs. John Pickett would truly be so dire a fate."

"Julia!" exclaimed Lady Dunnington, torn between amusement and horror. "You cannot be serious! He would never be received anywhere, and you would be ostracized from all good Society."

"I know," confessed Lady Fieldhurst. "But I hate what this annulment must do to him, particularly since it was I who set the whole dreadful thing in motion. Oh, how I wish I had never set foot in Scotland!" she groaned.

"It is unfortunate that such a thing should have happened, of course," Lady Dunnington acknowledged, "but if that is the only way for you to be released—" She looked at her friend sharply. "You do *want* to be released, don't you?"

"Of course I do, but not at the cost of crucifying someone I—"

She broke off abruptly, and Lady Dunnington regarded her with eyes narrowed in suspicion. "Someone you *what*, Julia?"

"Someone I esteem very highly, and to whom I owe a great debt," insisted Lady Fieldhurst.

But the words sounded feeble, even to her own ears.

Pickett's anger had burned itself out by the time he reached the environs of Bow Street, leaving in its place only abject misery. So sunk was he in despair that he didn't hear the voice calling his name until a small hand in a raveled fingerless glove of black netting slipped through his arm and clutched his sleeve. Looking down, he saw the crown of a purple bonnet of surpassing hideousness. He didn't have to see the face beneath it to recognize Lucy Higgins, the Covent Garden strumpet who'd had designs on his virtue since the night when, as a nineteen-year-old newly minted member of the foot patrol, he'd arrested her for prostitution.

"Why the long face, John Pickett?" She peered up from beneath the brim of her bonnet, a pert young woman with flashing dark eyes and dusky curls. "You look like you've just lost your last friend."

157

He nodded a half-hearted greeting. "It isn't that, Lucy, it's just—" He broke off abruptly. "Lucy! You're just the person I need!"

"Finally!" exclaimed Lucy, who needed no urging to follow when he grabbed her hand and half-led, half-dragged her into the nearest tea room.

"Two," he told the proprietor as he plunked Lucy down at a vacant table near the window.

"Might I have a drop of Blue Ruin instead?" Lucy asked hopefully.

Pickett grimaced. "That stuff rots your insides. Tea," he repeated in a voice that brooked no argument.

"Is this going to take long?" Lucy asked, while Pickett waited silently as the proprietor set two steaming cups before them. "I don't mean to rush you, ducks, not when I've waited so long, but I'm a working girl, you know, and—"

"Lucy, I'm married to her ladyship." And to his horror and shame, he found himself blurting out the entire story of his irregular marriage to Lady Fieldhurst, and what was required of him in order to set it aside.

"Oh, you poor thing!" breathed Lucy, wide-eyed. "No wonder you've turned me down all these years. If I'd had any idea, I never would've—"

"It isn't *true*!" insisted Pickett, indignant.

"It might as well be, for all the good it does me," muttered Lucy.

Pickett propped his elbow on the table and sank his chin in his hand. "It isn't funny, Lucy."

"I'll say it's not! Now I'm never going to—*say*," she leaned across the table as a new thought occurred to her. "You'd really like to stay married to her ladyship, wouldn't you?"

Pickett sighed. "What I would like has nothing to say to the matter."

"You wouldn't have to *say* anything."

"What do you mean?" he asked, fearing very much that he already knew.

"Half an hour with me, ducks, and there goes her ladyship's grounds. I could show up in court bewailing my seduction and abandonment by a sweet-talking rogue—that would be you—and there would be nothing her bleedin' ladyship or her fusby-faced lawyer could do about it." She spread her hands in satisfaction. "I get what I want, you get what you want, and everybody's happy."

Pickett had spent five years rebuffing Lucy's advances, but at that moment he was seriously tempted to succumb. If by bedding one woman, he could be eternally bound to another . . . Granted, Lucy was not the woman he wanted, but he liked her and she was attractive enough. He was reasonably certain she would see to it that he enjoyed the experience, and perhaps more to the point, he would be able to come to his wife with some knowledge of what he was doing. Still, there was one flaw in Lucy's argument, one too big to ignore. "And what about Lady Fieldhurst?" he asked. "What about what *she* wants?"

Lucy dismissed the viscountess with a wave of one gloved hand. "She's had it all her own way long enough, hasn't she?"

"You'd be surprised."

To be sure, Pickett thought, Lady Fieldhurst must appear to Lucy to live a charmed life, with money, servants, and all the luxuries Lucy could never afford even if she spent the rest of her life on her back. But he knew it had not been at all pleasant for her ladyship, first being bound to an unfaithful husband, and then being suspected of murdering him. Lord Fieldhurst's death had given her an unexpected reprieve from an unhappy marriage, but not without considerable cost to herself; he would not trap her in another, no matter how great the temptation.

Quickly, before his resolution failed, he pushed his chair back and rose, tossing sufficient coins on the table to cover the cost of their tea. "Stay as long as you like, Lucy, but I have to be getting back to Bow Street. Mr. Colquhoun will be wondering what's become of me."

And there, he reflected, was yet another interview he would have preferred to avoid.

Mr. Colquhoun, deep in discussion with Mr. Foote when Pickett entered the Bow Street Public Office, took one look at that young man's face and immediately dismissed the elder Runner.

"What's happened, John?" he asked without roundaboutation.

At least, having unburdened himself to Lucy, Pickett felt no compulsion to do the same with his mentor. He summoned a feeble smile. "Good news, sir. According to Lady Fieldhurst's solicitor, we should be able to obtain an annulment."

"Good news, eh?" echoed the magistrate skeptically, regarding Pickett with ominously lowered brows. "And on what grounds is this annulment to be granted?"

"G-grounds, sir?" stammered Pickett, stalling for time and in the process, had he but known it, confirming his magistrate's worst fears.

"I did a little reading up on marriage laws while you were in Leicestershire," Mr. Colquhoun informed him. "I know there are only three acceptable grounds for annulment—fraud, incompetence, and impotence. Now, as far as I can tell, none of them apply here, unless, of course, you have difficulties of a personal nature of which I am unaware—"

"It's—it's not the sort of thing a man likes to talk about, sir," Pickett said miserably.

"No, I don't suppose so, particularly if he were himself unaware of the problem until quite recently—say, within the last hour or two."

"Mr. Colquhoun, sir—"

"Let me remind you, Mr. Pickett, that you have a duty to uphold the law. If I find you have any intention of perjuring yourself—"

"None at all, sir," Pickett assured him hastily. "I'm told I will not—will not have to testify, or even appear in court at all."

Mr. Colquhoun made a noise in the back of his throat that sounded vaguely reminiscent of a growl.

"And Lord Fieldhurst—" Somehow the suggestion that he should be willing to accept money in exchange for his co-operation seemed even more insulting than all the rest. "—Lord Fieldhurst was kind enough to offer me the sum of two hundred pounds to compensate for any indignities I might suffer."

Mr. Colquhoun's bushy white brows drew together in a formidable frown. "It must be nice, being able to buy one's way out of any difficulty. What did you say to his lordship's generous offer?"

"I threw it back in his teeth," Pickett confessed.

"Hmph. I can't say I don't think all the better of you for it."

"If—if you will excuse me, sir, I should like to get to work. I must return Lady Dunnington's property to her." He gestured toward the porcelain shepherdess still adorning the magistrate's bench. It seemed a very long time since he had discovered it in Mr. Kenney's possession. He realized that he should have seen to its return before his hasty departure for Leicestershire, not so much for Lady Dunnington's sake as for the peace of mind of her maid, Dulcie, who had been suspected of stealing it. Unfortunately, both females had been forgotten in his eagerness to see Lady Fieldhurst before setting out. He reached over the wooden railing and picked up the porcelain figurine.

"It's a pity you have to return her," Mr. Colquhoun remarked. "I've grown rather attached to her—she lends the place a certain air of distinction."

Pickett smiled rather half-heartedly. There was, he thought, really nothing at all funny about having to give up a woman who was never yours to keep.

CHAPTER 14

In Which John Pickett Goes A-Courting

Having wrapped the porcelain figurine in brown paper for safekeeping and tied it with string, Pickett retraced his steps from the Bow Street office to the more fashionable suburb of Mayfair, where he presented himself at Lady Dunnington's house in Audley Street. The door was opened to him by the maid Dulcie, who seemed quite pleased to see him.

"Why, it's Mr. Pickett from Bow Street!" she exclaimed, opening the door wide to admit him. "Do come in, sir, but if you're wanting to see her ladyship, I must tell you that Lady Dunnington is not at home."

"To tell you the truth, Miss Monroe—"

"Dulcie," she reminded him.

"Dulcie, then, my business here concerns you as much as it does her ladyship," said Pickett.

"Me? But how—?"

He handed her the paper-wrapped parcel. "Open it."

"For me?" Turning quite pink with pleasure, she began ripping the paper to expose the porcelain shepherdess within.

"Oh, Mr. Pickett, you found her! And here I thought she must be gone for good. How terribly clever of you!"

It was perhaps inevitable that a young man with a wounded vanity would be particularly susceptible to the admiration of an attractive young woman, and Pickett's vanity (never robust even at the best of times) was very, very wounded indeed. He blossomed under her attention like a flower seeking the sun.

"I didn't do anything, really," he demurred modestly. "In fact, you might say she found me."

"I am sure you do yourself less than justice," Dulcie insisted. "Pray, where did you find her?"

"Mr. Kenney found her in the pocket of his greatcoat," he told her. "I should have returned her a week ago, but I was obliged to make a trip to Leicestershire, and have only just returned."

"I had wondered where you'd been keeping yourself," she confessed. "But are you saying Mr. Kenney took her?"

"Not intentionally. Apparently he is in the habit of carrying a pistol for self-defense, and when he returned to his lodgings after Lady Dunnington's dinner party, he discovered his gun had been stolen, and this thing put in its place."

"How very strange! Who would have done such a thing?"

"Presumably the same person who shot Sir Reginald."

"And—and do you know who this person is?" she asked, her eyes wide with mingled hope and fear.

"No, but it's early days yet, and these things take time. Are you still frightened?"

She gave him a timid smile. "Not so very much, knowing you are on the case."

Quite unexpectedly, the words of the roguish Irishman floated to the surface of Pickett's brain. *Make sure you claim a hero's reward.* . . . Dulcie was indeed a pretty girl, and much the same size as Lady Fieldhurst, the crown of her head just topping his shoulder. But her eyes were brown, not blue, and her hair, though blonde, was more wheat-colored than golden. He recalled having similar thoughts about Sir Reginald's daughter, and wondered fleetingly if it was his destiny to go through life comparing every female he met to Lady Fieldhurst—and finding them all wanting.

"I am glad you can no longer be thought to have stolen her, in any case," he said.

"Oh, that!" Dulcie shook her head, dismissing the notion and at the same time setting her curls bouncing. Pickett noticed for the first time that she was not wearing the ruffled cap and apron that constituted her usual costume.

"I believe her ladyship felt quite badly about saying such a thing to me," the maid continued, "for she has given me a half-day off today without my even having to ask. In fact, I was on my way out when I heard your knock."

"In that case, I hope you will allow me to escort you," Pickett replied promptly.

"Oh, but I couldn't ask such a thing of you, sir!"

"You didn't ask; I offered."

"I am sure you must have a hundred more pressing things to do," she protested.

"More pressing, perhaps, but surely none more pleasant."

Dulcie struggled mightily for a few seconds before succumbing with a dimpled smile. "Very well, Mr. Pickett, since you insist."

Having settled the matter to the satisfaction of both, he offered her his arm. "If I am to call you Dulcie, I think you had best call me John."

"I couldn't possibly call you John!" she objected, taking his proffered arm nonetheless.

"Yes you can, for you just did," he pointed out.

"Why, so I did!" she exclaimed as they stepped out onto the portico. "Shall I tell you what I think, Mr. Pick—I mean, John? I think you are a shocking flirt!"

He laughed at that, but did not deny it. Surely it was better to be thought a flirt than to be thought—but he would not think about that now, not when the sun was shining, the weather

165

was unseasonably mild for November, and a pretty girl was clinging to his arm and gazing up at him as if he were her one hope of heaven.

"Where shall we go, Dulcie?"

After some discussion, it was agreed they should go to Hyde Park, where they might watch the fashionables promenade and throw breadcrumbs to the ducks that were always to be found swimming on the Serpentine. It soon transpired that Dulcie was an avid follower of the Society pages, and she took great pleasure in pointing out to Pickett all the leading lights of the *beau monde,* many of whom she had served, since they had been guests of Lady Dunnington at one time or another.

They had been engaged in this pleasant pastime for some half an hour when the sight of an elegantly dressed young couple in a high perch phaeton caught Dulcie's attention.

"Oh, look! That is Miss Granger-Hix and her betrothed, Sir Anthony Caldwell. Are they not a handsome pair? It said in the *Morning Post* that they are to marry in the spring." A shadow crossed Dulcie's pretty face. "I wonder what will happen to Sir Reginald Montague's daughter, now that she is in mourning. I daresay they will have to call the wedding off."

Pickett could not agree. "I should think getting married, even if one had to do it quietly, would be more important than having a fashionable wedding. I saw Miss Montague and her fiancé together on the night Sir Reginald was shot—I was obliged to convey the news to his family—and they appeared to be quite devoted to each other."

"Perhaps, but appearances can be deceiving. Miss Montague's fiancé is a marquess, and the heir to a dukedom. He might not wish to be associated with a family tainted by the scandal of a murder."

Pickett, far from being shocked at such cynicism, knew only too well how quickly those in Society could turn on one of their own, having seen Lady Fieldhurst fall victim to this phenomenon in the days following the murder of her husband. "Will you think me very rag-mannered if I say I hope you are wrong? I should rather think that Miss Montague's fiancé, if he loves her, would want to be in a position to support her through such a trying time."

"Love!" Dulcie echoed with unwonted bitterness. She tossed her final morsel of bread onto the ground, where it was immediately set upon by a trio of greedy ducks. "Their kind doesn't fall in love, John, they only use one another for social advancement. Only look at my Lady Dunnington and her husband, who never see one another except to quarrel. And then there is her friend Lady Fieldhurst, who married a viscount and then stabbed him to death!"

Pickett could not allow this slander of his lady to go unchallenged. "I can assure you, Lady Fieldhurst did not kill her husband!" he said with some indignation.

Dulcie hastily corrected herself. "No, of course she did not, for you proved her innocence, didn't you?" she said, patting his arm placatingly. "But it certainly appeared for a time as if she had, and that she would hang for it."

"No one could be in her ladyship's presence for five minutes and still believe her capable of such a thing!" insisted Pickett, refusing to be placated.

"Forgive me, John. I meant no disrespect toward her ladyship." She cast a slanting look up at him. "I believe you are much attached to Lady Fieldhurst's interests."

Pickett did not deny it. "I have had the honor of being of assistance to her on more than one occasion."

"And yet I suspect there is rather more to it than that, is there not?"

"I know my place, Dulcie, and it is not with her ladyship," he said in a flat voice.

Her large brown eyes filled with tears of sympathy. "I am sorry for you, John, truly I am. But there are other women, you know, women who know how to value the love of a good man."

So saying, she stood on tiptoe and kissed him on the cheek.

He did not return her kiss, but gave a little squeeze to the hand resting in the curve of his elbow. By unspoken agreement, they talked of other things, and by the time they completed their circuit around the park, they were once again on easy terms.

Over the next few days, Pickett made a habit of seeking out Dulcie whenever his investigations took him to the smart district of Mayfair. He found her company both comforting and nonthreatening: unlike Lady Fieldhurst, she was not above his touch, and unlike Lucy, she had no designs upon his person. It occurred to him that this was perhaps not entirely fair to Dulcie, to appear to be courting her when he feared he would never be able to give her his whole heart. But to one whose manhood was being called into question, her obvious admiration acted as a balm to his bruised spirit, and so his footsteps turned with increasing frequency in the direction of Audley Street. Upon arriving at that fashionable address, he did not approach the front door, but took the steps down to the servants' entrance below street level and asked for Dulcie. She was always eager to hear about the progress of his investigations, and was gratifyingly appreciative of his cleverness in even the most mundane of discoveries.

On one such visit, Pickett was emboldened to go a step further.

"Dulcie," he began, twisting the brim of his hat in his hands, "I wonder if I might—that is, I wonder if you would—would consent to—to—"

Seeing him floundering helplessly, Dulcie came to his rescue.

"If I would consent to what, John?"

He took a deep breath, and the words came out in a rush. "I wonder if I might see you on your day off."

Dulcie smiled. "I would like that very much."

"Do you like the theatre?" Pickett asked, much encouraged. "Mrs. Church is to make her farewell appearance on the Drury Lane stage this Wednesday. I should—I should be honored if you would accompany me."

"My day off is not until Thursday next," Dulcie confessed. "Still, I would love to see Mrs. Church on the stage. I shall ask my Lady Dunnington if I might swap with Polly. May I let you know tomorrow?"

Pickett agreed that tomorrow would be a wonderful day for such a communication and, after an awkward hesitation, bent and kissed her lightly on the cheek.

He was feeling rather better about the world in general and his place in it as he climbed the servants' stair up to street level—and almost ran into Lady Fieldhurst as she approached Lady Dunnington's front door.

"My lady!" He felt strangely guilty, as if he had narrowly escaped being caught in some act of betrayal. But theirs was not a real marriage and never would be, so there was no reason—no reason at all—for him to feel that by kissing Dulcie he had somehow been unfaithful to the lady who was nominally his wife.

"Are you coming in, Mr. Pickett?" asked Lady Fieldhurst, gesturing toward the front door.

"No, I was just—just leaving."

"Oh," she said, rather daunted. "Well then, I shan't keep you."

"My lady," he said quickly as she turned away, "I—I owe you an apology. I lost my temper—I said some things—"

"You had every right to be angry, Mr. Pickett. You still have,

169

for that matter. It is unconscionable, what Mr. Crumpton is—
no, what *I* am asking of you. I don't blame you for ripping up at
me."

"But I shouldn't have—"

She took a deep breath. "Mr. Pickett, there is something I
must tell you. Lady Dunnington left the dinner table that night
because her husband had called and insisted upon seeing her.
They quarreled quite audibly, and apparently Emily fears he
may be—involved—in Sir Reginald's death."

Pickett pondered this confession for a long moment, less
surprised by the revelation than by the fact that she had made it
at all, given her determination to remain silent on the subject.
"And what do you think, my lady?" he asked at last. "Do you
believe Lord Dunnington capable of murder?"

Her brow puckered as she considered the question. "I truly
don't know. I am not well acquainted with Lord Dunnington. I
fear they were estranged long before I met Emily, so I have only
her stated opinions of him with which to form an impression.
And those opinions, I might add, are usually far from compli-
mentary. Indeed, I wonder that she should be so—but you will
not arrest him, will you?"

"I will certainly question him, but I will make no arrest, of
Lord Dunnington or anyone else, without substantial evidence
to back it up—and so you may tell her ladyship. But—forgive
me, my lady, but why do you tell me this now, when you
steadfastly refused to do so when I asked you before?"

She made a helpless little gesture with her hands. "Because—
after what happened—the meeting with Mr. Crumpton—I am
reminded that there is no one in the world more worthy of my
trust than you, Mr. Pickett."

"Thank you, my lady. I am—honored—by your faith in me.
And yet there is one instance in which I failed to keep my word
to you, and for which I must beg your pardon."

"Is there?" she asked, puzzled. "I fear I don't remember—"

"When I kissed you in Scotland, I promised you it would not happen again," he reminded her. "I can hardly fault you for being less than honest with me, when it appears I lied to you."

"Pray do not refine too much upon it, Mr. Pickett. Being kissed by you is not so dreadful a burden, I assure you."

And giving him an uncertain little smile, she turned and knocked on Lady Dunnington's front door.

"I saw Mr. Pickett leaving as I approached your door," Lady Fieldhurst told Emily Dunnington some few minutes later, when they had settled themselves in the drawing room and rung for tea.

"Your Mr. Pickett was here?" asked Lady Dunnington, taken aback by this revelation. "Just now?"

"He isn't 'my' Mr. Pickett," Julia said, not for the first time. "Yes, just now. Coming up the servants' stair, in fact."

"If he wished to question the servants, he might have asked me first," grumbled the countess. "What if Dulcie were to blurt out the truth about Dunnington?"

"Emily, I have a confession to make," said Lady Fieldhurst, twisting the drawstrings of her reticule around her fingers. "*I* blurted out the truth about Dunnington, just now."

"Julia!" cried Lady Dunnington, stricken. "How *could* you?"

"He must find out sooner or later," Lady Fieldhurst pointed out. "Surely it will look much better if it appears we have nothing to hide."

"Nonsense! There was no reason why he should ever have had to know about it at all—had you not told him!" she added, an odd mixture of fear and defiance in her voice.

"But Emily, there were half a dozen witnesses! You cannot expect them all to keep silent, especially if they are under investigation themselves. The temptation to divert suspicion would surely be too great to resist."

"Witnesses?" The countess seized upon the word. "But no one saw Dunnington except for myself and Dulcie!"

"Not *saw*, perhaps, but I can assure you everyone at the table *heard*." Seeing Emily's horrified countenance, she explained, "You were only in the next room, you know, and neither of you was making any effort to keep your voice down."

"Then—then you all heard what he said? About how he would 'put a stop to it,' no matter what it might take?"

"Yes, but those words could mean a great many things other than murder. Or they could mean absolutely nothing. I can assure you Mr. Pickett will be well familiar with masculine bluster; after all, I have met his magistrate! Depend upon it, he will not leap to any conclusions where Lord Dunnington is concerned."

Lady Dunnington twisted her wedding ring around on her finger. "I wish I could share your confidence in him. Or in Dunnington, for that matter. You may speak of masculine bluster, but Dunnington is not one to make idle threats."

"Do *you* think he killed Sir Reginald?"

"I—I don't know! I only fear I may have provoked him too far this time. I knew how he felt about Sir Reginald. In fact, that was my whole reason for pursuing the man—to make Dunnington jealous."

"He has never seemed to be troubled by jealousy where any of your other lovers were concerned," observed Lady Fieldhurst.

"I know," Lady Dunnington said mournfully. "I was at the end of my rope! I didn't know what else to do but find a man so thoroughly unsavory that Dunnington would *have* to take notice! And now Sir Reginald is dead, and if Dunnington ends up hanging for murder, I shall—I shall *kill* him!"

Lady Fieldhurst would have pointed out the illogic of this declaration, but another, far more important idea drove it from her mind. "Emily," she demanded with dawning comprehension, "do you *love* Lord Dunnington?"

The countess's mouth worked, and she cast her gaze wildly about the room. "I—I—"

Lady Dunnington was spared the necessity of making a reply by the arrival of Dulcie with the tea cart. Even after cups were poured and distributed and a plate of cakes offered, the girl remained standing awkwardly at her mistress's shoulder.

"Yes, Dulcie?" asked Lady Dunnington. "What is it?"

"Begging your pardon, your ladyship, but—but I wonder if I might make a request."

"Well, go ahead then, make it."

"The actress Mrs. Church is to make her final appearance in Drury Lane on Wednesday, and my young man has asked me to accompany him to the theatre that night. I know it's not my usual day, ma'am, but I wonder if I might swap days with Polly, just this once."

"Your young man?" echoed Lady Dunnington archly. "Why, Dulcie, I didn't know you were walking out with someone. You've scarcely been in my employ for six months. Am I to lose you so soon?"

"It's much too early to be thinking of that, your ladyship," Dulcie protested, but her coy blushes told their own tale.

"Nonsense! It is never too early for females to be thinking of marriage," the countess observed. "Very well, if Polly has no objections to swapping days with you, I suppose it's all the same to me. Only do not stay out too late—and *no* unpleasant surprises two or three months hence, if you please!"

Dulcie did not pretend to misunderstand her. "Why, no ma'am!" she exclaimed, shocked at the very suggestion. "Thank you, ma'am." She bobbed a curtsy and betook herself from the room.

"Well!" exclaimed Lady Dunnington once the two ladies were alone. "It's nice to know that *someone's* romantic intrigues are proceeding apace. Perhaps our problems would be more easily solved, Julia my dear, if we were members of a lesser class."

"Perhaps they would," Lady Fieldhurst murmured.

A faint shadow of disquiet crossed her mind. Mr. Pickett had just been here, downstairs in the servants' quarters, in fact, and he knew Mrs. Church well from their ill-fated adventure in Scotland . . . Nonsense, she told herself, pushing away the thought. There were doubtless many people eager to see Mrs. Church's final performance, and Dulcie was pretty enough that she might have any number of young men eager to court her. Mr. Pickett would never do such a thing—not now, not when he knew how much depended upon his remaining chaste until the annulment was granted.

And yet the troubling idea, once admitted, would not be so easily dismissed.

CHAPTER 15

In Which John Pickett Renews an Old Acquaintance,
with Unsettling Results

Pickett had intended to return to Bow Street, but in the light of Lady Fieldhurst's revelation, he instead called on Lord Dunnington at his town house in Park Lane. Pickett's luck was clearly in on this particular day, for in addition to his successes with the female of the species, he caught Lord Dunnington just before he left the house.

"John Pickett of Bow Street," he informed the butler, while looking over this individual's shoulder at a well-dressed man of late middle age engaged in donning gloves and high-crowned beaver hat.

Upon hearing the caller's words, the earl sighed, removed his hat, and began stripping off his gloves. "I had wondered when I might expect the honor of a visit from Bow Street," remarked Lord Dunnington, his voice dry. "Never mind, Figgins, I can always look in at my club later. I suppose you'd best come in, Mr.—Pickett, was it?—and let us get it over with."

In spite of this unpromising beginning, Lord Dunnington ushered Pickett into a sitting room decorated according to masculine tastes with dark wood paneling and button-backed leather armchairs. The earl, a man as sober in appearance as his countess was flamboyant, sat down in one of these and gestured for Pickett to take the one beside it.

"In truth, Mr. Pickett, I had expected to see you long before now," confessed Lord Dunnington. "I need not ask, of course, how you came by the information that I was present, however briefly, on the night of Sir Reginald's demise. I daresay she delighted in offering up my head on a platter, as it were."

"I believe you do her ladyship a disservice, my lord," Pickett protested. "I assure you, she took no pleasure in providing the information. In fact, she told me just today, and only because she felt she owed it to me for personal reasons unrelated to the case."

"I see." Lord Dunnington frowned. "I should have thought you were a little young for her."

Pickett stiffened. "I fail to see what my age has to do with it, sir."

"You are probably right. You are male, after all, and as far as her ladyship is concerned, that would appear to be enough."

Pickett shot to his feet. "I take offense, my lord! I have the greatest admiration and respect for Lady Fieldhurst, and I will not sit and listen to you or anyone else malign her in such a fashion!"

"Lady Fieldhurst?" echoed Lord Dunnington incredulously. "Who the devil said anything about Lady Fieldhurst? Oh, sit down, man! Am I to understand that it was *not* my wife who told you of my visit to Audley Street?"

Deflated, Pickett sat. "No, my lord, it was Lady Fieldhurst who did so, and that, as I said, only because she felt herself to be indebted to me for reasons that have no bearing on the case. In fact, your wife has been lying like a cheap rug in an effort to keep me from finding out about your presence that night."

"Has she, now?" Lord Dunnington drummed his fingers on the arm of his chair, an arrested expression on his face. "Has she, indeed?"

"Of course, you realize I must ask why you called in Audley

Street that night."

"Oh, of course," his lordship said. "I called in Audley Street that night for the only reason I ever call in Audley Street: to quarrel with my countess."

Pickett blinked at such plain speaking. "And the reason for the quarrel?"

"My good fellow, I rarely need a reason. My wife usually finds the mere fact of my presence to be sufficient provocation for an exchange of, shall we say, pleasantries. On this particular occasion, however, I had reason enough and to spare. My wife, as you may already be aware, had the fixed intention of entering into an intimate liaison with Sir Reginald Montague. I came to Audley Street to inform her I would not tolerate it; I believe my exact words may have been 'I will put a stop to this, whatever it takes.' " He grimaced. "Believe me, I am fully aware of how damning those words are, in the light of what followed."

"Then what exactly did you mean by them, if you had no intention of killing Sir Reginald?"

"In truth, Mr. Pickett, I hardly know myself. I daresay I meant to cut off her funds or some such thing. But even that would have been an empty threat. After all, one hardly wishes to force one's wife to beg for her bread, or to drive her into the arms—and consequently the bed—of a benefactor."

"But I believe this was not—forgive me!—the first time your wife had taken a lover, and you apparently saw no need to intervene before. Please correct me if I am wrong."

"No, no, you are quite right."

"Begging your pardon, my lord, but how can you have been so accepting of the situation for so long?"

"It is the way of our world, young man, and she understands it as well as I. Had our children been girls, of course, it would have been a different matter altogether, but once a lady has given her husband an heir—or perhaps two, in case of illness or a tragic accident—she is usually allowed to follow the inclinations of her own affections."

Pickett, astounded by this casual attitude toward adultery, thought of Lady Fieldhurst and wondered if, had she been capable of bearing her husband children, she would have ended by drifting from one man's bed to another. The thought made him feel more than a little ill, and he was conscious of an entirely selfish relief that she had remained childless.

"And yet you chose to intervene when Sir Reginald was the lover in question," Pickett noted. "Why him, and not the others?"

Lord Dunnington's eyebrows rose. "My good fellow, if you have done any investigating at all into Sir Reginald's character, I wonder you should have to ask! I am aware that the ladies found him attractive, but then, they had no knowledge of the depravities that were frequent topics of conversation—and occasionally cause for duels—at the gentlemen's clubs. No, nothing good could have come of such a liaison, but a great deal of harm might have done, and much of it redounded to my wife's discredit. Can you wonder that I wished to prevent her from becoming intimate with such a man?"

Pickett blinked as the significance of these words began to dawn. "Am I to understand, then, that you—that you care for her ladyship?"

"Care for her? Mr. Pickett, I shall love her until I die—which I quite realize may be sooner than anticipated, given my presence in Audley Street on the night Sir Reginald was murdered."

Pickett hardly heard the last part of this speech, so flabbergasted was he by the first. "You say you love her, and yet you stand by without a word while she bounces from bed to bed like a—"

"I should choose my next word with care if I were you, Mr. Pickett." Lord Dunnington did not raise his voice, but the atmosphere in the room grew decidedly wintry in spite of the fire burning in the grate.

"But—but—damn it, man, she's your *wife*! Aren't you going to—to fight for her?" Pickett knew he was overstepping his bounds rather badly, but something about Lord Dunnington's situation touched a nerve.

The earl regarded him with mild curiosity. "And how would you suggest I do so, Mr. Pickett? By putting a bullet through her lover, perhaps?"

The wind having been taken from his sails, Pickett flushed. "I beg your pardon, my lord. I—I should not have spoken in such a way."

"Apology accepted," said the earl, inclining his head. "As I said, it is the way of our world. I would not expect you to understand."

It was the best argument Pickett could think of for going through with the annulment, however humiliating the process. Were he and Lady Fieldhurst to remain married on such terms, it would shatter him into a million pieces the first time she took a lover.

"After this quarrel, then," Pickett said, dragging his attention back to the matter at hand, "what did you do?"

"I did not know, of course, that someone else was about to solve the problem for me. I stormed out of the house—I fear I can offer no witnesses to my departure, as I did not wait for my wife to summon a servant to show me out—and then I took myself off to my club to drink myself into a stupor. The porter at White's should be able to confirm my arrival there."

Pickett made a note of it. "I shall have to follow up on it, of course, but I am inclined to believe you." He stared down at his notes for a long moment, then spoke very deliberately. "I am going to ask you a question that you will not like, but I hope you will give me an honest answer. Do you believe it possible that Lady Dunnington shot Sir Reginald herself?"

Lord Dunnington bristled. "Emily, shoot a man in cold blood? Balderdash! If she were capable of such a thing, I should have been dead years ago. Besides, why the devil should she?"

"I'm afraid you're asking the wrong person, my lord. I don't pretend to understand women," Pickett said with a shrug, and rose to take his leave.

On Wednesday evening, Pickett donned his best coat of black wool and set out for Lady Dunnington's house on Audley Street. He had just received his wages for the week, and he treated himself to the unaccustomed luxury of hiring a hackney to convey him to Mayfair and thence, with Dulcie, back to the Theatre Royal at Drury Lane. It was not Dulcie, however, but another lady who filled his thoughts as the bustling Covent Garden district gave way to the manicured residential streets of Mayfair. *Being kissed by you, Mr. Pickett, is not so dreadful a burden.* . . . He could not suppress the rather foolish smile that stole across his face at the memory of Lady Fieldhurst's words. Still, kissing was one thing; marriage was quite another, and he would do well to remember it.

The hackney lurched to a stop before Lady Dunnington's house. Pickett requested the driver to wait, then descended the servants' stair to the entrance below street level and knocked on the door. It opened a moment later to reveal Dulcie, not in the apron and mobcap in which he was accustomed to seeing her, but in a high-waisted print dress and with a blue satin ribbon threaded through her pale blonde curls. She had obviously taken pains with her appearance, and he was glad he had worn his best coat.

"Are we to ride in a carriage, then?" she asked when they reached the top of the stairs and she saw the waiting vehicle. "Such extravagance, John!"

"It's a special occasion," he reminded her as he handed her up into the hackney. "Mrs. Church's farewell performance. Did I tell you I recently had the honor of being of assistance to her?"

"I see I shall have to keep a close eye on you," she scolded with mock severity. "First Lady Fieldhurst, and now Mrs. Church. It seems to me you have the honor of being of assistance to entirely too many beautiful women!"

"I hope you will count yourself as one of them," he said, seating himself beside her.

Her dark eyes shone in the lamplight filtering through the carriage windows. She tucked her hand through the crook of his arm and gave it a little squeeze. "I think you are very sweet, John."

It soon transpired that they were obliged to walk in any case, for when they reached Drury Lane, they found the street in front of the theatre so choked with traffic that Pickett was forced to dismiss his hired equipage and escort his fair companion the rest of the way on foot. Once inside the theatre, they found places in the pit that offered a reasonably good view of the stage (a good view, in this case, meaning one with no large bonnets or tall men to block it) and took their seats. As Pickett had seen Mrs. Church's Ophelia once before already, his attention was prone at times to wander, and all too frequently his gaze was drawn upward toward the rows of boxes overhead, where those wealthy enough to pay five shillings per seat congregated to survey the performance and each other.

"What is the matter?" asked Dulcie during one of these intervals. "What are you looking for?"

Pickett shook his head, somehow both disappointed and relieved to find the Fieldhurst box unoccupied. "Nothing."

Perhaps feeling a bit guilty for this lapse, Pickett turned to Dulcie when the final curtain had fallen. "Would you like to meet Mrs. Church?"

"Can you *do* that?" asked Dulcie, her eyes wide with awe.

"I can try. I told you, I once—"

"—Had the honor of being of assistance to her," she finished for him. "Yes, I remember. But will she agree to see you?"

"I don't know. There's only one way to find out."

Grabbing Dulcie's hand to keep from losing her in the throng, he squeezed his way backstage, where a dozen or more gentlemen bearing large floral bouquets had assembled outside the actress's dressing room.

"Yes, your Grace," a harried assistant to Mr. Sheridan, the theatre manager, assured an elegantly dressed man cradling two dozen autumn roses in his arm. "Mrs. Church has been informed of your arrival. If you will be patient—"

"Excuse me," Pickett said, tapping the much put-upon underling on the shoulder. "Will you please tell Mrs. Church that John Pickett requests the honor of a meeting?"

The duke shot Pickett a contemptuous glance, and a dashing officer in scarlet regimentals made a dismissive snort, but the theatre assistant, heaving a sigh, consented, albeit without enthusiasm. "I will, young man, but I make no promises."

Pickett nodded. "I understand."

The underling rapped on the door and then slipped inside, closing it quickly behind him before the more aggressive of the gentlemen callers could push their way inside. A moment later, the door opened again. Instead of the harassed assistant, a beautiful woman with heavy stage makeup and raven-dark hair appeared in the aperture.

"Mr. Pickett! How lovely to see you again! Do come in! Oh, good evening, Major Richardson. Yes, your Grace, I see you brought me flowers. It was very kind of you, and I shall thank you directly, but first I must have a word with my very dear friend Mr. Pickett. Do forgive me, gentlemen. Come in, Mr.

Pickett!" She reached out to take his arm and pull him through the crowd into her dressing room.

Pickett could not resist the urge to bestow a rather smug smile on the assemblage as, guiding Dulcie before him with a hand at her waist, he passed them all en route to Mrs. Church's *sanctum sanctorum.*

"Pray shut the door, Mr. Pickett, and lock it, if you would be so kind," urged Mrs. Church once they were safely inside.

He did so, and the noise outside was muted to a dull roar. "It is good to see you once more before you leave London," he told the actress. "Mrs. Church, may I present my friend, Miss Dulcie Monroe?"

"I hope you enjoyed the performance, Miss Monroe." Mrs. Church nodded at the young woman, but regarded Pickett with a quizzical smile.

"Oh, yes indeed! This was my first visit to the theatre," Dulcie confessed, blushing.

"But not your last, I hope. Tell me, how would you like to meet our Hamlet? Mr. Bracegirdle," she addressed the harried assistant, "pray take Miss Monroe to meet Mr. Brereton. Tell him I would be much obliged to him if he will see her. Thank you! You are an angel!"

Having shut the door behind Dulcie and the much-harassed angel, she turned the full force of her considerable charm on Pickett. "Now we may be private," she declared, giving him her hands and kissing the air on either side of his face. "It is indeed lovely to see you again, Mr. Pickett, but I must ask: who is this Miss Monroe? What, pray, has happened to Mrs. Pickett?"

Pickett flushed, thinking that perhaps his plan to dazzle Dulcie with his exalted connections had not been such a good idea after all. "I think you know that any 'marriage' between myself and Lady Fieldhurst was merely a masquerade."

She raised a knowing eyebrow. "Not in Scotland, it isn't."

183

He sighed. "Yes, we're finding that out."

"And?"

"And her ladyship's solicitor is already making arrangements to have the marriage annulled."

"And you're *letting* him? Forgive me if I am overstepping, Mr. Pickett, but it is obvious to the meanest intelligence how you feel about the lady! Surely you cannot mean to let the annulment go through without lifting a finger to stop it!"

"That's not all I won't be lifting," muttered Pickett, then blushed crimson as she burst out laughing. "I beg your pardon—I should not have spoken so to a lady."

"Ah, but you know I am not much of a lady—and you, I believe, have a greater claim to the title of gentleman than many who are born to it. If I can see that, I daresay a certain lady of our acquaintance has recognized it as well."

"I can't speak for her ladyship's feelings on the matter, but I cannot believe she would want to remain tied to a thief-taker with nothing but twenty-five shillings a week!"

"Have you asked her?"

Pickett bristled. "I would not so insult her!"

"If she required a fortune to be happy, she should have been ecstatic with her viscount," the actress pointed out. Seeing he was not convinced, she added, "Trust me on this, Mr. Pickett: life is too short and love is too precious to waste on things that don't matter—not really, not when one's future happiness is at stake. You are familiar enough with my own story to recognize I know whereof I speak. If you love her, don't give her up without a fight."

His own words to Lord Dunnington came floating back to him. *She's your wife! Aren't you going to fight for her?* But the two cases were completely different. Lady Dunnington had promised to love, honor, and obey, and however lightly she may have taken her vows in the years that followed, she had taken them knowingly and voluntarily. Lady Fieldhurst had done neither. It would be wrong of him to try to hold her to a commitment she'd had no intention or knowledge of making.

"I am glad for you, and hope you and your husband will be very happy together," Pickett said. "But things are different between Lady Fieldhurst and me. Even if the difference between our stations were unimportant—and it isn't, not by a long chalk!—she could have any man she chose. Why on earth would she want *me*?"

She gave him a long, calculating look. "Do you know, I don't think I shall tell you. It seems to me that a great part of your charm springs from the fact that you are utterly unaware of your own appeal. I should hate to spoil it. No, Mr. Pickett, if you desire an answer to that question, you must ask the lady herself."

"Mrs. Church," he said with some exasperation, "I tell you, I—"

"Oh, please call me Miss Kirkbride," she interrupted.

"Miss Kirkbride, then, I can't possibly—she would never—"

He got no further, for at that moment the door opened and Dulcie re-entered the room. Pickett hardly knew whether to be sorry or glad for the interruption.

"Thank you, Mrs. Church, that was quite wonderful! Mr. Brereton even kissed my hand." Dulcie held up her right hand as if to admire it. "I'm sure I shall never wash it again!"

So thrown off balance was Pickett by his aborted conversation with Mrs. Church that his farewell speech to the actress was disjointed almost to the point of incoherence. Once outside the theatre with Dulcie, however, he was obliged to focus all his attention on the problem of procuring a hackney when half of London seemed to be entertaining the same ambition, with the happy result that by the time they returned to Audley Street he was much himself again. He escorted his fair companion down the stairs to the servants' entrance, and she paused at the door and turned to face him.

"Will you not come in for tea, or perhaps coffee?" she asked, looking up at him with her large, doe-like eyes.

He shook his head. "Thank you, but I'd best get home. I have to be back at the Bow Street office in the morning."

"I understand," she said, obviously disappointed. "Well, thank you for a lovely evening, John. I do hope all goes well with your investigations."

"I don't know," said Pickett, considering the matter carefully. "If things go *too* well, I'll have no further reason to call in Audley Street."

"You don't need a reason, John." She ducked her chin and looked up at him through her lashes. "Whatever may be happening above stairs, you may always be sure of a welcome from me."

"Thank you, Dulcie."

He took her hand and would have raised it to his lips, but she slipped it out of his grasp.

"Not there! That's the hand Mr. Brereton kissed." She lifted her face ever so slightly to his. "I guess you'll just have to find something else to kiss."

Pickett, nothing loth, drew her into his embrace and lowered his mouth to hers.

But when he closed his eyes, it was not Dulcie in his arms.

CHAPTER 16

In Which John Pickett Tries His Hand at Matchmaking

Pickett arrived at the Bow Street Public Office the next morning to discover that Mr. Crumpton had been busy about his work. A message had been delivered for him there, and when he opened it, he was instructed that Dr. Edmund Humphrey had agreed to see him at his practice in Harley Street promptly at eleven. Pickett, glancing up at the clock over the magistrate's bench, saw that he had some time to make inquiries before presenting himself in Harley Street. In fact, he was more than a little surprised by the summons; when Mr. Crumpton had assured him that the results of the doctor's examination would be falsified (for a consideration, of course), he had assumed there would be no need for a face-to-face meeting. Now that he was made aware of his error, he approached the magistrate with some trepidation.

"Mr. Colquhoun, sir," he began, "I'm afraid I must be out of the office for much of the morning, with your permission."

Mr. Colquhoun regarded him from underneath beetling brows. "Does this concern the investigation, or the annulment?"

Pickett sighed. "Both, I'm afraid. I do have a few inquiries to make regarding the investigation, but as for the annulment, it seems there is the matter of a—a medical examination—"

"Good God, what next?" grumbled the magistrate. "I have been thinking, Mr. Pickett, and it seems to me I had best remove

187

you from the Sir Reginald Montague case altogether."

"Remove me from the case, sir?" echoed Pickett, surprised and not at all pleased. "But why?"

"I should have done so from the very beginning; the fact that you are at least nominally married to one of the parties involved might be construed as a conflict of interest, to say the least. But now, given the shambles that is your personal life at the moment—"

"Lady Fieldhurst may have been present at dinner that night, sir, but she is hardly 'involved'! There is no question of her being guilty, as she was with Lady Dunnington at the time the shot was fired."

"And has it not occurred to you that the Ladies Fieldhurst and Dunnington are one another's only alibi? It appears you are slipping, Mr. Pickett, or else you are so distracted by the annulment process that you can no longer give the investigation the attention it deserves."

"In fact, sir, it had indeed occurred to me. But as I am, as you say, acquainted with one of the parties in question—"

"Most people would consider marriage much more than a mere acquaintance!"

"—I know Lady Fieldhurst to be incapable of such an act, and in this case her innocence would seem to exonerate Lady Dunnington, since for one of the ladies to lie about the matter would require that the other lie as well." Of course, Lady Fieldhurst had certainly been less than truthful on the subject of Lady Dunnington's ten-minute absence from the dinner table, but since she had recently made a full confession about the matter (which had occurred quite some time before the murder in any case), Pickett saw no need to make Mr. Colquhoun a gift of this information.

"Nevertheless, Mr. Foote has expressed an interest in being dispatched to Mayfair on some of these cases involving the aristocracy—"

"Begging your pardon, sir, but Mr. Foote hates me and would like nothing better than to advance his own career at my expense!" Pickett put in with some asperity.

"If by that outburst you mean he is envious of you, of course he is, and who can blame him? You have established in less than a year a reputation that it has taken him the better part of a decade to achieve. But Mr. Foote is efficient, although by no means brilliant, and no one can accuse him of having close 'acquaintances' among the aristocracy. If you will hand over your notes on the case to him, he should be quite capable of picking up the investigation where you left off."

"Mr. Colquhoun, sir, *please* don't take me off this case," said Pickett, not above begging.

"Can you give me one good reason why I shouldn't?"

Pickett sighed. "At the moment, sir, it seems to be the one area in which my—my competence—is not being called into question."

Mr. Colquhoun looked into his youngest Runner's anguished face and felt himself weakening. It would not do for him to be perceived as favoring one Runner above all the others—much less the one with the least experience of any on the force—but John Pickett was already being put through hell over this annulment without his adding to the lad's burden.

"Oh, very well," he said reluctantly. "I'll give you a little longer, but if I don't see some real progress being made toward an arrest, I will have no choice but to remove you and put Foote in your place. Is that clear?"

"Very clear, sir. Thank you. Now, if you please, sir, may I— may I go? There is the—the matter of the physician's examination later this morning, and I have a line of inquiry I should like to pursue in the meantime."

Mr. Colquhoun made a flapping motion with his hands. "By

all means, be off with you."

"Thank you." He had not gone half a dozen steps when he turned back. "Oh, and sir?"

"Yes, what is it now?"

"After the case of Sir Reginald Montague is resolved, you may give Mr. Foote all the Mayfair assignments he wishes. I have no desire to visit the area again."

The magistrate scowled at him. "Are you sure? Aside from the fact that most of the well-paying commissions come from that part of Town, you seem to have a gift for dealing with the upper classes. Not that you blend in, precisely, but at least you don't set up people's backs. I fear Mr. Foote will be hard pressed to duplicate your success there."

"I am flattered by your confidence in me, sir, but I am quite sure. I—I think it best if, once this case is settled, I don't see her ladyship again."

The magistrate's eyebrows rose. "Very well, Mr. Pickett, if that is what you wish."

"It is, sir. Thank you," said Pickett again, and left the Bow Street office.

Mr. Colquhoun, watching him go, muttered, "Damn the woman," then snapped the head off a hapless member of the foot patrol who had the misfortune to choose that moment to ask a perfectly innocuous question.

Having obtained his magistrate's permission, if not his blessing, Pickett set out once again for Mayfair—specifically, for the Albany flat of Lord Rupert Latham. He could think of few places where he would not prefer to be (Dr. Humphrey's Harley Street office being a rare exception), and few people whose company he would be less desirous of seeking out. Still, Lord Rupert Latham was the only person he knew who would possess the knowledge he sought without having a personal stake in the dissemination of this information. And so it was that he came to be shown into Lord Rupert's flat just as that gentleman, gorgeously arrayed in a dressing gown of Oriental design, was sitting down to breakfast.

"My good fellow," he told Pickett, wincing at the sunlight emitted through the open door, "I am, as always, enchanted to see your happy smiling face, but at nine o'clock in the morning? Must you?"

As Pickett was neither happy nor smiling, he gave Lord Rupert's welcome all the consideration it deserved—which was to say, none at all. "I beg your pardon for calling so early, your lordship, but I have obligations later in the day, and wanted to see you first."

"Is the hour of my arrest at hand, then? Tell me, what reason have you uncovered that might inspire me to kill Sir Reginald? I should have imagined you would have lost interest in dispatching me to the gallows, given that you have contrived to wed Lady Fieldhurst against all odds. Or do you doubt your ability to hold her interest, and thus feel the need to eliminate the competition?"

"As for my marriage to her ladyship, you will no doubt be pleased to know that plans have already been set in motion for an annulment," Pickett said tonelessly, wishing he might be less sensitive to Lord Rupert's jibes.

"My dear Mr. Pickett, I am neither pleased nor displeased, having never really considered any other outcome," Lord Rupert assured him in bored accents. "But if I am not to be arrested, then to what, pray, do I owe the pleasure of your company?"

"Since you have no motive that I can see for wanting to kill Sir Reginald, I thought I could trust you to give me an honest opinion, if you would be so obliging."

Lord Rupert's face assumed an expression of exaggerated surprise. "Can it be that the child prodigy of Bow Street has come to me for help? Tell me, Mr. Pickett, why the devil should I wish to help you?"

Fortunately, Pickett had anticipated this response, and had prepared for it accordingly. "Consider, your lordship, that once the matter of Sir Reginald's death is resolved, I should have no reason for further dealings with her ladyship, at least not until our annulment comes up before the ecclesiastical court."

"There is that, of course," acknowledged Lord Rupert. "Still, that would presuppose that I consider you a threat to my own interests where her ladyship is concerned. Nothing could be further from the truth, I assure you."

"If I pose no threat to you, then surely it can do you no harm to favor me with your opinion," Pickett pointed out.

"Very true. I concede the point. And I might even indulge the hope that, once I have given you the benefit of my wisdom, you might go away and leave me alone. Yes, shockingly rude of me, I know, but I was at White's until very late, and have a throbbing head." As if in proof of this last statement, he reached for the coffee pot, refilled his cup, and drank it down black. "Very well, Mr. Pickett. What do you want to know?"

"I should like to know just how important a membership at White's is to your set."

Lord Rupert's eyebrows rose. "Are you thinking to persuade someone to put your name forward? I fear you are wasting your time. You are no better suited to be a member of White's than you are to be a husband to Lady Fieldhurst."

"I am thinking of Mr. Martin Kenney," Pickett said impatiently. "I believe he was once a member there?"

"You are well informed. He was indeed a member until quite recently."

"I understand he has Sir Reginald to thank for his expulsion from the club."

Lord Rupert nodded. "Correct again."

"Do you know what happened to cause Mr. Kenney to be blackballed?"

"Do I know? My good fellow, I was there at the time."

"Can you tell me what happened?"

Lord Rupert leaned back in his chair, rolling his eyes toward the ceiling as he cast his mind back to the night in question. "As I recall, Mr. Kenney was enjoying a prodigious run of luck, much of it at Sir Reginald's expense. Eventually Sir Reginald observed that Mr. Kenney seemed to be as familiar with the backs of the cards as with their fronts—the implication being, of course, that Mr. Kenney was cheating by using a marked deck."

"And was he?" Pickett asked.

Lord Rupert shrugged. "I saw no evidence of it. His luck was certainly in, but no more so than I had seen any other of a dozen men enjoy on any given night."

"Yet you said nothing in his defense," observed Pickett.

"My dear Mr. Pickett, why should I? Who would have listened to me? I daresay none of the men who voted to revoke Mr. Kenney's membership believed it either, but Sir Reginald is—was—a dangerous man to cross, and who was Mr. Kenney but an impoverished Irishman whose membership was no great credit to the club in the first place? No, I fear the poor blighter never stood a chance."

"And in your opinion, would being tossed out of White's constitute a motive for murder?"

"Only in a very highly strung individual, and I confess, I never received the impression that Mr. Kenney was so sensitive. However, since you have asked for my honest opinion, I must inform you that there was rather more to it than that."

"The young lady Mr. Kenney had hoped to marry," Pickett guessed.

"Oh, you know about that, do you?"

Pickett nodded. "Mr. Kenney told me himself."

"Mr. Kenney was certainly no prize before, although his birth was respectable enough. Still, the lady's father was inclined to look with favor on his suit simply because he doted upon his daughter, and she was smitten with the fellow. But the fond papa was in attendance that night, and, well, one can't have a scandal like that in the family, you know. Mr. Kenney might have won four hundred pounds at piquet, but the aptly named Miss Price and her forty thousand were forever lost to him."

"Hmm." Pickett frowned, deep in thought. Lord Rupert's account matched up on all major points with Mr. Kenney's, and yet, as disastrous as it was for the Irishman from a financial perspective, Pickett could not quite see it as sufficient motive for murder. He was aware, of course, that aristocratic males had a penchant for defending slights to their honor, whether real or imagined, by challenging one another to duels on Hampstead Heath or some other remote location; still, he failed to see how it might avenge one's honor to shoot an unarmed man in the chest at point-blank range. "Tell me, Lord Rupert, what sort of man is Mr. Kenney? What sort of husband would he make?"

Lord Rupert, in the process of taking another swig of coffee, paused with the cup poised halfway to his lips. "Are you thinking of cutting me out by choosing your own successor? I hate to disappoint you, Mr. Pickett, but at dinner your lady wife showed not the slightest interest in Mr. Kenney."

"Actually, I had another potential bride in mind," confessed Mr. Pickett, refusing to be baited. "One who stands in urgent need of a husband, thanks to Sir Reginald Montague."

"I hope this time you have found a female of your own class. Oh, I see! You meant another prospective bride for Mr. Kenney. You must be thinking of Lord Edwin's daughter, Miss Braunton."

Pickett stared at him, taken aback by this revelation. "You know about Miss Braunton's, er, condition?"

"My good man, when one considers Miss Braunton's abrupt departure from London in the middle of a Season in which she was touted as a diamond of the first water, followed almost immediately by her father's offering of a rather lavish financial inducement to matrimony to nearly every unattached gentleman in Town, one need not be a Bow Street Runner—forgive me!—for putting two and two together and arriving at the correct sum."

"Your opinion of Mr. Kenney, then?"

Lord Rupert leaned back in his chair as he considered the question. "I believe Mr. Kenney to be a good enough sort. No money, of course, but you knew that."

"And the gambling?"

"Most of the aristocracy does it, at least to some extent," said Lord Rupert with a shrug. "Still, I have never heard of Mr. Kenney dipping deeper than he ought; the cardinal rule of gambling, you know, is never to wager more than one can afford to lose. But if rumor is to be believed, Mr. Kenney's father left the estate heavily encumbered when he died, and I daresay living by his wits, as the saying goes, is the only way to make ends meet, at least until he can persuade some heiress to marry him. Yes, I believe such a marriage might serve very well, for both parties concerned. I confess, Mr. Pickett, before making your acquaintance I had no idea an instrument of the law would possess such a romantic streak."

Pickett, suspecting this observation concealed yet another dig at his own interest in Lady Fieldhurst, did not dignify it with a reply, but rose to his feet. "I thank you for your candor, your lordship. I will leave you now to enjoy your breakfast in peace."

Lord Rupert rose and followed him into the flat's small foyer, where his lordship's man was waiting with Pickett's hat and gloves. Pickett had taken these and was about to put them on when Lord Rupert spoke again.

"By the bye, about this annulment . . ."

"Yes?" prompted Pickett, fairly certain he would not enjoy the exchange that was about to follow.

"On what grounds is it to be sought?"

"I—I beg your pardon?" Pickett stammered, seeing his worst fears were about to be realized.

"Come, man, I am well aware that one cannot stroll into the ecclesiastical court and emerge half an hour later with a grant of annulment in one's pocket! It may surprise you to know that I was not always the ornament of Society who stands before you today. Once in my mad youth, I had some idea of being independent of my elder brother, and to that end began reading for the law. It would never have worked of course; besides the fact that it would have taken up far too much of my valuable time, I should have looked utterly ridiculous in a barrister's wig. Still, while I was by no means brilliant, I did retain enough to recall that there are only certain conditions under which an annulment may be granted. You are not underage, I believe, nor are you mentally incompetent—"

"Coming from you, my lord, I will take that as a compliment," put in Pickett.

Lord Rupert's eyebrows rose. "Will you? It was not intended as such, I assure you, merely a statement of indisputable fact. There is another option, however, much as one hesitates to mention it—"

Of its own volition, Mr. Pickett's right arm moved ever so slightly so that the crown of his hat covered the fall of his breeches.

Lord Rupert, observing this unconscious gesture, murmured, "Quite so." He continued in a somewhat louder voice, "Before my father passed, there was a certain quotation by Henri Estienne of which he was particularly fond. I can still hear him say with a sigh, 'If youth but knew; if age but could.' Were my father alive today, Mr. Pickett, I would assure him that the French philosopher had been overly optimistic, at least where youth's, er, capabilities were concerned."

Pickett, flushing crimson, held his tongue with an effort. It would do Lady Fieldhurst no good at all if he were to blurt out the truth every time he was challenged on the matter. "If you have nothing further to contribute on the matter of Sir Reginald, your lordship, I will bid you good day," he said, putting on his hat and turning on his heel.

"Oh, I'm sure I shall have a very good day, indeed," retorted his lordship, chuckling.

After his exchange with Lord Rupert, it was a relief to Pickett to seek out Lord Edwin Braunton, with whom he felt himself to be on rather surer footing. Upon being shown into Lord Edwin's study, he lost no time in coming to the point.

"It appears you have been holding out on me, your lordship," he began.

"Eh? What's that?"

"A week ago I sat in this room and listened while you enumerated reasons why several men might want to murder Sir Reginald Montague."

"Yes, what of it?"

"You failed to mention that you have your own reason for wishing to do him harm. I have recently returned from Leicestershire," Pickett explained, "where I had the privilege of meeting your lovely daughter."

Lord Edwin's face turned first pale, then crimson. "Now, look here, you'll leave my daughter out of this!"

"I mean Miss Braunton no harm, your lordship," Pickett assured him. "In fact, I am sympathetic to her plight, and hope I may be of some assistance. But first I would like you to give me the accounting that you did not give last time we spoke."

Lord Edwin slumped in his seat, looking suddenly older than his forty-odd years. "I hold myself partly to blame, Mr. Pickett. If she'd had a woman's guidance, if her mother had been alive to warn her, perhaps things would have gone differently."

Pickett shook his head. "From what I have heard, Sir Reginald could be very beguiling when he chose to exert himself. I believe ladies older and more experienced than Miss Braunton have been known to succumb to his charm," he added, thinking of Lady Dunnington.

"When I found out—when Catherine told me she was—was in a delicate condition, I didn't know what to do." Lord Edwin dug his handkerchief out of his pocket and mopped his glistening forehead. "I daresay you will say I should have cast her off, but how can a man do such a thing to a child he loves?"

"I should think not!" exclaimed Pickett, appalled. "Your lordship, I have seen what happens to those females who are cast off by their parents just when they need them the most. It is not a pretty sight. Those who survive childbirth are more often than not obliged to earn their living on their backs. They usually don't last long before dying of pox or the clap. I can assure you, your daughter has done nothing to deserve such a fate."

Lord Edwin nodded distractedly. "Would that there were more people who felt that way."

"So," Pickett asked diffidently, "what did you do?"

"I didn't kill Sir Reginald, if that's what you're thinking! My first thought was to try and find my Catherine a husband as quickly as possible. Her dowry is respectable, but not so much as to tempt a man to raise another's bastard as his own child. I went at once to my elder brother—the Duke of Wexham, you know—and told him in the strictest confidence how things stood. He's always had a fondness for my Catherine—he has no girls of his own, only the two boys—and he added a substantial sum to the dowry in the hopes of making it—and her—more attractive to a potential bridegroom. In the meantime, I've done my damnedest to force Sir Reginald into taking some responsibility for his actions. Obviously he couldn't marry her—and to be perfectly honest, I'm not sure I wouldn't rather see her ruined than married to such a man as he!—but he should have paid something for the child's upkeep, at the least reckoning."

"And to come to such an agreement, you obviously needed him alive," Pickett concluded. It made perfect sense, and for all Lord Edwin's bluster, Pickett could not picture him acting so rashly. No, Lord Edwin might well have been capable of killing Sir Reginald, and he certainly had reason enough for wanting to do so, but he would not have done the deed until he was sure his daughter's future was settled.

"But you said you might be able to be of some assistance? In what way?"

"Tell me, Lord Edwin, how well do you know Mr. Martin Kenney?"

"Not well. Oh, I know what everyone else knows—an encumbered estate in Ireland with no money to pay the mortgages, and of course that business at White's, but other than that—" Lord Edwin shook his head.

"According to your daughter, she met Mr. Kenney earlier in the Season and danced once or twice with him. They seemed to be quite taken with one another."

"I see," said Lord Edwin slowly. "You think he might be willing to marry my Catherine?"

"I not only think he might be willing to marry her, I think they might eventually be very happy together."

Lord Edwin heaved a sigh. "He's not what I would have wanted for her, Mr. Pickett, I'll not deny it."

"Very likely not, but neither of them is in a position to be overly nice in their requirements. As you know, sir, time is of the essence, particularly in your daughter's case. The fact that they were both wronged by the same man might incline them to look on each other with understanding and sympathy. Marriages have been built on less." Sometimes much less, Pickett thought. He could think of one that had been formed from nothing more than the casual enacting of a ruse in a country that happened to have laws about such things.

"Thank you for the suggestion, Mr. Pickett," said Lord Edwin with a more hopeful expression on his countenance than he'd worn since Pickett had confronted him with his daughter's dilemma. "I shall bear it in mind."

Having finished with Lord Edwin, Pickett decided he had just enough time to call on Mr. Kenney before presenting himself in Harley Street. He did not expect this call to result in much progress in the matter of Sir Reginald; in fact, it was not so much to gather information as to divulge it that he sought out the Irishman. Still, to Pickett's mind it was a call worth the making.

No one opened the door to his knock, but a pronounced Irish brogue from inside bade him enter. He did so, and found Mr. Kenney washing out his linens in a basin and hanging them before the fire to dry. Pickett was more than a little taken aback; even at his poorest, his landlady had always been willing to undertake this task for him, although there had been a few times, mostly in his early days with the foot patrol, when he'd been unable to pay her for this service as promptly as he would have liked.

"Come in, Mr. Pickett," urged Mr. Kenney, his voice surprisingly cheerful given the bleakness of his circumstances. " 'Tis laundry day, as you can see. It's gratifying to know that if my luck at cards should ever fail me, I can always support myself by taking in washing."

"You could," Pickett agreed, "or you could render a service

for a young lady in desperate need, and live quite comfortably for the rest of your life."

The wet cravat in his hand slipped through Mr. Kenney's fingers and landed in the basin with a splat. "What young lady? What are you talking about?"

"Are you acquainted with Miss Catherine Braunton? I believe you may have danced with her a couple of times earlier in the Season."

"Miss Braunton? Of course I remember her! A charming girl and a diamond of the first water but, alas, far above my touch. She is the granddaughter of the previous Duke of Wexham, and the niece of the present duke. And I—" He made an expansive gesture with dripping hands. "I am nothing but a fortune hunter, as every young lady with a sizable dowry is warned as soon as I show her the slightest interest."

"Mr. Kenney, what would you say if I were to tell you that Miss Braunton has been no less wronged by Sir Reginald Montague than you have yourself?"

"Wronged?" Mr. Kenney gave the sodden cravat a firm twist, sending a stream of water into the basin. "In what way?"

"In the worst way in which it is possible for a man to wrong a woman."

"I—see," Mr. Kenney said slowly. "And now?"

"Now Miss Braunton finds herself in desperate need of a husband, and her uncle the duke has increased her dowry substantially to aid her in the cause."

"You are asking me to marry Miss Braunton and raise Sir Reginald Montague's bastard as my own child."

"I'm not asking you to do anything," Pickett objected. "I'm merely pointing out that there might be a simple solution to both your problem and Miss Braunton's. If you find the idea interests you, it might be worth discussing the matter with Lord Edwin."

"I feel for Miss Braunton, truly I do. And yet—Sir Reginald's bastard—" The Irishman shook his head. "What sort of father would I be to the child if I couldn't look at him without seeing his sire?"

"The babe might be a girl who looks like her mama—who, between you and me and the lamppost, most men would consider it no hardship to face over the breakfast table for the rest of their lives," Pickett observed, and received an answering grin from Mr. Kenney. "Either way, it seems to me there might be a certain satisfaction—a kind of revenge, if you will—to be gained in raising Sir Reginald's child to be a better person than his father was—and for you and Miss Braunton to be happy together in spite of him."

"There might, at that," conceded Mr. Kenney. "And one hates to see an innocent child suffer for the sins of its father; after all, the poor little blighter never asked to be conceived. Tell me, do you happen to know Miss Braunton's feelings on the subject?"

"I confess, I did take the liberty of mentioning the matter to her, and it seems she remembers you kindly. I do not think I presume too much in saying that if you were to come to her assistance at such a time, you could be sure of commanding her admiration as well as her gratitude."

"And mighty oaks from such little acorns grow," concluded Mr. Kenney, drying his hands on a towel. "Thank you for stopping by, Mr. Pickett. Now, I do not wish to appear rude, but if you will excuse me, I believe I shall look in on Lord Edwin Braunton."

"Not at all, sir, and I wish you every success, with both Lord Edwin and his daughter," said Mr. Pickett, and took his leave.

CHAPTER 17

The Seduction of John Pickett

As Pickett left the unsavory environs of St. Giles, Lady Fieldhurst undertook a conciliatory call of her own. She feared Lady Dunnington had not yet forgiven her for confiding in Mr. Pickett regarding Lord Dunnington's presence in Audley Street on the night of Sir Reginald's death. And yet how could she have done otherwise, when Mr. Pickett was doing so very much for her?

Upon arriving at the countess's town house, she was not admitted by the maid Dulcie, but by Jack, the footman. She congratulated him on his return to good health and was soon ushered into the drawing room.

"Julia, my dear, do come in," urged Lady Dunnington, who seemed, Julia was relieved to note, happy enough to see her. "I'll ring for tea, shall I?" the countess offered, reaching for the bell pull.

"Tea sounds lovely," Lady Fieldhurst assured her, taking her usual chair before the fire. "But tell me, Emily, have you heard any word from Lord Dunnington?"

"No, and truth to tell, I hardly know whether to be sorry or glad," Emily confided. "On the one hand, I am agog to know what is going on. And yet if he had been arrested, Dunnington would have sent word to me—I think," she added doubtfully.

"I am genuinely sorry to have given you cause to worry so,"

said Lady Fieldhurst, knowing all the while that, had she been forced to make the decision again, she must have done exactly the same thing. It was perfectly dreadful, being pulled between two dear friends with diametrically opposed agendas. "In fact, I had no notion you were so concerned for Lord Dunnington's sake. If you will forgive me for asking, Emily, how—how did things between the two of you come to such a pass?"

Lady Dunnington shrugged. "How do these things ever happen? Shortly after Kit's birth, I discovered quite by accident that Dunnington had taken a mistress. I was distraught at first, but when I confided in my mother, she told me I was making a great to-do over nothing. She said I had fulfilled my obligation to Dunnington by giving him two sons, and now we were both free to follow our own inclinations, just as she and my father had done for the past two decades—which was news to me, I assure you! So I took a lover of my own, although I confess it was less a matter of inclination than it was an attempt to give Dunnington a little of his own back." Overcome with restless energy, she leaped up from her chair and grabbed the poker from the hearth, then began jabbing at the coals. "I might have saved myself the trouble. If he noticed at all, he never let on."

"Emily, how old is Kit now?"

"He is twelve, and Robin—Viscount Brey, I suppose I should call him, but he will always be Robin to me—Robin is fifteen." Emily smiled as she thought of her sons, both of whom were in school at Eton. Whatever her failings as a wife, she was a doting mother, and had been so from the moment her husband's tiny heir had been placed in her arms.

Twelve years, thought Lady Fieldhurst. A dozen years of trying to break through the apathy of a husband she still cared for. It all seemed such a waste. Was that what her own future would have been had her husband lived, had she been able to give him the heir he had wanted so desperately?

She was still struggling for something to say that might comfort Lady Dunnington when a light scratching on the door interrupted their conversation.

"Lord Dunnington, my lady," announced Jack Footman, and stepped back to allow Emily's lord and master to enter the room.

"Dunnington!" Emily exclaimed, dropping the poker. "Never say you have been arrested!"

He blinked at her vehemence. "If I had been arrested, my dear, I doubt I would have been allowed to call on you to inform you of it in person."

She put a hand to her forehead. "No, of course not. What am I thinking? Do come in, Dunnington. I believe you are acquainted with Lady Fieldhurst?"

The earl executed a bow in Julia's direction, but addressed himself to his wife. "I have endured a visit from that Bow Street fellow. He had the gall to ask me if I believed you were capable of murdering a man in cold blood."

"Did he? And what did you say?"

Lord Dunnington did not wait to be invited, but seated himself on the sofa. "What else? I told him that if you were capable of such a thing, I should have been dead these past ten years and more."

"Really, Dunnington!" chided Emily, choking back a laugh in spite of herself. "You will give him the oddest notion of me!"

"He seems to have more than a few odd notions already," remarked the earl, frowning at the memory of the interview. "But he said one thing that I found curious. He told me you attempted to withhold the information that I had interrupted your dinner party that night. I should like to know why."

Thus cornered like a fox at the hunt, Lady Dunnington fluttered one hand in agitation. "The scandal, you know—we must think of the boys."

"The boys. Of course," drawled the earl.

"My lord, I fear it was I who told Mr. Pickett of your presence on that night," confessed Lady Fieldhurst. "I would not have done so, had I not the greatest confidence in Mr. Pickett's discernment."

"No, no, you did quite right, my lady," Lord Dunnington assured her, then turned back to his wife. "Emily, as much as I appreciate your attempt to protect—the boys—I believe it is usually best in these matters to be truthful, insofar as one is able. Nevertheless—" He broke off and sat frowning into the fire.

"Nevertheless what?" prompted Lady Dunnington.

"If that fellow comes around harassing you and suggesting you might have had a hand in Sir Reginald's death, you have only to send for me and I shall lodge a complaint against him with his magistrate."

Emily nodded. "Thank you, Dunnington."

"Surely such a thing will not be necessary," protested Lady Fieldhurst.

He bent what Julia felt was a rather fierce scowl in her direction. "I am not surprised that you would come to his defense, my lady. You appear to have a rather ardent champion in young Mr. Pickett."

She would have given much to know what Mr. Pickett had said to inspire such a remark, but she could hardly ask. Instead, she merely nodded. "He—he has been a very good friend to me."

In fact, he had been much more than that—and was being very shabbily repaid for his many kindnesses to her. Perhaps she should have fought harder for him, should have demanded that Mr. Crumpton find a solution to their dilemma that did not require the humiliation of an innocent and honorable man. Just what that solution might be, she did not know, but surely the solicitor could have thought of something, given the lavish retainer he was paid out of the Fieldhurst estate. She should have insisted upon it.

At that moment the door opened to admit Dulcie with the tea tray. "Oh your ladyship, I've only brought two cups!" she exclaimed in dismay upon seeing Lord Dunnington. "I'll run downstairs and fetch another, shall I?"

"No, no, that won't be necessary," the earl objected, rising to his feet. "I shan't intrude on your tea party, Emily, but you will send for me if you should need me?"

"Yes, Dunnington, I will. Thank you." After he had gone, she sat staring at the door through which he had passed. "Well, well," she murmured, her voice almost a purr. "What do you make of that?"

As he left Mr. Kenney's cheap lodgings, Pickett could not help but be satisfied with the interview, however little it might have achieved toward discovering the identity of Sir Reginald's killer. Although his magistrate might beg to differ, Pickett considered it a morning well spent. But now the morning was far advanced, and he had an appointment to keep.

Since Pickett had not expected to be obliged to actually undergo an examination, he had given little thought to what such an assessment might entail. But as he made his way on foot toward Harley Street, he began to wonder. How might one prove (or disprove, as the case might be) such a thing as Mr. Crumpton had suggested?

Alas, he was soon to find out. Upon reaching the tall brick structure in which Dr. Humphrey both lived and practiced, he was met at the door by the physician himself, who smiled toothily at him. It should, Pickett reflected later, have been his first clue.

"Ah, Mr. Pickett, is it?" the doctor greeted him cheerfully.

"Yes, I've been expecting you. Come in, come in!"

Once inside, he led Pickett to a small back room furnished much like a modest drawing room, with a sofa centered against one wall and a desk and chair in the corner.

He gestured toward the sofa. "Have a seat, Mr. Pickett, and we will begin. Girls," he called to someone apparently in another room, "Mr. Pickett is here."

Pickett sat on the sofa and watched with an increasing sense of foreboding as a side door opened to admit two women, one dark and one fair. Neither was in the first blush of youth—Pickett estimated them to be in the early thirties, at the least reckoning—but both were still remarkably attractive. As the women advanced into the room, sunlight from the windows filtered through their filmy, low-cut gowns, revealing the fact that they wore very little, if anything, underneath. He was very much afraid he was about to find out which.

"These lovely ladies are Electra and Persephone," the doctor explained. "They will be assisting with the examination."

Pickett looked from one woman to the other and tried hard not to let his gaze drop lower than the ladies' chins. He wondered fleetingly if they were each being paid a consideration too. "Which—which one is Electra, and which is Persephone?"

"I am," they chorused in unison.

The doctor seated himself at the desk, prepared to observe the proceedings with clinical detachment. The two women took places on the sofa, one on either side of Pickett, and each looped one hand through his arm while the other hand roamed at will.

Pickett whimpered.

The half-hour that followed was the most humiliating experience in a life already undistinguished by any great degree of dignity. Pickett managed to escape the ordeal with his virtue intact, but he took very little satisfaction in the doctor's conclusion that, yes, it appeared the examination results must indeed be falsified. Crimson with mortification, utterly embarrassed and deeply ashamed, he left the Harley Street medical district, but he could not bring himself to return to Bow Street; he could not face his magistrate's too-astute questioning or too-perceptive gaze. Instead, he turned his steps toward Audley Street, and was soon pounding on the below-ground servants' door with a strength born of desperation.

"Yes, yes, I'm coming!" called Dulcie impatiently as she opened the door. "What is the—*John!*"

She had no idea why he had called or what had happened to him, but the look of utter devastation on his face told its own tale. She opened her arms to him, and he fell into her embrace.

It was for comfort that he had sought her out, but comfort soon turned to desire, and desire to passion. Within minutes, he had pinned her against the wall and was kissing her with all the frustrated longing he felt for another. She returned his kiss with the same intensity (if for an entirely different reason), and it was several minutes before some slight noise from overhead penetrated his consciousness. He broke the kiss and looked up.

Lady Fieldhurst stood on the pavement above, staring down at him through the black wrought iron railings.

Lady Fieldhurst, leaving Lady Dunnington's house some ten minutes after the earl's departure, was not so much shocked as amused at a glimpse of one of the countess's housemaids in a passionate embrace with her young swain. But in the next instant she recognized both the girl and her admirer, and all traces of amusement vanished. Her strangled cry was enough to alert the pair that they were no longer alone. The male half of the couple looked up, and her world tilted on its axis.

She had never expected him to be utterly without feminine companionship; after all, he was young and personable, and if she could see this, surely the females of his own class were equally aware of it. In fact, she had seen him once before in the company of a young woman, a dark-haired, sharp-faced girl wearing a ghastly purple bonnet. She had been dismayed by his choice at the time, knowing he deserved better than a female who was obviously Haymarket ware. But Dulcie! Dulcie was lovely and sweet and demure. And at that moment she hated the girl with an intensity she had never felt for the most brazen of Frederick's mistresses.

Breaking eye contact with Pickett, she whirled away from the embracing couple and burst through the front door without knocking, to the shocked disapproval of Jack Footman, who had returned to his post just that morning only to discover that the world as he knew it had fallen apart while he lay on his sickbed. First murder in the hall, and now visitors charging in and out of the house without so much as a by-your-leave!

"Sick!" gasped her ladyship, clapping both hands to her mouth. "Sick!"

Correctly interpreting this cryptic message and its accompanying gesture, Jack snatched a bouquet of autumn roses from the crystal bowl adorning a side table, and thrust the bowl under her ladyship's nose. He was only just in time before she was violently ill.

"Julia, is that you?" Lady Dunnington, having heard the commotion from the drawing room, came into the hall to investigate. "Good heavens! What is the matter? Here, Jack, give me that bowl. I shall tend to Lady Fieldhurst while you fetch a glass of water for her."

Having dispatched the footman on this errand, she steered the trembling viscountess to the drawing room and seated her on a chair, placing the bowl on her lap.

"There, my dear, now you may be easy. Perhaps it was merely something you ate, and you will feel much more the thing for having got it off your stomach. Unless—" Her eyes widened as a new thought occurred to her, and she did a few rapid calculations on her fingers. "It is only six months since Frederick died. Julia, my dear, is it possible that at last you are—?"

"Of course not!" Lady Fieldhurst said impatiently. "Do I *look* as if I were six months gone with child?"

"No, but it often happens that one does not begin to show with one's first until quite late, and with moderate lacing of the stays—but if not that, then what has happened to make you ill? Don't tell me there is another dead body lying about!"

"No!" Lady Fieldhurst shook her head vehemently. "Worse!"

"Worse than a dead body?" Lady Dunnington wracked her brain. "*Two* dead bodies?"

"There were certainly two of them, but they were very much alive."

"What then, Julia? My dear, you are frightening me!"

"My Mr. Pickett was kissing your Dulcie!" she cried, and burst into tears.

"*Your* Mr. Pickett? When you have been telling me for this age that he is *not* yours!"

"He isn't," sobbed Lady Fieldhurst. "He's *hers!*"

"Do you mean *Mr. Pickett* is the young man she is walking out with? Why, I'll wager she didn't even know him until the night Sir Reginald was killed. The shameless hussy! She certainly didn't let any grass grow beneath her feet, did she? Shall I give her the sack?"

Lady Fieldhurst fumbled in her reticule for a handkerchief. "No, you must not do so for my sake," she said, controlling her tears with an effort. "I have no real claim on him, so he is free to pursue any female to whom he might take a fancy. Besides, if you dismiss her for encouraging his attentions, he might very well feel himself obligated to marry her, for that is just the sort of noble, unselfish—" Words failed her, and she succumbed to a fresh bout of tears.

But at the sound of a light tapping upon the door, years of training came to the fore. She dried her eyes and dabbed at her nose, and when Pickett appeared in the doorway, she was able to meet him with some semblance of composure.

"Your ladyship," Pickett addressed himself to Lady Dunnington, "may I have a word with Lady Fieldhurst? In private, if you please."

Lady Dunnington's eyebrows rose at this high-handed treatment. "Are you ordering me from my own house, Mr. Pickett?" Receiving a pleading glance from Lady Fieldhurst, however, she rose to her feet and whisked the bowl away. "Oh, very well, if you insist. Thank you for your assistance, Julia; I daresay I must have eaten something that disagreed with my stomach. I shall be in the next room, so if you should need me, you have only to call."

Pickett stepped into the room and nodded to her ladyship as she exited by the same door he had just entered. He closed the door behind her, and the viscountess and her thief-taker husband were alone. She found herself staring at his mouth. She had long thought he had the mouth of a poet, with a perfect Cupid's bow above and a full lower lip below. Was it her imagination, or was it slightly fuller now, swollen from his recent . . . activities? She was possessed of a sudden urge to find a wet cloth and scrub his lips raw.

Pushing aside the thought, she ventured a rather weak smile. "I have only to call, if I have need of her," she said. "Really, I wonder what she thinks you intend to do to me?"

"My lady," said Pickett, ignoring this admittedly feeble attempt at humor, "what you saw out there, it was—you need not distress yourself over—"

She raised a trembling hand to forestall him. "Pray say no more, Mr. Pickett. I realize I have no claim on you, aside from a legal one formed by the merest mischance. You need not answer to me for anything."

"I just want to assure you, my lady, that I have done nothing—with Dulcie nor anyone else—that would jeopardize the annulment in—in any way."

The annulment? She could not tear her gaze from the man's mouth, and he thought she was worried about the *annulment*? But surely it was better that he should continue to labor under this misapprehension.

"Thank you, Mr. Pickett," she said stiffly. "It—it is kind of you to let me know."

There seemed to be nothing more to say after that. They remained there for a long moment and pretended not to stare at one another, he standing just inside the door, she seated on the chair where Lady Dunnington had placed her. At last Pickett took an awkward step backward in the direction of the door through which he had entered.

"I'd best be going," he said, gesturing vaguely toward the front of the house.

Going where, she wondered. To Bow Street, or back downstairs to Dulcie? She desperately wanted to know, but had no right to ask, no right at all. She nodded a farewell—she did not trust herself to speak—and when she looked up again, he was gone.

CHAPTER 18

In Which John Pickett Wins the Day, but Loses at Love

Pickett plodded down Audley Street in a slough of despond, the indignities he had suffered in Harley Street driven from his thoughts by a greater calamity. If he had harbored doubts before about his courtship of Dulcie, he now had his answer. She had made it plain enough that she was not averse to receiving his attentions, but it was wrong to encourage her to hope for more than he was able to give. He would not marry where he could not give his whole heart, and he could never give Dulcie his heart; that organ belonged, irretrievably, to a woman he could never have. If he lived to be a hundred, he would never forget the stricken look on Lady Fieldhurst's face as she stared down at him from between the wrought iron railings . . .

His usually brisk stride grew slower as he pondered the image emblazoned on his brain for all eternity. He could still see her face . . . *He could see her face!* His steps came to a halt as the implications of this recollection began to dawn. James, the footman from the house three doors down, had seen no one leave the house. Nor, for that matter, had anyone in any of the houses across the street. Yet he had seen Lady Fieldhurst, foreshortened, it was true, due to the fact that she stood just slightly above street level while he was positioned several feet below. But he had seen her quite clearly nevertheless.

He turned abruptly and strode back up the street. He did not stop at Lady Dunnington's house, but walked straight past it and counted one, two, three doors beyond. He darted behind the wrought iron railing and descended the stairs to the servants' entrance, then knocked on the door. While he waited for someone among the reduced staff to answer his summons, he withdrew his occurrence book from the inside pocket of his coat and rifled through the pages. By the time a wide-eyed kitchen maid opened the door, he had found the information he sought.

"Is this the Fanshaw residence?" he asked urgently.

Her head bobbed up and down. "Aye, that is, it's their Town residence, but the master and mistress have gone back to Yorkshire for the winter."

"That's all right, I don't need—" Realizing he was getting ahead of himself, Pickett stopped and tried again. "John Pickett of Bow Street, miss. I believe there is a footman named James who works here. I should like to see him, if you please."

"Bow Street's come for our James?" cried the girl, her voice rising on a screech.

"James is not in any sort of trouble, I assure you," Pickett put in hastily. "I should merely like to speak to him, if I may."

"I don't know if I ought to let you in, without the master or missus being present," confessed the girl. "Still, if you'll wait here, I'll send him out to you."

"That will be fine."

Darting a last, mistrustful glance at Pickett, the girl shut the door. It opened again after a brief delay, this time to reveal the same footman he remembered from the night of Sir Reginald's death.

"James, isn't it?" asked Pickett, although he already knew the answer from the notes he'd made on the night of the murder.

"Yes, sir. You're from Bow Street, aren't you? I remember you, but I'm afraid I don't recall your name."

"Pickett, but it isn't important. I have a question to ask you regarding the murder of Sir Reginald Montague."

"I'll be happy to answer it if I can, but I'm afraid I've already told you everything I know."

"If I ask you anything you don't know, you have only to say so. Now, I want you to think back to that night, if you will. You said—" Pickett consulted his notes. " 'I heard the shot, and a moment later this thing came flying over the railing. It clattered down the stairs and landed almost at my feet.' " Pickett looked up at the footman. "Is that correct?"

James nodded. "Yes, it is. It's not the sort of thing a fellow would be likely to forget."

"Think carefully, if you will. Did you see anyone leave the Dunnington house immediately after the shot?"

"I didn't see no one," the footman insisted. "I swear to God, I didn't."

"Oh, I believe you," Pickett assured him. "Now what I want to know is, *why* didn't you see anyone? Did you look up when you heard the gunshot? I understand your attention was, er, otherwise occupied at the time."

James grinned. "I'll not deny my Polly is plenty distracting, but I can't imagine the female that would make a fellow fail to notice a gunshot practically right over his head—especially when he's afraid for a moment that the gun might have been aimed at him! No, Mr. Pickett, I was occupied right enough, but hearing that gun—well, I shoved Polly back inside, but I'll swear my eyes never left the railing up there, for fear the next ball might find its mark! But I never saw no one, just the gun, like I said."

No one had seen anyone leave the house following the shot, and yet Pickett knew—indeed, would he ever forget?—that anyone leaving the house should have been easily visible to James, standing in almost the very same spot where he had stood only moments ago and seen Lady Fieldhurst. The logical conclusion—no, the *only* conclusion—was that no one had been seen leaving because no one had left. The person who had shot Sir Reginald had still been in the house.

"Thank you, James, you have been more helpful than you know."

"Will I—will I get to be a hero?" James asked hopefully, apparently not only resigned to having his rôle in the little drama made public, but by this time actually looking forward to the experience.

"I think there is a very good chance you will be called to testify in court," Pickett told him.

The footman seemed highly satisfied with this answer, and Pickett suspected James would lose no time in notifying Lady Dunnington's kitchen maid Polly of this gratifying turn of events. Pickett frowned at the thought. It would not do for word to get out before he was fully prepared. As he passed Lady Dunnington's house, he would stop in and—no, he would not. Lady Fieldhurst would still be there, and he could not allow himself to be distracted, not at this stage of the investigation.

And so it was with mixed feelings that he strode past Lady Dunnington's door and made his way straight to Bow Street.

"John!" exclaimed Mr. Colquhoun, who had been waiting more impatiently than he cared to admit for his youngest Runner's return from his appointment in Harley Street. "How did it go?"

"Very well, thank you," Pickett said distractedly, his attention fully engaged in dashing off a note to be delivered to Lady Dunnington as quickly as might be arranged.

Mr. Colquhoun's eyebrows rose. From what he had learned while looking into the annulment process, he could quite see how some young men of four-and-twenty might find the experience pleasurable enough (particularly if they knew themselves to have no difficulties in that particular area), but he had not thought his rather naïve young protégé would have been among their number. In fact, he had feared the boy would return to Bow Street more than a little traumatized by the ordeal.

"Have you a moment, sir?" Pickett asked. "I think—I very much think I will need you to make out an arrest warrant."

The magistrate regarded him keenly. "You've discovered something."

"I believe so, sir."

"Would you care to enlighten me?"

Pickett did so. At the end of his recital, Mr. Colquhoun wagged his head. "I don't know, John. You may be right—in fact, I think it very likely you are—but most of your evidence appears to be circumstantial. I'm not sure the charges would ever hold up in court."

"I'm aware of that, sir, but I don't think any more concrete evidence exists."

"An unprovable case, then."

"Perhaps not, sir. In fact, I am hoping to force a confession."

"Are you?" The magistrate's bushy white eyebrows drew together over the bridge of his nose, and he regarded his youngest Runner sternly. "And what if you fail?"

Pickett sighed. "Then I am afraid I shall make rather a fool of myself, and the case will remain unsolved."

"That wouldn't be the idea, by any chance, would it?"

Pickett stiffened at the suggestion. "To make a fool of myself? Oh, I see: to allow a killer to escape justice. I trust I know my duty, sir."

"Very well," Mr. Colquhoun conceded with obvious reluctance, "you shall have your arrest warrant. I don't like taking such a risk, mind you, but I'm afraid you're right when you say it's our only hope of getting a conviction."

"Thank you, sir. And can you spare a couple of men from the foot patrol to accompany me?"

"Certainly, if you wish, but why? Do you expect the situation to be dangerous?"

"No, sir, not dangerous, but it might be—awkward."

The magistrate chuckled. "Yes, I can see how it might." He signed the warrant with a flourish, then shook sand over the paper to absorb the wet ink, rolled it up, and handed it across the railing to Pickett. "Good luck to you, then. I shall expect a full report in the morning."

Pickett nodded in agreement, then took the warrant, tucked it into his hollow wooden tipstaff, and returned to the note he'd been writing. He had a busy evening ahead, and its success or failure might well depend on Lady Dunnington's cooperation.

He arrived in Audley Street that night accompanied by two members of the foot patrol clad in the signature red waistcoats that had given them the sobriquet of Robin Red-Breasts. Everyone who had been in attendance at the fateful dinner party was already assembled in the drawing room, including Lord Dunningon, the uninvited guest; Lady Dunnington had not disappointed him, although the signs of strain about her eyes and mouth suggested she took little pleasure in carrying out his request. In fact, as he was announced Pickett glimpsed a sudden movement and realized his hostess had grabbed her husband's hand and now gripped it so tightly that her knuckles turned white. Lord Dunnington, Pickett was pleased to note, patted her hand with his free one, all the while glaring at Pickett as if daring him to make any accusations against her.

"Do have a seat, Mr. Pickett," Lady Dunnington urged him. "I understand you have something important to tell us. I assure you, we are all agog with curiosity."

"Agog" was hardly the word he would have chosen. His gaze instinctively sought out Lady Fieldhurst, whom he found sitting stiffly on a chair near the fire, looking up at him with a stricken expression in her blue eyes. He wondered if she was thinking about Sir Reginald's murder at all, or about his own seeming betrayal earlier that afternoon. Lord Edwin Braunton and Mr. Kenney sat side by side on the sofa; Pickett wondered if their united front indicated they had come to an agreement concerning Miss Braunton. Captain Sir Charles Ormond looked faintly annoyed at being called away from his regiment on such a pretext, Lord Rupert appeared bored, as usual, and Lord Dernham fairly bristled with hostility.

"Excuse me, sir," murmured a feminine voice at Pickett's shoulder. "Would you care for a drink, Mr. Pickett?"

He looked down and saw Dulcie proffering a silver tray laden with glasses of sherry. Although she addressed him formally and with eyes modestly downcast, she peeped up at him through her lashes with a secretive smile. Pickett was somewhat surprised to realize that she had no idea it was all over between them.

He shook his head. "No, thank you." As Dulcie removed herself to a discreet corner of the room, Pickett seated himself in the only vacant chair remaining, leaving the men of the foot patrol to take up stations on either side of the door. "I thank you all for coming, and at such short notice. I thought that, since most of you have been under suspicion at one time or another, you would all be eager to know the results of the investigation." There was more to it than that, of course, much more, but that was all they needed to know, and it appeared to be enough.

"Are you saying you know who killed Sir Reginald?" demanded Lord Dernham, leaning forward in his seat.

"I believe so, yes."

Half a dozen pairs of eyes darted about the room, gazes colliding briefly before shying away to encounter another speculative glance. *Is it you?* they seemed to ask each other. *Is it you?*

"From the beginning it was clear that almost all of you had

reason to hate Sir Reginald, yet it seemed to me that two of you, Lord Dernham and Captain Sir Charles, had more compelling reasons than the others." He turned to address the captain. "I confess, Captain, you were at the top of my list for a time. You might have made things a great deal easier on both of us if you had thought to mention that your horse threw a shoe on your way back to the barracks after leaving Audley Street."

The captain gave a grudging laugh. "I beg your pardon, Mr. Pickett. The omission was not deliberate, I assure you. I can only plead distraction, as the review the next morning drove the event from my mind."

"Quite all right, sir. There was another problem with your motive, as far as I could tell, which also held true for Lord Dernham's perfectly understandable hatred of Sir Reginald."

"The timeline," guessed Lord Dernham.

Pickett nodded. "Exactly. I suspect both of you thought longingly of doing Sir Reginald an injury when your losses were fresh, but that was three years in your case, my lord, and almost a decade in the captain's. I couldn't understand why either of you would have taken revenge now, when you had managed to restrain yourselves at the time. I wondered what in Sir Reginald's recent past might have recalled your injuries to your mind to such an extent—not that they were ever forgotten, of course—" he added quickly, anticipating Lord Dernham's objection. "—But the only momentous event I could find in Sir Reginald's life of late was the upcoming marriage of his daughter to the Marquess of Deale, eldest son and heir of the Duke of Covington."

"Murder as a method of preventing a marriage?" drawled Lord Rupert skeptically. "I can certainly see how one might be tempted, Mr. Pickett, but surely the bridegroom would be the more logical target in such a case?"

Pickett could not have failed to understand the subtext, but had more pressing concerns at the moment. "I assure you, Lord Rupert, it made no more sense to me than it does to you. Still, it was enough to send me off on a search for mare's nests." He glanced at Lord Edwin, but saw no reason to drag the disgraced Miss Braunton into the discussion.

"So Miss Montague's marriage had nothing to do with it, after all?" asked Mr. Kenney.

"I didn't say that," objected Pickett. "But I'll get to that in a minute. There was something else, too, that puzzled me. James, the footman at the Fanshaw residence three doors down, was standing at the servants' entrance below the street, but although the gun nearly hit him, he never saw anyone fleeing the house. Nor did any of the servants across the street see anyone leaving. It was not until earlier today"—he cast an apologetic glance at Lady Fieldhurst—"when I had occasion to be standing in that same spot myself, that I realized anyone leaving the house should have been clearly visible from that vantage point. The obvious solution, then, was that no one had left. Whoever had shot Sir Reginald was still inside."

"Now, see here, fellow!" blustered Lord Dunnington. "If you are suggesting that Lady Dunnington—"

But Pickett paid him no heed. Instead he rose from his chair and turned to Dulcie, who moved discreetly along the perimeter of the room refilling glasses. "I'm sorry, Dulcie, but in the name of His Majesty, King George the Third, I am placing you under arrest for the murder of Sir Reginald Montague."

"Me?" exclaimed Dulcie, her tray wobbling wildly enough to set the glasses on it rattling. "How can you say such a thing?"

"You were the only one who would have known Mr. Kenney had a gun in his coat pocket, much less had the opportunity to remove it and substitute a porcelain figurine in its place. You weren't summoned to show Sir Reginald out, but you very well could have waited for him in the hall, shot him, thrown the gun out the door, and then been watching in apparent shock and horror from the top of the servants' stair when the others arrived on the scene."

She set the tray down with a *thunk*. "But John, think what you are saying!" she said cajolingly. "You know me, you've courted me, you've kissed me! Even if I had the opportunity, as you say, why should I do such a thing?"

"Because Sir Reginald was your father," Pickett replied. "I know you follow the Society pages faithfully. It must have been hard, reading about your half-sister—who looks very much like you, by the bye—marrying the heir to a dukedom with all pomp and ceremony at St. George's, Hanover Square while you were reduced to earning your living as a housemaid."

She brushed past Lady Dunnington and Lord Rupert Latham, then slipped her hand through Pickett's arm and looked up at him with huge, pleading eyes. "But John, even if it were true, you wouldn't arrest *me*, would you? You couldn't— you love me!"

Pickett, in agony, shook his head. "I'm sorry, Dulcie."

Her hand fell from his arm, and she stepped back as if stung. "I see what it is!" Her soft, coaxing voice grew shrill and accusing. "It's *her*, isn't it? You wouldn't let *her* hang when it was *her* neck about to be stretched! Are you really such a fool as to believe she'll ever love you in return? She's been using you all along!"

"You would know best about that," replied Pickett, pale but resolute. "But Sir Reginald wouldn't let you use him, would he?"

"All I wanted was a settlement, enough to let me live in comfort," Dulcie insisted, her voice rising on a note of hysteria. "When he came to dinner that night, I told him who my mother had been, and that he had an obligation to me. He told me I was entitled to nothing. Nothing! Not even a paltry five pounds a month, when I'll bet his other daughter's wedding gown cost ten times that amount! When I took Mr. Kenney's coat a few minutes later, I felt the gun in his pocket, and thought I could persuade my dear father to change his mind."

Mr. Kenney made a convulsive movement at the mention of his name, but neither he nor any of the other guests made any sound. No one dared interrupt the scene being played out before them.

"I took the gun, just as you guessed, and put the porcelain figurine in its place in the hope that Mr. Kenney wouldn't notice it was gone. Then when Sir Reginald left, I confronted him in the hall. When he refused me again, I pointed the gun at him. He laughed at me." She gave a short, bitter laugh of her own. "He's not laughing now."

Pickett made a silent signal in the direction of the foot patrol, and both men came forward and took Dulcie by the arms. She shrugged them off.

"Yes, I'll come peacefully, but there's something I must do first."

Pickett nodded, and they released her.

She gave him a long, steady look. "Something to remember me by."

She seized his cravat and dragged his head down, then pressed her mouth to his. He could not bring himself to return her kiss (especially not with Lady Fieldhurst watching), but he allowed it. He owed her that much, as an apology for the demands of duty and the wayward heart that was no longer his to give.

"Goodbye, John." She darted a smug, triumphant glance at Lady Fieldhurst, then took the arms of the waiting foot patrol like a lady accepting the escort of two rival suitors and allowed them to lead her from the room.

The little drama concluded, the assembled company sat in

stunned silence for a long moment, until at last Lord Rupert Latham rose to his feet with lithe grace. "Accept my compliments, Mr. Pickett," he said with grudging admiration. "That cannot have been easy for you. Of course, she might have borne the loss of your fickle affections more easily had she only known—what we both know."

Pickett, utterly drained, collapsed onto his chair without responding at all, not even blushing. A hand fell softly on his shoulder, and he looked up to find Lady Fieldhurst standing beside him offering a glass of sherry. He accepted it gratefully and tossed it off in one gulp.

Lord Edwin Braunton and Mr. Kenney exchanged brief nods, then rose as one. "Best be pushing off," said Lord Edwin, obviously speaking for both of them. "We leave at first light for Leicestershire, you know."

Pickett summoned a smile. "I did not, sir, but I wish you both well. Please give my best regards to Miss Braunton."

"I will." Lord Edwin lowered his voice. "And if all goes well, I'll be sending you a small token of my appreciation. I realize playing matchmaker is not part of your duties."

"That won't be necessary, my lord," Pickett protested. "I am happy to have been of service."

"I must be on my way back to the barracks." Following the others' example, Captain Sir Charles Ormond heaved himself to his feet. "Not that it wasn't fascinating, Mr. Pickett, but I can't quite see why my presence—or anyone else's, for that matter"—he made a sweeping gesture that took in the entire company—"was necessary."

"I'm afraid I must plead guilty there," said Lord Dernham, addressing himself to the captain. "I told Mr. Pickett I wanted to be informed as to the identity of the person—although I believe I said 'man' at the time—who avenged my wife's death."

"Since most of you have been suspects at one time or another, it is only natural that you should all want to know," Pickett said. "But it was rather more complicated than that. It was a footman from a neighboring house who provided the final piece of the puzzle. But he's been keeping company with Lady Dunnington's kitchen maid, and I was afraid word would get back to Dulcie that I had solved the case. I didn't want her to get the wind up, so I asked Lady Dunnington to summon everyone who had been present on that night. I felt certain that, with so many guests expected, Dulcie would not be allowed to leave even if she requested permission to do so."

"Was *that* the reason?" demanded Lady Dunnington. "And here I thought—" She broke off abruptly.

"What did you think, Emily?" asked her husband.

She shook her head. "Never mind."

"Then there was the fact that I had absolutely no proof," Pickett continued. "My only hope was to persuade her to confess, and if she did, I would need plenty of witnesses."

Lord Dernham sighed. "I can't help feeling sorry for that unhappy young woman. It would be useless, I daresay, to offer to pay for her defense counsel since she has acknowledged her own guilt, but I feel I must make the gesture. You will inform her, Mr. Pickett?"

Pickett nodded. He would send word to her, informing her of Lord Dernham's offer, but he had no desire to see Dulcie again. He would be obliged to do so all too soon, at her trial.

One by one the guests took their leave, until at last only the Dunningtons, Lady Fieldhurst, and Pickett remained.

"Thank God that's over!" Lady Dunnington leaped to her feet and began pacing restlessly about the room. "I can see I will need to use more caution in the future when choosing a new lover—or hiring a new housemaid, for that matter."

Lord Dunnington cleared his throat. "About this lover, Emily. Might I make a suggestion?"

Startled, she ceased her pacing. He joined her before the fire and placed his hands on her shoulders.

"Instead of a new lover, would you perhaps consider an old husband?"

Her lower lip trembled. "What are you saying, Dunnington?"

"I've missed you very much, my dear. Maybe it's time you came back home."

To the utter astonishment of her audience, Lady Dunnington cast herself onto her husband's chest and burst into tears. "Oh, Dunnington! I was so afraid you were going to hang for murder!"

For the next several minutes there was no intelligent conversation at all, the Dunningtons communicating almost entirely in that nonverbal dialogue euphemistically known as billing and cooing. Pickett and Lady Fieldhurst, embarrassed witnesses to this exchange, tried hard not to look at either the Dunningtons or each other. Pickett, however, had an obligation to return to Bow Street and prepare the report he would make to his magistrate the next morning. Seeing no other way of separating the earl and his lady long enough to take formal leave of them, he gave a discreet cough.

Upon hearing it, Lady Dunnington emerged from her husband's embrace long enough to turn and look at the pair of them, blinking as if surprised to see them standing there. "What, are you still here? Run along, children. Or shall I summon the footman to show you out?"

"I'm sure we can find our own way, Emily," Lady Fieldhurst said with a smile.

She and Pickett made their way to the hall, where they stopped before the door and regarded one another in rather embarrassed silence.

"Well, there's one good thing that has come of it," observed Lady Fieldhurst.

"Yes. It appears to me Sir Reginald did more good dead than he ever did while he was alive."

"Does it?" she asked in some surprise. "I was under the distinct impression that most of the credit should rightfully go to John Pickett."

He shrugged. "All they needed was the opportunity to unite against a common enemy—in this case, me."

"If either of them thinks of you as an enemy, it only shows how little they know you. Am I correct in thinking you never really suspected either of them, but allowed them to believe you did in the hope that this very thing might happen? It was kind of you to take the trouble, Mr. Pickett."

Pickett smiled rather sheepishly. "If only I could manage my own affairs half so well!"

A shadow crossed her face. "About that girl—Dulcie. You—you lov—" She could not bring herself to say the word. "You cared for her. I am sorry for your sake, Mr. Pickett."

Pickett considered this thoughtfully. "I am sickened by the waste of a girl's life, and I feel ten times a fool for being taken in by a trick as old as Eve, but my heart was never really in danger. It—it has not been in my possession for quite some time," he added ruefully.

The air in the hall suddenly seemed very close, while as for Lord and Lady Dunnington in the next room, they might have been on another planet.

"Will you think me very selfish," asked Lady Fieldhurst, her voice hardly more than a whisper, "if I say I am glad?"

"Shall I say it, my lady?" He took a step in her direction, but made no move to touch her. "Shall I say it just once, and then speak no more of it?"

"Yes, please," she said breathlessly.

He let out a long sigh, as if relieved to abandon the unequal struggle. "I'm in love with you, my lady. I have loved you from the moment we met, and my feelings have only grown stronger in the months since. And *that,* my lady," he concluded with a regretful little smile, "is why I can never be your lover."

Her mouth worked, but no words would come. What did one say to such a declaration, when marriage—*real* marriage—was not an option?

"You need not answer," he assured her. "I know there is no hope for me, and I am not asking you to return my regard. I know nothing can come of it. I—I will not see you again. I have asked Mr. Colquhoun not to send me into Mayfair on assignment in the future."

"But—our court appearance—"

He shook his head. "Mr. Colquhoun strongly advises me to be absent in order to avoid any possible charges of perjury, and I think he is probably right. You will send word when—when it's done?"

She nodded, unable to speak. Dulcie was gone, but he was lost to her all the same.

"My lady, I hope—I hope you will think of your second husband with kindness from time to time. I can assure you that he will never forget you."

He gave her an uncertain little smile and turned toward the door.

"Mr. Pickett, would you please kiss me?" She had not meant to ask, much less beg, but the words came out in a rush, refusing to be held back.

"My lady, are you *trying* to torture me?" he asked in mingled exasperation and very deep affection.

"No," she said miserably. "But I can't bear seeing you go away with that—that female's kiss on your lips."

Pickett apparently saw nothing to dispute in this line of reasoning, for he turned away from the door. He did not take her in his arms, but cupped her face in his hands and lowered his mouth to hers. It was a long kiss, long and slow and agonizingly sweet—and it held goodbye in every brush of his lips, every wisp of his warm breath.

She clutched the lapels of his brown serge coat. "Will you not kiss me like you kissed *her*?"

Having committed himself this far, Pickett threw caution to the wind. He crushed her to his chest and plundered her mouth with his own. Her hands were pinned between them, but she tugged one free and buried her fingers in his hair, returning his kiss with fervor until at last he drew back, breathless and panting, and released her.

"Goodbye, my lady."

And then he was gone. Lady Fieldhurst sagged against the door, her heart racing and her legs suddenly unwilling to support her weight. *I know there is no hope for me . . . I am not asking you to return my regard . . .*

"Oh, but I do," she whispered. "I do."

And in a matter of—what? Days? Weeks? Months?—she would have to convince an ecclesiastical court that he was incapable, this virginal man who could make her knees weak with his kisses, who could ravish her with the sound of his voice.

She had a bad feeling about this annulment.

She had a very bad feeling indeed.

AUTHOR'S NOTE

Readers who have written to me over the years thanking me for the wholesomeness of my books may be a bit shocked by certain events described and/or insinuated in Chapter 17. I'm sorry if this is the case, but in my own defense must refer you to File "Y," under "You Can't Make This Stuff Up." The legal requirements for obtaining an annulment in Regency England were, as far as I was able to ascertain through research, exactly as I have portrayed them here, with one exception: in fact, the couple would be required to live together for three years without consummating the marriage before an annulment could be granted. But since I believe there is such a thing as stretching tension too far (let alone the fact that poor John Pickett had suffered enough), I chose to overlook this prerequisite for the purpose of the story.

ABOUT THE AUTHOR

At age sixteen, **Sheri Cobb South** discovered Georgette Heyer, and came to the startling realization that she had been born into the wrong century. Although she doubtless would have been a chambermaid had she actually lived in Regency England, that didn't stop her from fantasizing about waltzing the night away in the arms of a handsome, wealthy, and titled gentleman.

Since Georgette Heyer was dead and could not write any more Regencies, Ms. South came to the conclusion she would have to do it herself. In addition to the John Pickett mysteries, she has also written several Regency romances.

A native of Alabama, she now lives in Loveland, Colorado. She loves to hear from readers via email at Cobbsouth@aol.com or her Facebook author page.